KING OF
THE DEAD

TOR BOOKS BY JOSEPH NASSISE

THE JEREMIAH HUNT CHRONICLE

Eyes to See
King of the Dead

KING OF THE DEAD

JOSEPH NASSISE

TOR®

A TOM DOHERTY ASSOCIATES BOOK

NEW YORK

This is a work of fiction. All of the characters, organizations, and events portrayed in this novel are either products of the author's imagination or are used fictitiously.

KING OF THE DEAD

Edited by James Frenkel

A Tor Book
Published by Tom Doherty Associates, LLC
175 Fifth Avenue
New York, NY 10010

www.tor-forge.com

Tor® is a registered trademark of Tom Doherty Associates, LLC.

Library of Congress Cataloging-in-Publication Data

Nassise, Joseph.
    King of the dead / Joseph Nassise. — 1st ed.
        p. cm. — (The Jeremiah Hunt chronicle ; bk. 2)
    "A Tom Doherty Associates book."
    ISBN 978-0-7653-2719-2 (hardcover)
    ISBN 978-1-4299-4683-4 (e-book)
    I. Title.
  PS3614.A785K56 2012
  813'.6—dc23

                                    2012024535

First Edition: November 2012

Printed in the United States of America

0 9 8 7 6 5 4 3 2 1

For Maria

KING OF THE DEAD

1

HUNT

Life as an interstate fugitive isn't easy. It's not being on the run itself that's so difficult: mankind has been wandering from place to place since the dawn of human existence. No, it's the constant state of fear and anxiety that wears on you, little by little, bit by bit, until you're ready to turn yourself in to make it all stop.

Being on the run turns you into a virtual prisoner; all that's missing are the steel bars. You can't go out without worrying about being seen in public. If you do go out, you end up having a terrible time because you're constantly looking over your shoulder, wondering if you've been recognized. Then, when you've finally buckled under the strain of it all and retreated to whatever hole-in-the-wall you're calling home that week, you spend the entire night waiting for that knock on the door, the one that heralds the arrival of the police who've come to drag your ass away to jail for the rest of your natural born life. All that and I didn't even mention the never-ending itch between your shoulder blades, that constant sense you're being hunted, tracked, like a fox fleeing before the hounds.

Fact is, life as a fugitive pretty much sucks.

You'll have to take my word for it when I tell you that it's even tougher when you're blind.

I know. Cry me a river, right?

We, meaning Dmitri Alexandrov, Denise Clearwater, and I, had been on the run for the last three months. We'd left Boston in early September, just a half step ahead of an FBI agent named Robertson. Mr. FBI was convinced I was the serial killer known as the Reaper, a particularly vicious monster he'd been hunting for more than a decade. He also thought I was responsible for the death of a homicide detective named Stanton. To be honest, I did have to take some responsibility for Miles's death; he wouldn't have been following me and ended up getting himself killed if I hadn't broken out of a holding cell at One Police Plaza.

Then again, if I hadn't been illegally imprisoned and accused of multiple homicides that I couldn't possibly have committed, I wouldn't have had to break out of jail in the first place.

Oh, what a tangled web we weave.

It all started with the kidnapping of my daughter, Elizabeth, five years before. I didn't know it then, but she'd been snatched by the supernatural equivalent of the man with a thousand faces: a doppelganger, or fetch as they were sometimes called, that could take the form of any creature it came into contact with. The fetch was the magically created twin of a sorcerer named Eldredge, who had been locked away in a mystical prison somewhere around the time the American colonies won independence. Eldredge eventually died, but not before he used the power that bound him to become a shade.

Shades are nasty business—incorporeal spirits imbued with the intelligence and power that they had in life, with no expiration date for their hatred or their craving for vengeance. With the right ritual and no small measure of arcane energy, a shade can even regain its physical form, or, in the words of *Star Trek*'s Spock, create life from lifelessness. All Eldredge needed to do was track down and slaughter the last living relatives of those who had originally sealed him away in that mystical prison beneath the earth and he'd be home free.

It had taken him more than a decade but he'd made good use of the time, sending his doppelganger crisscrossing the country, killing as it went. By the time I'd entered the picture he was down to the final four or five.

If the doppelganger hadn't kidnapped my daughter, he probably would have succeeded.

Instead of completing the ritual and waltzing off into the sunset, he'd been forced to fight for his life and, in the end, the three of us had cleaned his clock and put him down like the rabid dog he was.

Before we had, though, his pet fetch had disemboweled Stanton and nearly killed the three of us as well.

We'd survived and had taken out Eldredge, something a powerful group of sorcerers two centuries before hadn't been able to do. The fairy-tale ending I'd hoped for never materialized, though. I soon found out that while Elizabeth had been kidnapped by the fetch at Eldredge's command, she died in an accident almost a year before.

Sending her ghost on to the rest she deserved was one of the hardest things I'd ever done.

And what did we get for all our trouble?

Three months of living as fugitives, with no end in sight.

Which was why we were parked in an empty lot in the warehouse district at midnight, trying to buy a set of fake IDs from a gangbanger named Carlos. He'd been recommended to us by the friend of a friend of someone Dmitri knew, which didn't put him too high on the trustworthy list, but at least it gave us a place to start. We needed those IDs. With them, and the security of being able to do simple daily tasks, we could start to build some semblance of a life. It wouldn't be what we'd had before; there was no way we could ever go back to that, but at least it would better than what we had now.

Things had been going pretty well, too, until the punk in front of me stuck his gun in my face.

I was standing next to the door of my car when he arrived in his low-riding Impala, the booming beat of a bass drum pumping out of his open windows. I had to struggle to conceal my smirk as he got out of the car and sauntered over to me. He'd killed his headlights before doing so and that had allowed me to give him the once-over from behind my sunglasses without making it too obvious.

He was five seven, maybe five eight on a good day, which put him four inches shorter than me. He was dressed in a pair of baggy pants that were belted on halfway down his ass, revealing the top of his boxer shorts, and a dark formfitting long-sleeved shirt, the kind the bodybuilders wear. The whitest sneakers I'd ever seen and a red bandanna tied around his left arm completed his getup. He was trying too hard and it showed; he looked more like Hollywood's idea of a cholo than the real thing.

In the good ole days, before we had to run for the hills, Dmitri had owned and operated the best bar in all of Southie, which, when you think about it, was kind of unusual for a guy with the last name Alexandrov. But he'd successfully defended his territory against more than one attempt by the Irish mob to hone in on it, and it wasn't until I'd known him for a few years that I'd discovered why. Besides being a mean son of a bitch, Dmitri had been one of the best fixers in the business. Information and equipment were his stock in trade; if you needed something, anything at all, you went to Dmitri.

It was his safe house that we'd been staying in for the last several weeks and when it came time to establish a new set of identities for each of us, it was his expertise that allowed us to set up this meet.

Something went wrong, however. We were expecting a professional and ended up with the farm team instead.

This punk with the gun.

The acrid smell of gunpowder filled my nostrils, letting me know the weapon had been fired recently.

That wasn't a good sign, either. So far, our negotiations were off to a bad start.

I put my hands up without being asked and said in a soft, non-threatening tone, "Easy, man. No need for that."

Carlos must have thought he was now the big man on campus for he turned his wrist so that the weapon was practically upside down and waggled it back and forth in front of my face. "Shut up and give me the money," he said with a sneer.

Nobody with an ounce of brains would fire a gun from that position and expect to hit anything with any degree of accuracy, so I could tell he was more bark than bite. If I could stall him for just a bit longer, I knew we could turn the tables on him, so I played the clueless white guy, full of indignation and completely out of his element.

"But we had a deal," I whined. "Two sets of IDs for ten grand."

Carlos grinned so wide that I could see the gold teeth in his mouth.

"I'm changing the deal, shithead. Give me the money before I put a cap in your ass!"

My whining tone did the trick. All he saw was some gringo in way over his head, which was exactly what I wanted him to see. It kept him focused on me and not on what was silently lumbering up behind him on all fours.

"Okay, okay. Take it easy," I said, looking down and to one side, signaling my submission in a way he'd instinctively understand. "I'm going reach into my pocket and . . ."

"Stop talking and just do it, fool!"

I reached into the pocket of my coat and withdrew a thick envelope. I started to hand it over to him and then pulled back.

"The IDs . . ."

Carlos practically snarled as he snatched at the envelope in my hand. "Give me that!"

I pulled my hand back just enough to keep it out of his reach. The charade had gone on long enough. I glanced over his shoulder, saw what I was looking for, and dropped the scared gringo act.

"You might want to look behind you first," I said, letting the boredom I was feeling with the whole situation color my voice.

Surprisingly, Carlos caught the change in tone. Maybe he was smarter than I was giving him credit for or maybe he just had a finely tuned sense of survival, I don't know, but he seemed to recognize he was no longer in control of the situation. His eyes narrowed, and I could almost see the wheels turning in his head as he tried to figure out where the danger was coming from.

It didn't take long.

From directly behind him came a roar that suddenly split the night in two, shockingly close and loud enough to make my knees tremble involuntarily, despite the fact I'd known what was coming.

Poor Carlos didn't have any such warning and he nearly wet his pants as that cry sounded from directly behind him, so close that he could probably feel hot breath on the back of his neck. His eyes got as round as saucers and he frantically spun around and tried to bring his gun to bear at the same time.

Whatever it was that he expected to see there, I'm pretty sure that a ten-foot-tall polar bear wasn't it.

In the aftermath of my daughter Elizabeth's disappearance I'd tried everything I could think of to discover what had happened to her. When, after a few years, I'd exhausted the usual methods, I'd delved into more esoteric ones. Things like divination, witchcraft, and black magic. It was in the course of those "investigations" that I'd encountered the Preacher.

To this day I'm still not sure who or what he actually was or why he appeared to me, but it was through his help that I located a ritual that would let me see that which was unseen, and I'd used it in an effort to locate Elizabeth.

As is typical of dark magick, the ritual did exactly what it promised to do but not in the way I'd expected. Rather than helping me locate what was missing, it stole my natural sight and replaced it with something else, something I've come to call my ghostsight. Among other things, it lets me see the supernatural denizens of the world around me. It doesn't matter what they were, I can see them all: the good, the bad, and the scares-me-shitless.

I'm not completely blind. I can actually see better in complete darkness than most people can in broad daylight. I can no longer see colors—everything comes out in a thousand shades of gray—but at least I can see. The minute you put me in the light, however, everything goes dark. Direct sunlight is the equivalent of a complete whiteout for me; I can't even see the outline of my hand if I hold it directly in front of my face. All I see is white. Endless vistas of white. Electrical lights are almost as bad, though if I use a pair of strong UV sunglasses I can see the vague shapes and outlines of things around me.

Which was why I was standing in a dark alley at night wearing the darkest sunglasses I could find.

Thanks to my sight I'd known that Dmitri wasn't just a simple bartender, but I hadn't been able to pierce the glamour around him to know exactly *what* he was. It was when I was hunting for the fetch earlier that fall that I'd discovered that he was a berserker.

First mentioned in the Norse saga Vatnsdoela, the berserkers were described as elite warriors that wore animal pelts on their heads and charged into battle in a ravaging frenzy, fighting so hard that they were nearly unstoppable. Of course, the bards hadn't quite gotten it right, never realizing that the berserkers were actually warriors that were so in touch with the totem spirits of certain animals that they could assume the physical properties of those beasts in battle, borrowing their strength, cunning, and senses to accomplish things they never could have done as mere humans.

Dmitri and I decided to play it safe for tonight's rendezvous, arriving early and having only one of us meet our intended contact. While I did that, Dmitri would remain out of sight, ready to come to my assistance if necessary.

Now we were glad that we'd taken the extra precaution.

Dmitri reared up on his hind legs, towering over Carlos. He opened his mouth and let loose another ground-shaking roar of challenge. That close, his teeth seemed bigger than my clenched fist.

To his credit, Carlos stood his ground and tried to bring his gun to bear, though what he thought a pistol was going to do against a brute like Dmitri was beyond me.

He needn't have bothered. Before he'd even managed to move his arm a few inches it was intercepted by the swipe of a massive fur-covered paw. The impact sent Carlos spinning to the ground and the gun went flying off into the darkness. Dmitri lumbered forward, straddled Carlos's body and clamped his teeth firmly onto the back of the gangbanger's neck.

A few more ounces of pressure and bye-bye Carlos.

For the first time all night, our would-be thief did the smart thing. He froze.

Smiling now, I put one hand on Dmitri's broad back and squatted down next to Carlos so that he could see me without having to move his head. This close I could smell the stink of urine and feces that was coming off of him in waves. From the smell I knew he'd be a bit more receptive to our needs now that we'd gotten the preliminaries out of the way.

Good thing, too, since I was done dicking around.

"One word from me and my friend here will crush your head like an eggshell. *Comprende*, amigo?"

He opened his mouth, only to find that his fear had stolen his voice. He gaped like a fish a few times, vainly trying to get something out.

I took that as a yes.

"Where are the IDs?"

This time he managed to find his voice.

"Glove box," he gasped out.

I patted Dmitri on the back, rose to my feet, and walked over to the lowrider. I slid into the front seat, leaned over to the other side, and opened the glove box. Inside I found another pistol and a manila envelope containing the driver's licenses and passports that Carlos's organization had agreed to provide. I put the new IDs back in the envelope and then tucked that and the pistol into the pocket of my jacket.

Carlos had left the keys in the ignition, perhaps in anticipation of a quick getaway after screwing us over. I took them with me as I got out of the car and threw them into the darkness as far as I could.

Once I had, I signaled for Dmitri to let Carlos up.

Dmitri growled low in his chest, expressing his annoyance at the idea and eliciting another whimper of fear from Carlos, but with a little encouragement Dmitri eventually backed off, moving to sit on his haunches at my side. Even seated, he towered over me.

"Not a particularly bright play, Carlos," I said, packing all the disdain for his intelligence that I could into the words. "But today must be your lucky day, for I've decided to let you go. Now get the hell out of here and don't even try to come back for your car."

Carlos didn't need to be told twice. He scrambled to his feet and ran off, never once looking back.

Dmitri turned his shovel-shaped head in my direction and grunted something.

Having no idea what he'd just said, one roar sounding pretty much like the next, I just stared at him blankly.

Another growl, a quick sensation of movement, and before I had time to look away, Dmitri was back in human form, standing in front of me completely naked and seemingly not bothered by it at all.

Catching a glimpse of what he was carrying around with him, I could understand why.

Some guys just get all the luck.

He walked over to Denise's car, a black Dodge Charger we'd borrowed for the evening's activities, and pulled on the extra set of clothes that he'd brought along for that purpose. I got in the passenger side, he slid in behind the wheel, and we took off in a spray of dirt and gravel.

Dmitri drove for a few blocks and then pulled into the parking lot of an all-night diner, finding a spot beneath one of the few streetlamps illuminating the lot.

"Give 'em here," he said.

I passed him the envelope containing the fake IDs.

Besides limiting my vision, the Preacher's ritual had also robbed me of my ability to see photographs or paintings of any kind. I could see the spot on the IDs where the images were supposed to be, but the images themselves were just flat black squares, making it impossible for me to judge how well the passports and driver's licenses had turned out.

Dmitri looked them over for a few minutes, even going so far as to hold them up to the light one at a time and turn them this way and that, before dropping them back into the envelope.

"Good enough, I think," he said, passing the envelope back to me, and I let out the breath I didn't know I'd been holding. If we'd gone through all this trouble only to end up with useless junk . . .

But we hadn't and that was good. Really good. Having the IDs would at least provide us some small measure of protection, allow us to do simple things that other people took for granted, like cashing a paycheck or signing a long-term lease on a piece of property. Even opening up a bank account or getting a line of credit was now possible, though I didn't think I'd want to put our IDs up to that level of scrutiny unless it was absolutely necessary.

Dmitri started the car and pulled out into traffic, while I took out one of the prepaid cell phones we'd been using to communicate with one another and called to let Clearwater know we were on our way home.

If I'd known what she was going to drag us into less than seventy-two hours later, I might have tossed the phone out the window and told Dmitri to head south at the fastest possible speed, do not pass Go, do not collect two hundred dollars.

Unfortunately, I didn't.

2

CLEARWATER

Around her, the city burned.

She ran through the streets, the buildings on either side engulfed in writhing sheets of flame, tongues of green and blue danced with those of red and yellow, evidence of the eldritch energies mixing with the natural ones. The heat pouring off of the fire was intense; even from the middle of the street she could feel it beating against her flesh, sending rivulets of sweat running down her face. Smoke and soot and ash filled the air, limiting her ability to see as she ran, searching for something, though she couldn't remember who or what it was that she sought. Behind her, lost in the smoke and ash, something searched for her in turn.

She stumbled forward, looking for a street sign or some other landmark that would give her a better sense of her location, but all such markings seemed to have been removed, if they'd ever existed at all.

The thing behind her drew closer. She didn't know how she knew; she *just did. The first twinges of panic rose to the surface of her mind, but she fought them back down. Giving in was not an option; the thing behind her would catch her and that would be the end.*

Of everything.

She couldn't let that happen!

The smoke grew thicker, darker, and she was forced to hold her arm over her mouth as she stumbled forward. Her breath was coming in short, sharp gasps as she struggled to draw enough oxygen from the polluted air, but she bravely fought forward.

Something moved in the ruins to her left and she turned in that direction, eyes straining to make out what it was in the glare of the flames, but it was gone as swiftly as it had come.

A wailing cry sounded from close behind, just beyond the nearest curtain of smoke, and her heart pounded to hear it.

Faster! You have to run faster! *a voice shouted at her from deep inside her mind.*

She pushed herself, drawing on the last of her reserves. Sweat poured down her face and plastered her hair against her scalp, while her clothing seemed weighted down with falling ash. She dodged wrecked cars and the shattered remains of crumbled homes, racing deeper into the darkness, searching for a way out.

She didn't see the jagged crack in the pavement until it was too late. Her foot caught on the edge and she fell, her hands coming up to protect her face as she slid across the harsh surface, leaving flesh and blood in her wake.

Already an inner voice was shouting at her, Get up! Get Up! Get Up!

She tried, really tried, but her right leg wouldn't support her and she fell back to the pavement, crying and screaming in pain and fear. She must have broken her ankle in the fall.

Unwilling to give in, she used her arms to pull herself forward, dragging her wounded leg behind her.

That wailing cry sounded again, this time from immediately behind her, and she knew she'd been found. She rolled over, bringing her hands up before her in defense, as she caught a glimpse of something monstrous looming against the darkness of the smoke surrounding them.

She screamed as the thing descended . . .

>+—<

The vision departed as swiftly and as unexpectedly as it had come. In its aftermath, Denise found herself standing before the big bay window in the living room. She was clad in the loose-fitting pajamas she'd pulled on when she went to bed earlier that evening, and she shivered in the cold air. A portion of the window had been fogged over, as if someone had just breathed on it, and the outline of two words were clearly visible on its surface.

NEW ORLEANS.

Just seeing the words there made her nervous and so she reached up, intending to wipe them away. *Out of sight, out of mind,* she thought, rubbing her fingers across the glass, only to recoil in fear when the words did not disappear.

They couldn't.

They were written on the *outside* of the glass.

A shiver of arctic cold ran up her spine, and she took a few steps back, unable to tear her gaze away from the letters as they slowly faded from view, seeming to mock her as they did so. Her thoughts raced through all the ways those words could have ended up on the window in front of her, each one more dangerous than the last . . .

"Are you okay, Denise?"

She screamed.

She couldn't help it. So great had been her concentration that she hadn't heard Hunt enter the room behind her. His sudden voice in the silence of the room shocked her almost as much as seeing the words on the window.

Almost.

She knew he'd react to her fear and so she quickly turned, waving her hand and intentionally laughing to keep him from learning how upset she actually was.

"Gaia, Hunt, you startled me!"

Moonlight spilled in through the windows, letting her see his face. His white eyes seemed to gleam of their own accord in the partial darkness and she wondered, not for the first time, exactly what the ritual he'd undergone had done to him.

"You looked like something scared you," he said. "Well, before I did, I mean."

She shook her head. "It was nothing—a bad dream, nothing more. I'll be fine. Your voice just surprised me, that's all. I didn't hear you come into the room."

He glanced past her to the window but apparently didn't find anything there to make him suspicious since he turned his attention back to her.

"You're sure?"

"Yes, of course. Go back to bed. I'm sorry I woke you."

Now it was his turn to brush it off. "You didn't. I was up anyway. Memories, ya know?"

She did know. She'd been there when the ghost of his daughter Elizabeth had asked him to use his power to release her into whatever it was that came next. It was the glimpse of the man she'd seen in that moment, the one who would have gladly given his life to save that of his little girl, that convinced her to join him when he was forced to flee the city.

"Really, I'm fine," she said, and smiled again to show that she meant it.

Whether he believed her or not, she couldn't tell, but he said good night, turned, and wandered off back in the direction of his bedroom at the rear of the house.

She stayed up after Hunt had gone to bed, settling onto the couch and staring out into the night's darkness, considering her next move. The visions had started two weeks before, and there was no denying the fact that they were coming more regularly now. Each time it was the same: she was trapped in the burning city while magick ran amuck around her and something dark and twisted stalked her through the smoke and flames of the city streets.

She couldn't ignore the summons much longer. And there was no doubt about it, that's what it was—a summons. Gaia needed her assistance again, just as she'd been needed when the fetch and its master had begun slaughtering people in Boston, intent on disrupting the natural order of things. Then, like now, she'd begun having visions, images of her and Hunt and Dmitri wrapped up in their efforts to put a stop to what was to come. Most of those visions came true, as she knew they would. The longer she waited, the more fixed those events became in that future timeline, as if her willingness to act sooner rather than later made a difference to the ultimate outcome. And maybe that was the point. You couldn't ignore a call from the Earth Mother any more than you could ignore gravity, not if you wanted to continue as a practitioner of the Art, and doing so could have dire consequences.

So why was she resisting?

The answer was right there, simply waiting for her to acknowledge it, and this time she did so.

She was afraid.

Facing off against the shade of Eldredge and his deadly fetch had nearly killed her and her friends. Going back into battle against the unknown a second time wasn't high on her list of favorite things right now.

What if this time they weren't strong enough?

No matter how long she sat there, she couldn't come up with an answer that satisfied her.

3

HUNT

A few days after our adventure in Newark, the weather finally broke, clearing away the gray overcast that seemed to be an ever-present feature of a New Jersey winter and giving us a glimpse of blue sky, with temperatures higher than they'd been for months.

It was the third week of December and the thermometer was hovering in the low fifties.

God bless global warming.

By noon it had turned into a beautiful day.

Or, at least, it seemed that way to me, though I'd be the first to admit that my viewpoint might have been a little off, given that I'd already consumed a six-pack of a Mexican ale with a name I wouldn't have been able to pronounce properly when sober, never mind in my current state. I was sitting in a lawn chair at the ocean's edge, an array of fishing poles stuck in the sand in front of me and a now partly empty beer cooler close at my feet.

Given his particular line of work, Dmitri knew he might one day have to run, and he'd planned ahead, buying a little place on the Jersey Shore. Why he'd picked Jersey was a mystery to me. I mean, come on, who wants to hide out in New Jersey, for heaven's sake? Florida, the Bahamas, maybe even Costa Rica, sure, places like that made sense.

But New Jersey?

I had to give him credit though, the place he'd chosen was practically ideal, if you ignored the fact it was in Jersey. The town was small, the kind of community where people kept to themselves and didn't stick their noses into other people's business. Dmitri's infrequent comings and goings were met with complete indifference, especially now that it was the middle of December.

The little house stood in the dunes not far from the water's edge and from the front porch you could look out at the Atlantic and practically see forever. I'd been doing just that each night for the last several weeks, trying to come to grips with what I'd learned about my daughter's death and the events that had led me to hiding out like a common fugitive rather than the respected Harvard professor I'd once been.

Funny how all it takes is one little curveball to turn your world upside down, isn't it?

A few newscasts and a little bit of Internet research had let us know that I was currently occupying a spot pretty high up on the FBI's Most Wanted List. There were half a dozen terrorists ahead of me, but I'd made the top twenty without difficulty. According to the FBI, I was a serial killer known as the Reaper, responsible for a killing spree that stretched from coast to coast and went back ten years or more. In my lighter moments I was amused by it all, but the truth was that if the cops ever got their hands on me it would probably be a long time before I was anywhere but inside a six-by-six cell.

Dmitri wasn't on the list, but there was no doubt he was the focus of the same kind of manhunt that I was; hacking into my police file had revealed that he was listed as a known accomplice of mine.

As far as we knew, neither the police nor the FBI had connected Denise to either of us. It was something we were thankful for, because it meant one of us could still move around freely without worrying about being recognized.

We weren't too far from Atlantic City and we were making occasional use of Clearwater's ability to influence the natural world to win at the craps tables from time to time. Not enough to call attention to ourselves, but enough to keep the heat on and pay the grocery bill. But while Denise was out and about, Dmitri and I were trapped in a beachfront cottage with nothing better to do than watch endless *Seinfeld* reruns and play cards.

Trust me. It wasn't as exciting as it sounds.

The fishing poles had been Denise's idea. She had picked them up for us one night after a particularly good run at the tables, and we'd been waiting for more than a week for the freezing rain to stop so we could try them out. Finding the sun out when we'd risen this morning had caused us to start acting like a couple of giddy schoolgirls and it didn't take us long to stake out a spot at the water's edge.

Now, a couple of hours later, we'd moved past mellow and were well on our way to being more than a bit under the influence.

As a result, neither of us was all that quick on the uptake when Denise showed up.

She wandered over without our realizing it, and the first we knew she was there was when she said, right out of the blue, "New Orleans."

I turned my head and glanced over in her direction, surprised to find her out there with us. I couldn't see her, the brightness of the midmorning sun rendering me as blind as a cave newt for all practical purposes, but normally I would have at least heard her approach.

I considered what she'd said and then decided that maybe my ears were playing tricks on me.

"Come again?" I asked.

"We need to go to New Orleans."

I shook my head. "No, we don't."

"Yes, we do." She said it slowly, as if talking to an errant child.

I reached over to my left and nudged the monster dozing in the lawn chair next to mine.

"Want to go to New Orleans?" I asked him.

Dmitri grunted. "Leave this lovely weather behind? Are you nuts?"

I smiled up at Denise, ignoring the glare I felt her leveling in my direction even though I couldn't see it. "See? New Orleans is a bad idea; even Dmitri thinks so."

I snatched a beer out of the cooler to my right and held it up to her. "Pull up a chair and have a cold one instead."

My offer was met with silence. I could feel the temperature around me drop a good ten degrees beneath the weight of her stare.

Not good.

I tried again.

"Come on, relax, Denise. Sit down and we'll talk about it, okay?"

I might as well have been talking to myself for all the good it did.

Her voice was calm and controlled, but I could hear the strain behind it as she said, "I'm leaving in the morning, with or without the two of you."

The sound of her steps as she made her way across the sand told me the discussion was over.

"Sounds like you managed to piss her off," Dmitri said. His tone held more than a touch of amusement.

"You think?" I shot back, but my heart wasn't in it. A cold feeling was forming in the pit of my stomach. Something was wrong; I could feel it in my bones.

I started to get up out of my chair and then hesitated. The joking with Dmitri aside, one thing I'd learned to respect in the few months we'd been living together in our little cottage was Clearwater's temper. She was pretty slow to boil, but when she went off, it was like Krakatoa in full eruption.

In other words, she was volatile as hell.

And right now, it seemed like she was on the verge of blowing her top.

Under the best of circumstances, pissing off a woman was usually not a good idea. Doing so to one who could turn you into a cockroach was even worse.

"Any idea what that was all about?" I asked Dmitri, my ass half in and half out of the chair beneath me as I wavered in indecision about whether just to let her cool off or to follow her back up to the house in the dunes behind us.

"Not a clue. But if I were you, I'd go find out."

"Turning into a regular Dr. Phil, aren't you?"

Snagging the beer from my hand, he replied, "I'm much better looking than Dr. Phil. Besides, somebody's got to keep the two of you from killing each other."

Great.

I grabbed hold of the guideline that he'd strung for me when we'd first arrived and, with one hand on the rope, followed it back up the beach to the house. It stood a good ten feet off the ground on a raised platform, designed that way in order to provide some protection from the angry Atlantic in the midst of the winter storms.

The wooden steps leading up to the front door were smooth be-neath my bare feet—worn down by the water, wind, and the passage of time.

Noise coming out of Denise's bedroom at the end of the hall led me in that direction. I found her inside and didn't need my eyesight to know that she was tossing what few belongings she had with her into a suitcase and preparing to do just what she said she would.

Leave us behind.

"What's going on, Denise?"

I was honestly bewildered. Sure, I'd been a bit of a wiseass back on the beach, but that wasn't anything unusual; wiseass was practi-cally my middle name. My behavior certainly didn't deserve this strong a response.

I thought of how I'd seen her late last night, standing before the big bay window at the front of the house, staring off into the dark-ness outside, a look of fear on her face.

"Decided you've had enough?" I asked.

She stopped throwing things around, and I knew she'd turned to face me when I felt the weight of her stare.

"Is that what you think?" she said, her voice trembling with sud-den anger. "That I can't handle it anymore?"

I raised my hands in surrender and took a step back. "I don't know what to think, Denise. That's the problem. You've been tense for days; you're short-tempered, you won't talk to us, and now you suddenly declare, completely out of the blue, that you're going to New Orleans with or without us. I mean, come on, what am I sup-posed to think?"

I waited for the explosion I knew was simmering beneath the surface, but, much to my surprise, it never came. Instead, I heard a sigh of frustration and the sound of the bedsprings as she sat down on the bed.

I walked over and sat beside her, quietly waiting.

"Sorry," she said eventually.

"No problem." And it wasn't. She'd been under a lot of stress lately, we all had, and the fact that we weren't ready to kill each other by now was a minor miracle. A little temper tantrum now and again was expected, in my view.

Besides, she was my friend. It had been a long time since I'd been able to say that about anyone.

"Want to tell me about it?"

A long moment of silence followed and I thought she wasn't going to say anything, but she surprised me again. "I'm having visions."

I tensed. The last time she'd had visions, we'd ended up facing off against a doppelganger and the vengeful shade of the sorcerer that had created it. The three of us had almost died in the process.

"Visions?" I asked, already knowing I wasn't going to like the answer.

I knew she was nodding, even though I couldn't see it. "I'm in New Orleans and something is chasing me through the streets, something horrible. I don't know what it is; all I know is that I can't let it catch me, no matter what."

Sometimes I hate being right. "Sounds to me like you'd be better off avoiding New Orleans altogether," I said.

She sighed. "That's the problem. I can't."

"Why not?"

"Because it just isn't done. Ignoring a summons from Gaia is like driving the wrong way down the highway at rush hour. There's only one way it can end and that's in disaster."

Gaia. Now there was a concept I was still having trouble wrapping my head around. Best I could understand, Denise believed that the Earth itself was alive, that it was the embodiment of an ancient goddess spirit, and that all life, human or otherwise, was linked to it through some kind of mystical web of interconnectedness. It was this divine spark of energy that powered her magick, she explained once, when I asked her about it.

Telling me she tapped into the Force would have made about as much sense. Then again, I wasn't the one who had to believe.

Still, just because she was content taking directions from Mother Nature, didn't mean that I was too.

"Needs you how?" I asked.

She thought about it for a minute, and I got the sense that she was choosing her words with care. "I'm not . . . really sure," she said. "I think I'm supposed to prevent something from happening, something really major, but I'm not quite sure what that is."

She explained that each of her visions had shown her the city of New Orleans wrapped in some kind of apocalyptic scenario. Destruction by fire and water featured fairly prominently, but she'd also seen it destroyed by war, famine, and plague. Clearly, they were all a warning of some danger to come and a summons for her to prevent it, if possible.

"But how do you know that?" I argued. "What if they're just lucid dreams brought on by something you read? Or something you saw on television?"

"Because dreams don't write on windows," she replied, but then seemed to regret doing so and wouldn't elaborate any further when I pressed her.

Write on windows? *What the hell did that mean?* I wondered.

We sat in silence for a few minutes until I decided to try a different tack. "Okay, I've seen some really strange shit over the last few months, so let's say I buy into the whole 'message from the Earth Mother Goddess' thing you got going on here. How do you know you're interpreting it right?"

Her answer was pretty quick and to the point.

"It's pretty hard to misinterpret apocalyptic disasters, don't you think?"

She had me there.

In for a penny, in for a pound, I guess.

"Okay, New Orleans it is."

She suddenly went still, like a deer caught in the headlights of an oncoming car. I felt that she was watching me carefully, trying to gauge whether I was serious or not.

After a moment, she said, "You'll go with me?"

I shrugged. "You followed me to New Jersey. Least I can do is return the favor and go with you to New Orleans."

My motivation was more than that, but now wasn't the time to explain it to her, as I wasn't yet sure that I could put it into words. Just thinking about her leaving made me anxious; it simply wasn't an option as far as I was concerned. If that meant following her half-way across the country, then so be it.

She turned and wrapped me in a hug, something she had never done before, and I responded in kind. I was acutely aware of her scent in my nostrils and the warmth of her body beneath my hands; it had been a long time since I'd held a woman.

"Thank you, Jeremiah," she whispered in my ear, before pulling away.

I let her go, wondering if she felt the same reluctance to end our embrace that I did.

HUNT

Denise called Dmitri inside and filled him in on what we'd just discussed. Upon hearing her reasons for wanting to leave, he agreed that it was a wise move. Ignoring the visions, he told her, could have disastrous consequences, and not just for the people of New Orleans. So with that settled, we got down to some serious planning, figuring out what we needed to do in order to close up shop here, deciding just how we intended to get there and what to take with us.

Given our decision to hit the road, I thought I'd be able to skip my afternoon tutoring session, but I soon found out I was sorely mistaken.

After we'd fled Boston together, Denise had taken it upon herself to improve my education with regard to the ways of the supernatural world around us, and not a day had gone by since then that we hadn't spent an hour in "class," trying to bring me up to speed as quickly as possible.

Our sessions ranged from formal lectures on how to identify a nukekubi in the middle of the day while it was in its human form to hands-on workshops like the time she had me track a wererat around the Newark shipyard in the middle of the night after three straight days of no sleep. That was anything but fun. Dmitri would occasionally sit in, giving his own unique perspective on the topic at hand, but more often than not it was just Denise and me.

Some days I looked forward to my lessons. Denise was a good teacher, with what seemed to me to be an encyclopedic knowledge of the unusual and the arcane, which meant that I always came away from our time together a little more informed than before. At other times it just felt like a colossal waste of energy. With the police on my tail, I didn't expect to remain free long enough to encounter a Malaysian Pennagglan, never mind need to know that the only way to kill it was to pour broken glass into its empty neck cavity while the head and internal organs were off feeding on someone in the dead of night.

Heading into today's session, I was pessimistic about it all.

Cross Mr. Miyagi, Yoda, and Merlin the Magician and you've got some sense of what it was like having Denise as an instructor. Learn by immersion, that was her motto, particularly for our hands-on sessions. She had a habit of giving me specific instructions without explaining the hows or whys behind whatever it was we were doing, expecting me to pick it up as we went along. What that really meant was that I'd usually fail the first few times, often spectacularly, and usually at my own expense. At that point she would patiently tell me what I had done wrong, walk me through the steps necessary to correct it, and then grill me mercilessly over and over again until I had it right. More often than not, this went on for days, as I tend to be a slow learner.

The whole "wax on, wax off" approach got on my nerves, I must admit.

That afternoon, after telling me there was no way we were going to miss our session, Denise led me back down to the beach. While we'd huddled about our trip, the good weather had slowly slipped away, leaving a gray sky and a chill wind that blew off the ocean with a vengeance. The smell of the mud flats on the wind told me the tide was out.

Denise brought me to the water's edge and then stepped back, saying, "Tell me what you see."

Cloud cover or not, I couldn't see a thing; I never could, not in broad daylight. Denise knew that and I knew she knew, so she must have been asking me to look at the world around me in a different fashion.

Confident that I'd solved the first of the lesson's challenges, I triggered my ghostsight.

The snow white blindness faded, leaving me looking out into a hazy world of gray. I could just make out the suggestion of the things around me, like faint sketches only half-drawn; the long rise of the beach to my left, the roll of the waves off to the right, and the blurry outline of Denise standing several yards away.

"What do you see?" she asked again.

This time, I answered her.

"Ghosts," I said.

And I did. About half a dozen of them stood a few feet away, watching us with the unblinking stares of the dead. They were surrounded by a faintly luminous silver white glow that made them seem to pop out against the gray haze of their surroundings, clear and distinct to my eyes, though whether the glow was something that they projected themselves or simply an aftereffect of the use of my special sight, I didn't know.

"Call one of them over to you," Denise instructed.

Since most of my work lately had been targeted at increasing my control and connection to the spirits around me, I wasn't surprised by her request, though I did wonder why we were doing this down on the beach. The dead followed me wherever I went. We could have done this just as easily from the warmth and privacy of the beach house's kitchen.

Yours is not to question why, I thought to myself, as I pulled my harmonica out of my pocket.

There is a theory in certain circles that ghosts feed off the emotions of the living, that by doing so they can regain, at least for a little while, some of what they have left behind. I don't know if that's true or not. What I do know is that they react to my music like it's a drug of some kind, a balm to the soul that helps them ease the pain they're feeling at being stranded between this world and the next. Like a junkie who refuses to give up his fix, some ghosts will sit there for hours listening to me play, until they have exhausted all of the energy it takes for them to manifest and they fade away into nothingness.

I spent a moment listening to the sounds of the world around me, the crash of the waves, the low murmur of the wind, trying to get a feel for the place, to sink into the here and now. That was one of the tricks Denise had taught me, and it had made this process a whole lot easier than it had been before. When I thought I was ready, I brought the harmonica to my mouth and began to play.

I'm not sure how it is that I know just what to play in times like this. I just do; the music just comes to me, like it's been sitting down there deep in my soul, just waiting for the right moment to come out, and this time was no exception. A low mournful tune filled the air, and as I watched, one of the ghosts, a tall, thin man with thinning hair, dressed in a cheap suit and carrying a battered briefcase, stirred and began walking in our direction, following the sound of my music.

I kept playing until he stood within arm's reach.

"Now borrow his sight, Jeremiah."

That, too, had become old hat. I reached out to put my hand on his shoulder, but Denise stopped me.

"You don't need that anymore, do you?"

She was right; I didn't. Where once I'd had to touch my target in order to borrow its sight, the weeks of practice had shown me how to do it from across short distances. The closer I was to the ghost, the easier it was to make the connection, and this distance should be no trouble for me at all.

I let my hand fall to my side and focused my thoughts. There was a moment of dizziness, startling in its intensity, and then the taste of bitter ashes flooded my mouth and I was looking out through the eyes of a dead man.

It's not what you'd think and certainly not what I ever expected. There's this incredible explosion of color, ten times brighter and more vivid than anything I remember from the days before I lost my normal sight. And the things they can see! The supernatural denizens of the world are clearly visible to ghosts. They see everything, from the fallen angels that swoop over the narrow city streets on ash gray wings to the changelings that walk among us unseen, safe in their human guises. The glamourlike charms that supernatural entities use to conceal themselves from human sight are no match for the eyes of a ghost.

But what has always struck me as the cruelest irony is that ghosts can see emotions pouring off the living as plain as day. It's like each one has its own wavelength, its own unique color, the same way light does when seen through a prism. And if that isn't bad enough, then there's the fact that it isn't just the living that give off emotions the dead can no longer feel for themselves, but average everyday objects, too. If it was important to someone for some reason, an object would soak up whatever emotions the living attached to it. A child's teddy bear might glow with the pure white light of unconditional love, while the hairbrush used to brush a woman's long glossy hair might reflect the scarlet eroticism felt by her husband as he wielded it night after night over twenty years of marriage. The more important the object was to its owner, the brighter the glow.

Down here on the empty beach there weren't any objects to focus on, and I'd long since gotten used to seeing Denise through the eyes of my sight. So I was starting to wonder what this was all about.

Thankfully, Denise didn't keep me in suspense. "This is a test of control," she said. "No matter what happens, I want you to maintain the link, all right?"

"Sure."

Piece of cake, I thought.

Which just goes to show how blasé I'd been getting about my lessons lately.

When I'd first met Denise I'd thought her talents had been restricted to simple things like fortune-telling and scrying. What I used to think of as parlor tricks. The term *hedge witch* just didn't conjure up images of Gandalf the Grey, if you know what I mean. But during our confrontation with the fetch and its sorcerous master, I'd seen some of what she was really capable of and had come to understand that Denise was a force to be reckoned with, a power in her own right. An affinity with nature wasn't just about plants and healing poultices. After all, earthquakes, tsunamis, and hurricanes were all part of the natural world as well. I just wasn't expecting to run into any of them on a sandy beach in New Jersey.

After all I'd been through over the last few months, you'd think

I would have taken Oscar Wilde's famous quote, "Expect the unexpected," to heart by now.

Denise retreated up the beach toward the dunes, leaving me standing by the water's edge with the ghost at my side. I could feel his interest waning now that the music had stopped, so I brought the harmonica back to my lips and played for a bit, strengthening the ties between us. Just when I was starting to wonder what Denise was up to, I caught sight of something moving down the beach toward me.

Or should I say under it.

Imagine a massive worm tunneling just beneath the surface, causing the ground to rise up several feet as it was displaced by the creature running beneath it, and you'd have some idea of what I was looking at. The fact that there were four of them headed in my direction didn't help matters either. My entire being screamed at me to run.

I fought down the urge while doing what I could to maintain my link to the ghost beside me, reminding myself that this was a test of control. If I lost my vision now . . .

The ground beneath my feet began to shake and tremble as the things drew closer, but I planted my feet and simply willed myself to stay upright.

Fifty yards.

Twenty.

Ten.

I was sweating by this point, wondering if I had made the right decision, as those four humps churned toward me with remarkable speed, and I prayed that I wasn't about to become lunch for some supernatural denizens of the deep that I hadn't yet learned about. Denise would have warned me if I was in trouble, wouldn't she?

At the very last second, the creatures, if that's what they were at all, dove deep beneath the surface, leaving the ground to shake for a moment beneath my feet. Then that too quieted down and grew still.

I grinned; my link with the ghost beside me remained intact, and I used my borrowed sight to focus on Denise and wave to her good-naturedly.

No sooner had my hand gone up than I was pummeled by a hurricane-like wind that seemingly sprang up out of nowhere. It knocked me to the ground and forced me to cover my eyes from the sting of the sand and grit that were carried along with it, but I recognized it for what it was, another test, and focused my concentration on maintaining my link to the ghost serving as my lab partner. The wind howled around me in a voice like a thousand banshees, but I refused to be distracted, and after a moment it died down as quickly as it had sprung up.

Still able to see, I climbed to my feet and turned to look toward the dunes. I saw Denise standing high atop one of them, watching my performance.

"Is that all you've got?" I shouted at her, grinning madly all the while.

Bring it on, sister, I thought.

Big mistake.

Denise raised her arms slowly over her head, and as she did the sound of the surf behind me suddenly faded. Instead of the crash of the waves against the shore, there was nothing but silence. At the same time, a dark shadow fell across the beach, blotting out the sun.

I turned to see a massive wave looming above me, a good fifteen feet in height. It hung there, trapped in that moment just before breaking, like a bull straining to break out of the rodeo gate.

Fuck me.

The wave broke.

Knowing I was about to be pulverized by a half ton of water

caused my concentration to slip. The connection allowing me to borrow the ghost's sight shredded like a wet tissue, and I found myself surrounded by a fog of brilliant white. I had time to take two or three stumbling steps in the direction I thought the dunes lay, and then that massive wall of freezing water crashed down upon me. The force of the wave knocked me off my feet and carried me up the beach in a twisting, tumbling roll before depositing me at the foot of the dunes and receding back into the sea as if it had never existed.

Spitting out seawater and gasping for air, never mind trying to remember which way was up after being tossed around like a rag doll, I pulled myself into a seated position, my head hanging between my legs, both literally and figuratively.

A voice called down from the top of the dune above.

"Looks like you lost your concentration, Hunt."

I spat up what felt like another lungful of seawater and answered with what was left of my dignity.

"Nag, nag, nag. You just wait. I'll get you for that."

Denise laughed, the first genuine laugh I'd heard from her in over a week. "Whatever you say, Grasshopper," she said lightly. "I think that's enough for today."

I waited until I heard her footsteps moving away from me before I muttered beneath my breath.

"Watch it or I'll sic a poltergeist on your ass."

Her honey-and-steel voice came floating back across the dunes.

"I heard that . . ."

I smiled. *Maybe things were going to turn out okay after all*, I thought.

Unfortunately, the universe had other ideas.

5

HUNT

We made good time that next day, driving west on I-78 across New Jersey and into Pennsylvania. There we picked up I-81 South and passed through Maryland and West Virginia.

We stopped to get some dinner in a mom-and-pop place just north of the Virginia state line. After weeks of TV dinners and fast food joints, a sit-down meal done the old-fashioned way tasted like heaven. Still, we didn't dare linger too long; you never knew who might be watching.

After eating, I convinced the others to give me a turn behind the wheel. Driving long distances has always been a monotonous chore for me, and being trapped in the car for so long with nothing to do but sit there and listen to the radio was driving me crazy. Besides, the two of them had both taken a turn at the wheel and needed the rest. Denise was reluctant at first, convinced that the lights of the oncoming cars would cause me problems, but I pulled out my trusty shades, slapped them on my face and told her I'd be just fine.

"Besides," I said with a grin as I took the keys from her hands, "I'm the one who can see in the dark, remember?"

Dmitri didn't care one way or the other, provided he got to stretch out in the backseat. Without his support, Denise's objections soon crumbled. Muttering beneath her breath, she got into the passenger seat while I slid in behind the wheel. My eyesight turned the night's darkness into broad daylight, and I had no problem seeing as I pulled back out onto the road. I turned the car's headlights down as low as possible to minimize their impact. I considered turning them off entirely but decided that a black car racing through the night without headlights was a bit too much of an attention getter.

The Charger was the kind of car I'd have loved to have owned in the old days, all brute force and pent-up energy packed into a sleek design, the kind that was built to eat miles for breakfast and ask what was for lunch. It took me a little while to get used to the way it handled the road, but once I had, I just relaxed and enjoyed the passage of time as the white lines disappeared beneath the wheels.

We hit our first patch of trouble about fifty miles or so past the Tennessee state line, still headed south on Interstate 81. I had the cruise control set a couple of miles an hour over the speed limit and was humming along with the stereo, minding my own business, when I saw the patrol car sitting on the median between the north- and southbound lanes.

Most of the other drivers on the road with me probably never even saw it as they zoomed past; the cop was pulled up off the road, hiding in the darkness of the emergency lane that bisected the median. With my altered sight I could see him as plain as day from more than fifty yards out. By the time I went cruising past him, I had the accelerator pegged right at the speed limit and made sure not to do anything that would have made us look out of place.

Or so I thought.

I kept my eyes on him as I went passed and got a good look as he pulled onto the highway a minute later.

"Shit!"

Beside me, slumped in the Charger's passenger seat, Clearwater stirred at my outburst and in a tired voice asked, "What?"

"Cops."

As I watched, the cruiser moved out of the far left lane and slid in behind me as smoothly as a shark cuts through deep water. The darkened windshield and reinforced front end seemed to give it a certain sense of malevolent intent, though that might have simply been my paranoia talking.

I checked my speed, saw that it was a few miles beneath the limit now, and hoped the cops were just headed for the off-ramp coming up on my right.

They weren't.

They'd remained immediately behind me even when traffic had opened up enough to let them switch lanes. I started to get worried. I felt my heart accelerate and took a couple of deep breaths to try to calm myself. It wouldn't do to go into this out of control.

I managed to get another couple of miles down the road before the cops hit their flashers, indicating that they wanted me to pull over.

Not good.

"How many?"

The sleepiness was gone from Denise's voice. That one word, *cops*, brought her out of her quasi slumber to full wakefulness in a matter of seconds.

"Just one patrol car," I told her.

For now.

Out of the corner of my eye I could see her sitting up straighter, though she didn't look back at the cop car behind us.

"Not a lot of choice, is there?"

The red and blue flashers split the night, coating everything with their garish glow.

I sighed. "Nope."

Looked like we were going to test just how good my new ID was sooner rather than later.

We'd talked before leaving New Jersey about how to handle certain situations and this was one of them. We'd agreed that it would be best to comply with any official request until it looked like we were going to be taken into custody. If that happened, all bets were off and we'd use whatever means necessary to get us out of there as quickly as possible.

My hands tightened on the wheel as the squad car followed me across two lanes and onto the shoulder. I'd been hoping they just wanted me to move out of the way and let them pass, but that clearly wasn't the case. I put the car in park, rolled down my window, and turned off the engine.

Footsteps sounded outside the window and a shadow loomed.

"License and registration, please."

"Of course," I said, nodding. I reached into the center console where I knew Denise kept the documents, pulled them out and passed them through the open window. From my position I couldn't see the cop's face, but I did get a look at his name tag. HENDRICKS, it read.

As he was looking over the license and registration, I was struck by the sudden urge to say, "These are not the droids you are looking for," in a deep commanding voice and had to clamp my jaw shut tight to avoid the nervous laugh that threatened to pop out as a result. *Now was definitely not the time to be looking like a psycho*, I told myself sternly.

The beam of a flashlight suddenly pierced the shadowed interior of the car.

"Mind taking off those sunglasses, sir?"

I did. I minded a lot, in fact.

I tried to talk my way out of it. "I'd rather not, Officer, if that's okay. I have an unusual birth defect that renders my eyes susceptible to bright light. The sunglasses protect me from that."

He chuckled. "Oh, that's a new one, I'll give you that." He put one hand on the open window and the other on the butt of his gun. His expression got all serious. "Take off the sunglasses, sir."

Oh, for heaven's sake! I stomped on my irritation, knowing that getting mad wasn't going to help the situation, and took off my sunglasses, bracing myself as I did so.

Good thing, too, for no sooner had I done so than the flashlight beam was in my face as the cop tried to check my eyes to see if I'd been drinking. The bright light stole all vision from me and I instinctively put my hand up to shield them.

"Holy shit!" Hendricks exclaimed, making no move to take the light out of my face. "You weren't kidding, were you?"

I wanted to slug the asshole, but managed to restrain myself.

The light disappeared. "Where are you folks headed?" he asked.

"Denver," I replied, before Denise could say anything. No way was I going to give our actual destination. "Is there a problem, Officer? I didn't think I was speeding . . ."

I let my voice trail off, hoping he'd jump in, and he did so right on cue.

"Did I say you were speeding?"

He was back to being testy again.

"No, sir," I said, hoping to stay on his good side.

Apparently I was too late for that.

"Your left taillight is out. That's a hundred-dollar fine in this state. I'm going to have to write you a . . ."

He never got out the rest of his sentence. In the seat next to me, Denise started screaming.

6

HUNT

Her scream ripped loose, filling the air in and out of the car with the sound of someone being tortured mercilessly. Just the sound of it sent a twisting cramp through my guts and made my skin crawl. All I wanted to do was get as far away from that sound as I possibly could. I would have done anything to make it stop.

Her screaming had the same effect on Hendricks as it did on me. He swore and fumbled for his gun, dropping my driver's license and registration inside the car in the process.

One glance at Denise told me everything I needed to know. She was jerking and twitching in her seat like an epileptic in the midst of a seizure. Her hands were up in front of her face, as if she were trying to ward something off, and her eyes were open wide and staring at a scene only she could see. Clearly she was in the midst of one of her visions.

Unfortunately, there was no way for me to explain that to Hendricks. He was staring into the car at Denise, his eyes as wide as the headlights on his patrol car, his mouth open, and I could tell from his stance that if Denise didn't stop screaming soon he might pull that pistol and start blazing away, just to make that horrible noise end.

I did the only thing I could think of.

My hand shot out and grabbed his wrist, pinning it against the windowsill. At the same time, I gathered my will and with a great mental shove pushed it in his direction.

The thunderclap of noise that filled my head was accompanied by a moment of pain so strong that I almost doubled over. I knew if I surrendered to it we were in deep trouble, so I fought against the blackness that threatened to drown me in its grip and hung on for the few seconds it took for it to pass.

When it had, I could see.

Not in that strange, new way I had since my encounter with the Preacher years before, but actual, honest-to-goodness sight. The colors I was seeing were muted, faded, as if they'd stood for too long under a hot desert sun, but I knew it was just one of the odd side effects of borrowing sight from the living and wasn't concerned by it.

Officer Hendricks, on the other hand, wasn't taking things so calmly.

"Aaagggh!" he screamed, adding his voice to Denise's, his hands flying up to cover his face. "My eyes!" he screamed. "What happened to my eyes?!"

Denise had once told me that borrowing another's sight was just like anything else: with a little practice, I'd get better at it. She'd been right, too. My training session yesterday had been proof enough. Months ago I needed to make physical contact in order to effect the link, just as I had done with Whisper in the days before we'd fled Boston. But now I'd gotten to the point where I could forge the connection I needed across a good-sized room without much effort and could even maintain it for an hour or more. It was harder with the living; I still had to be in physical contact to make that initial link, and if I lost contact the connection would fade within minutes, but it was better than it had been a few months ago.

Besides, minutes were all I needed right now.

We never get over being alone in the dark, not really. We just learn how to control and manage it instead. Lock a person alone in the dark for a few days and you'll see how quickly even the toughest among us can be reduced to that whimpering child we used to be, staring at the closet door, terrified of what's waiting in the darkness on the other side. Kidnappers don't blindfold their victims to prevent them from seeing where they are going, but to create a sense of isolation and hopelessness. If we can't see what's coming, we naturally assume the worst. Fear like that can be crippling.

Hendricks was no different from the rest of us, law enforcement training or not. He stumbled away from the car, all thought of using his weapon forgotten as his fear over losing his sight overwhelmed him.

I had a minute, maybe two, before the link between us dissolved and his sight returned. I needed to make the most of it.

"Dmitri!" I yelled, never taking my gaze off of Hendricks.

"I got her," came the immediate reply, and I didn't wait for anything more. He'd know what to do.

Scrambling out of the car, I rushed the cop like an NFL lineman intent on sacking the quarterback.

He was partially turned away from me when I slammed into him, the momentum of my charge lifting him completely off the ground only to slam back down against it a moment later with my weight atop him. The link between us surged back into place the minute I touched him again. I used full advantage of it to be certain he wasn't going to be getting back up again any time soon.

As Hendricks's hand went for the gun at his side, I rose up, strad-dled him, and punched him sharply in the face. When that didn't do the trick and he continued to struggle beneath me, I did it again.

And again.

And again.

Okay, so Muhammad Ali I'm not. But by the time I let that fourth punch fly, the cop was lying unconscious beneath me. Breathing heavily from the exertion, I let the link between us die and my own sight return. The train roared through my head and I knew I was going to pay for my actions later when the energy drain caught up with me, but right now I had a job to do.

The whole fight had lasted only a few minutes, yet the fear and adrenaline pouring through my system were going to leave me shak-ing and exhausted before long. We weren't out of the woods yet, though, and so I staggered to my feet and stumbled back to the car.

Denise's screaming had stopped, but that didn't mean things were back to normal. Far from it. Dmitri had wrapped his arms around her from the rear seat, holding her in place, but she was still bucking and shaking like a bronco, trying to break his hold on her. Her eyes had rolled up in her head, showing only the whites in an eerie mimicry of my own eyes, and she was emitting a strange keening sound that made me think of nothing more than strangled kittens.

"Do something!" Dmitri grunted.

If I didn't do something soon, she was going to hurt herself, per-haps severely.

I'd never dealt with anyone having a fit before and I wasn't sure what to do. I just knew I had to do *something*. So I slid into the car, grabbed her shoulders just above where Dmitri held her secured, and tried to get her to wake up by gently shaking her.

I might as well have tried cleaning the Augean stables with a toothbrush, for all the good it did me. I tried again, shaking her a bit harder and calling her name, with no better results.

Officer Hendricks wasn't going to stay unconscious forever. I hadn't hit him that hard, by any stretch. Knowing time was of the essence, I reverted to more extreme measures with Denise.

I slapped her.

Just once, but hard enough that I winced when I did it.

Hard or not, it did the trick. One minute she was struggling to break free of Dmitri's hold on her, and the next she slumped against him, all of her energy spent. It was like turning off a light switch.

That was good enough for me.

It was time we got the hell out of there.

A glance out the window to my right showed me Hendricks still lying unmoving by the side of the road right where I'd left him. He was near enough to the road that a passing car would easily see him, but not close enough that he'd get hit by a careless motorist, so I was reasonably comfortable with leaving him there unconscious.

I sure as hell wasn't going to bring him with us. Assaulting a cop was one thing. I didn't need to add kidnapping to my list of felonies, thank you very much.

"Hold on to her," I told Dmitri and waited for his grunt of acknowledgment.

When I got it, I started the car and threw it into drive, stomping on the accelerator. The tires spun in the dirt and gravel, and then we shot forward, bouncing up over the edge of the asphalt and out onto the highway.

As soon as we were underway, I killed the headlights. I could see better with them off, so I took full advantage of that fact now, racing away from the scene down the deserted road.

The Charger responded as if it had been made for this kind of adventure, the engine purring with the increased rpms and the wheels hugging every curve of the blacktop. As I drove I frantically tried to figure out my next move.

Denise seemed to be doing okay; her breathing was steady, and when I put my fingers against her throat I found that her heart rate was fairly normal. A few quick glances told me she wasn't bleeding anywhere, which was a relief. As near as I could tell she'd come through the experience without injury, at least physically. She was still unconscious, and I had no idea when she was going to come out of it, but for now maybe that was for the best. Her body had been through a significant shock and had apparently shut down to protect her from what she'd been through. Some decent rest was probably the best thing for her.

With my fears allayed in that regard, I could turn my attention to our next step. We were in trouble; that was certainly clear. Once Hendricks woke up, he was sure to report what had happened. That would bring every cop in the surrounding area down on our heads.

It would also make him look like a bungling idiot.

That thought drew me up short. Hendricks seemed to get off on that power and authority shtick; the thing with the flashlight was a perfect example. Reporting that he'd been overwhelmed in the midst of a routine traffic stop would be humiliating. Having to explain how I'd managed to get out of the car and knock him unconscious when he was armed and I wasn't would be even worse.

So maybe he wouldn't report it at all.

No, I thought. He'd report it, he just wouldn't tell the truth. He'd make up some bullshit story, something that would not only allow him to keep his image as a tough guy but that might even enhance it a bit. The incident would go from a routine traffic stop to a confrontation with criminals intent on plugging him full of bullet holes.

Which would make us not just fugitives, but armed and dangerous ones to boot.

Just what we needed.

I tried to remember if he'd just glanced at the license and registration papers or if he had read them carefully. If it was the former, he wouldn't have much to go on. The license was a fake and wouldn't help him at all, except to indicate that I had something to hide, and that had become obvious by the way I'd reacted during the traffic stop. No, it was the car's registration papers I was worried about. If he'd gotten a good look at them, the police would know the Charger was registered to Denise. That would be enough to drag her into this mess on a level she hadn't had to deal with previously, and she'd be labeled a fugitive just like me.

This trip had started out poorly and was quickly going from bad to worse. Given that we were still some five hundred miles away from New Orleans, that didn't bode well for what we could expect when we reached our destination.

7

HUNT

I stuck to the highway at first, wanting to put as much distance between us and Officer Hendricks as physically possible. We couldn't
outrun the police radios but we could make it more difficult for the
cops to find us by widening the search area. Getting as far south as
quickly as I could was the best way of achieving that.

The next fifty miles were tense, to say the least. I kept waiting
for lights to flash in my rearview mirror and for a voice over a loud-
speaker to tell me to pull over. Or, even worse, to see a helicopter
floating over our heads while trying to force us off the road. Thankfully, none of that happened.

By the time I hit the state line and crossed into Georgia, I was
starting to breathe a bit easier. We'd left one jurisdiction behind
and moved into another, which meant any pursuit would have to go
through an entirely new set of channels. If they hadn't tied the three

of us to the events in Boston back in the fall, we were probably home free at this point.

"I think it's time we got off the highway," Dmitri said, and I agreed. I took the next exit and kept to the back roads, steadily working my way southwest as I kept my eye out for a place to hunker down for the rest of the night. It didn't take long: about ten minutes after leaving the highway behind, I came upon the Happy Acre Motel. The sign out front said VACANCY and there were a dozen or more vehicles in the parking lot.

I parked away from the office on the far side of the motel lot, since I didn't want the clerk looking out the window and seeing me get out of the Charger. Having a blind man behind the wheel unnerved people, I'd discovered.

Go figure.

Denise had slept like the dead through the ride, without twitching or groaning even once. Nor did she stir when I shut off the engine. Now that I had a chance to think about it, I realized it was kind of creepy, actually, and I took a minute to be sure she was still breathing. Thankfully, she was.

Dmitri started to get out of the car in order to get us a room, but I stopped him.

"Let me do it," I told him.

"You're blind, Hunt. The clerk's gonna remember that."

"Yeah, that's the point. No one is looking for a blind guy. And besides, that's all they see, my blindness. They don't notice any of the other details. But if you go in there, she'll remember you pretty easily. It's not like you blend in all that well, ya know?"

It was true. There weren't that many men his size on the road to begin with, and if Hendricks had gotten a decent look at him it wouldn't be hard to put two and two together.

"Besides," I told him, "if Denise starts thrashing around again, I'm not strong enough to hold her."

He knew I was right and reluctantly agreed.

"Yell if you get into trouble," he told me and I nodded in agreement.

I got out of the car and waited for Dmitri to pass me my cane from the floor of the rear seat. Now came the hard part. Getting a room without making the clerk too suspicious. If a BOLO, or "be on the lookout," had been issued with our descriptions, walking into that lobby could spell trouble. Of course, that was still preferable to sleeping in the car, especially after the day we'd had, so I decided on the lesser of two evils and headed for the front door, a story already forming in my head as my cane tapped the asphalt in front of me.

The lights coming from the lobby windows messed up my sight, and by the time I opened the front door I was once again drowning in a sea of white. A little bell sounded as I came in and a voice spoke from somewhere in the back room.

"Be right with you."

I marched up to the counter, pulled some cash from my pocket, and laid it on the counter under one hand where it would clearly be seen.

"Good evening, sir, how can I . . . Oh! I'm sorry, I didn't realize you were blind."

What do you say to something like that? "Gee, I didn't either?" Or maybe, "Bully for you?" I mean, seriously, that's got to be one of the most useless statements in a situation like this and yet I hear it all the time. I just didn't get it.

I decided the best course of action was to ignore it. "I'd like a room with two double beds, please. And one away from the street, as I'd like to sleep in late."

"Of course. No problem at all."

She was nervous; I could hear it in her voice. I was hoping that would mean that she wouldn't ask too many questions. I could hear her clacking away on her keyboard as she looked for a room that met my specifications.

"Ah, here we go. I can put you in room 27, which is around the other side of the building, away from the street. Would that be all right?"

"Fine."

"Very good. All I need is some photo ID and a major credit card, and I . . ."

I cut her off. "I left my wallet in the truck that gave me a ride. I've got cash, that's all. Is that going to be a problem?"

I put a bit of irritation in that last sentence, as if all I ever got was a hassle from people like her. The angry handicapped guy wasn't the only card in my deck, but right now it seemed like the one that was going to produce the results I wanted as quickly as possible.

As expected, she got flustered at my tone and backpedaled. "Ah, no. No problem at all. I'll just make a note on the record."

She busied herself with getting some paperwork together—I could hear it rustling between us—and then she set it down on the counter in front of me.

"If you would just sign . . ."

Her voice trailed off again.

I didn't say anything, just stared in her direction from behind my sunglasses, waiting to see what she would do. If she left the form where it was, I'd simply sign it with a false signature, but my preference was to not have to sign anything at all.

She swallowed. "Ah . . . I don't think we really need a signature. That's fine."

The paperwork disappeared.

Score one for me. No one wanted to inconvenience the blind guy, it seemed.

She handed me my key, told me that a couple of local places delivered if I was hungry, and let me know that checkout time was noon the next day. I thanked her and left before she changed her mind about that paperwork.

I returned to the car, gave my eyes a minute to adjust, and then drove around the motel and parked directly in front of our room. I was pleased to see that the lights in the adjacent rooms were off. For the moment we were alone and unobserved.

We didn't waste any time. I got out and unlocked the door to our room, while Dmitri carried Denise in from the car. Laying her on one of the beds, he slipped off her shoes while I got her out of her coat. After that it was simply a matter of pulling the covers up to keep her from getting a chill.

I stared down at her for a long moment, wondering what was to come, and then decided that the question was far too big to deal with at this time of night. Instead, I took a hot shower, washing the dirt out of my hair and picking small rocks and bits of debris out of the cuts on the knuckles of my right hand, cuts I'd apparently gotten in my tussle with Officer Hendricks. Though necessary, the cleaning started them bleeding all over again, so I wrapped a washcloth around my hand and knotted it in place with my teeth.

It wasn't the best of bandages, but it would do for now.

Finally feeling more like myself again, I changed into a clean set of clothes and then switched places with Dmitri while he went to take a shower of his own.

When he came out he took the empty bed while I stretched out next to Denise. Then we all tried to get some sleep.

Somewhere around three in the morning, I woke up to the sound of Denise calling my name, her voice full of fear and desperation.

"I'm here. Right here," I said gently, reaching out with my right hand to reassure her.

To my surprise, she moved in close, putting her head on my shoulder and her arm across my chest, clinging to me tightly.

For a moment, I didn't know what to do.

Then I let my arm slip around her shoulder and hugged her back. Her hair tickled my nostrils and the scent of jasmine and coffee, that unique scent that I associated only with her, filled my nose.

It would have been pretty damn close to perfect if she hadn't spoken up again, her voice thick with sleep.

"He's coming, Hunt. He's coming for both of us."

I had no idea who she was talking about.

"Who's coming, Denise?" I asked her gently.

She mumbled something under her breath.

"Say that again. I didn't hear you."

But her breathing slowed and then deepened, and I realized that she'd fallen asleep again without hearing my question.

I spent much of the rest of the night lying there with my eyes open in the darkness, thinking about her answer. No matter how many times I heard it in my head, it always sounded the same.

"Death," she'd said.

Death was coming for us.

8

HUNT

We rose before dawn, wanting to make an early start of it. I watched from the motel room window as Dmitri prowled through the parking lot with a pocket knife. Thankfully very few customers had gotten underway at that hour and there were still several cars in the parking lot. Choosing one of the cars at random, he used the knife to take off the license plate and put our plate back on the car in its place.

Last night's encounter had been too close for comfort. As far as we knew, Hendricks hadn't had time to run our plates, but that didn't mean that every cop for miles around wasn't going to be looking for us at this point. We didn't need to make it any easier for them to find us by driving around in the same car with the same license plate, Dmitri explained. By switching the plates, we could at least pass a general inspection without raising too many red flags.

Human nature being what it is, I knew that if Dmitri simply took the other license plate off the car and didn't put anything in its place, it would be noticed a lot faster than if he replaced the missing one with our own. The eye is trained to notice change; an empty spot where the plate should be was the kind of thing that caught your eye. But if the eye saw a license plate where a license plate was expected to be, then very few people would actually pay attention to what was on the plate itself.

In fact, it might take the owner of the other vehicle from several days to a week before they realized that something was different. A few days would be more than enough time for us to ditch the stolen plates and figure something else out.

Or so I hoped.

It was the work of only a few more minutes to put the stolen plate on the Charger. Back in the room I found Denise was already up and about, getting ready for the second leg of our trip, and so I asked about what she'd seen.

"What was it?" I asked.

"What was what?"

"Your vision."

Her silence spoke volumes.

"You don't remember?"

"No," she said, and I could hear the confusion in her voice. "I had a vision?"

At first I couldn't believe that she didn't remember, but after questioning her for several minutes, it was clear that she did not. Nor did she remember her comments in the middle of the night.

While she grabbed a quick shower, Dmitri and I studied the map and tried to figure out the best route for us to take. Given the fact that we weren't sure just how much interest local law enforcement would show in us, it seemed safer to stick to the back roads for a while longer, at least until we put another state line between us and the Tennessee state police. We were able to trace out a route that would get us across the western tip of Georgia and into Alabama without too much trouble.

By just after seven we were on the road, headed southwest once more. We had another five hundred some odd miles to go, which meant a good ten- to twelve-hour drive, depending upon what we ran into along the way, and we didn't have any time to waste.

The morning passed without incident and we decided to risk getting back on the main thoroughfares, picking up Interstate 59 after crossing into Alabama. That continued the diagonal route we'd planned, taking us through Birmingham and the middle part of the state. We stopped for a late lunch somewhere north of the Mississippi line, then crossed the rest of the state and entered Louisiana itself.

We caught the first news report about a hundred miles outside of New Orleans. I was flipping through the stations, looking for something other than country music, when I landed on the tail end of a broadcast.

". . . another strange case of that mystery illness in New Orleans, this time a young woman in her twenties. Local authorities tell us they suspect some kind of a flulike virus, maybe even a mutated strain of H1N1, but tests have so far been inconclusive. This is Tyler Jackson, reporting live from New Orleans."

I cocked my head, wondering if I'd heard correctly. Unknown illness? New Orleans?

Denise was having the same difficulty in making sense of it that I was. "Did he say New Orleans?" she asked.

"Yeah."

I spun the dial, looking for another newscast, but eventually gave up without finding anything. It seemed we'd have to wait a little longer to figure out what was going on.

I didn't like it, but there wasn't anything I could do about it, so why stress?

At least that's what I told myself.

Unfortunately, things didn't work that way. The closer we got to the city, the more anxious I became. It was like my body knew something that my head hadn't managed to figure out yet and it was doing its best to communicate that information with the only tools it had at its disposal. The increased heart rate, the difficulty breathing, the inability to sit still for more than a few moments, all of which were evidence that my body was trying to tell my brain it was making a big mistake.

It didn't matter what I did to try to calm myself: the anxiety wouldn't go away.

By the time the city loomed ahead of us, I was a nervous wreck.

9

HUNT

We entered New Orleans from the east, driving south through St. Tammany Parish to the shore of Lake Pontchartrain, and then into the city proper across the Causeway. In the setting sunlight I couldn't see, so I asked Dmitri to describe the Causeway to me as we drove across. It wasn't every day that you found yourself atop the world's longest continuous bridge over water.

Dmitri was his usual eloquent self. "It's a long stretch of road over a big muddy lake."

Apparently I wasn't the only one tired of the long drive. I settled for rolling down the window and letting the humid Louisiana air roll across my face, imagining I was poling my skiff through a cypress swamp while trees draped with Spanish moss soared high around me.

And they say I'm not a romantic.

The mental exercise had the added benefit of helping to calm the anxiety I had been feeling for the last hour. By the time we reached the other side of the lake and entered the city proper, I was back to my usual grumpy self.

Denise began to work her way through the part of New Orleans known as Metairie, not far from the infamous 17th Street Canal breach that played such a big role during the flooding after Katrina. Unlike the average individual, I hadn't been able to watch the news reports as they'd come in during the storm and so I hadn't seen the pictures of either the flooding or the aftermath. At the time, I hadn't particularly cared; all of my attention had been focused on my search for my daughter, Elizabeth. But now that I was here in person, I was struck by the desire to experience it for myself. Call it academic interest, call it morbid curiosity; all I knew was that I needed to see it for myself, to get a sense of the lay of the land before we got involved in whatever it was that Denise's patron deity had in store for us.

I tapped Dmitri on the shoulder from the backseat.

"Mind if I have a look?" I asked.

He must have been feeling apologetic for his surliness earlier, for I felt him shrug as he said, "Suit yourself."

I'd borrowed Dmitri's sight before and quickly made the connection. Borrowing the sight from a Mundane makes everything appeared washed out, like a colored shirt left too long in the sun, but borrowing the sight from one of the Gifted like Dmitri is the closest thing I've found to being able to see normally again.

It took me less than five minutes of looking around to realize something about New Orleans.

It was a city of ghosts.

And I don't just mean the literal kind, although there were plenty of those to go around, too. No, what I mean is that New Orleans has a way of haunting itself, a way of showing its true face to those who are smart and clever enough to look for it and of hiding it away from those who are not, like a spirit that can be seen only by those who truly believe in its existence in the first place.

First there was the City-That-Was, an ephemeral sense of a time gone by that still lingered in a kind of mystic echo, one that would suddenly rear its head in the glimpse of a face in the window of a Garden District plantation house or in the swagger of a sailor fresh off one of the boats along the lakeshore. From the narrow streets and wrought iron balconies of the French Quarter to the above-ground cemeteries that dotted the city haphazardly, the past cried out for recognition.

Then there was the City-That-Has-Been, the spirit that stubbornly refused to bend in the aftermath of disaster, the remnants of what was left after the devastation wrought by the ravages of Mother Nature and the greedy nonchalance of the men who believed that nothing could ever harm their precious jewel of a city, no matter the warnings or the dire predictions that came before. Hurricane Katrina did more than just destroy a few billion dollars of property: it stole the innocence of the city's residents and snatched away their hope of the future, one aspect of the city murdering its own descendant before it had even been born.

Five years after the disaster and still the evidence remained: Block after block of destroyed homes, some no more than moldering piles of debris, others still standing but forever branded with that discoloration at waist height that marked the high point of the water's reach and, just as often, the markings of the searchers themselves in the aftermath, those ubiquitous National Guard unit IDs and numbers spray painted on the outside of the families' homes, noting the presence of their dead and the number that each house contained. Neighborhoods in the midst of rebuilding. Families making do the best they could. Like a cancer that couldn't be cut out, the ghost of that city had burrowed in deep and haunted the souls of those who remained, just as it would for a long time to come.

Finally, there was the ghost of the City-That-Might-Yet-Be. You couldn't see it all that well just yet, for it remained cloaked in darkness, hiding from the light. But if you turned a corner in that precious moment when the sun was setting and night was only just beginning to fall, you could see it there, struggling to get out, to show us that the old girl had some life in her yet.

The ghosts of the past, present, and future, all vying for dominance.

Denise began scouting around for a hotel that wouldn't ask too many questions, where we could come and go at will without being noticed. After driving around for a half hour, we finally found a place that looked like it would suit our needs.

It was called the Majestic, which was the height of irony, for there was nothing at all majestic about it. I didn't even need my vision to tell me so. The crack of the decades-old linoleum underfoot in the central lobby, the stink of mold and body odor that wafted off the walls, the tepid air that barely stirred as we passed through it, all those things told me the dilapidated old place had probably never heard of better days, never mind seen them. Calling it a roach-infested dump was giving it way too much credit.

The lights in the lobby, though dim, were still bright enough to keep me from seeing much even with my sunglasses on, so I kept myself to the left of Denise and let her motion subtly guide me along. I could have used my cane, but I didn't want to make it obvious that I was blind. We were a long way from Boston, but the proliferation of shows like *America's Most Wanted* meant it was best if we kept as low a profile as possible. Besides, the FBI had placed a fifty-thousand-dollar reward on my head, and in this economy there were too many people who would consider that easy money.

Dmitri went over to the registration desk while Denise and I waited, our backs turned slightly so that the clerk couldn't get a good look at either of us. Dmitri came back with the keys to two rooms on the third floor and the news that the elevator was "out of service." Given the state of the place, I wouldn't have been surprised if it had been that way for the last few decades.

Our rooms were at the end of the hall, though not adjacent to each other. It didn't matter; we had no intention of using that first room anyway. We'd rented it simply to keep the desk clerk from asking too many questions or remembering us for all the wrong reasons. Dmitri let us into that second room, the one farther down the hall from the stairwell. There were only two beds, but that wasn't a problem for us; in a place like this, one of us was always going to be on watch while the others slept. The rougher parts of New Orleans had always been, well, rough, and in the aftermath of Katrina they'd gotten considerably worse. I wouldn't have put it past the clerk in the lobby to sell us out to some of the local riffraff as an easy way to make a few bucks. If they looked for us in the other room first, we'd hear them. If they tried this one . . .

Dmitri settled down in front of the door without a word.

"What are you doing?" she asked.

"Playing guard dog," he said.

Denise was a smart gal; she didn't need him to spell it all out for her. But I'd forgotten about her quick wit.

"Nice to see that you know your place," she said over her shoulder as she slipped into the bathroom. I could imagine the mischievous grin she was wearing as she closed it behind her.

"Laugh away, sweetheart, laugh away," he called after her. "But when a pack of ravenous zombies bursts through the door, you'll be happy that there's a food source between you and them."

I thought it was a pretty good comeback, but Denise obviously didn't. She yanked open the door and said, "Sweet Gaia, Dmitri! Zombies are nothing to joke about. Especially here in New Orleans. What's wrong with you?"

At which point she shut the door again, leaving the two of us to wonder if she was serious or having another joke at our expense.

As I settled down to catch some sleep, I hoped like hell it was the latter.

10

HUNT

Dmitri woke me just after midnight for my turn to stand watch. The room was dark and so I had no difficulty seeing him there, crouched over me where I slept on the mattress he'd tossed on the floor earlier.

"Any trouble?"

I kept my voice low, not wanting to wake Denise.

He shook his head. "Some shouting from down the hall earlier, but nothing that concerns us," he said.

I climbed to my feet as he slid into the bed I'd just vacated. I knew he'd be asleep in seconds; at some point in his life he'd learned the old soldier's trick of snatching sleep whenever he could get it. In our months on the run I'd seen him sleep through noise that could wake the dead.

In the end, the night passed without incident; the marauding packs of ravenous zombies must have gone elsewhere for the evening.

We took turns using the shower to freshen up from our cross-country odyssey. With my hair still damp and a fresh set of clothes on my six-foot frame, I was ready to play psychic detective and track down whatever Denise's vision had meant her to find.

Provided I got a cup of coffee in me first, of course.

We asked at the front desk where we might grab a bite to eat, and the clerk directed us to a quaint old place a few blocks from the hotel. It wasn't much to look at from the outside; the window from the street was intentionally soaped over in big white circles, preventing you from seeing in, and the sign on the door simply read EATS. But once inside I was overwhelmed by the rich, thick smell of roasted coffee and crisp bacon. My stomach grumbled hungrily in response.

It was too bright inside for me to see much of anything, but the presence of the ghost in the corner was as clear as a light in the darkness. He was a grizzled old man, dressed in the whites of a short-order cook, complete with a spatula in his hand. He watched us the way the dead always do, his gaze full of such longing that I had to turn away and pointedly ignore him.

We chose a table in the back and were halfway through our meal when I felt Dmitri stiffen. We'd been together long enough that I didn't need to be told that someone had suddenly taken an interest in us.

"How many?" I asked, without turning my head or giving any other indication that I'd noticed the newcomers' approach.

"Three," he said, sotto voce, and then, louder, "If you're looking for trouble, I'd reconsider if I were you."

There was a brief snatch of laughter, as if the newcomers weren't worried by Dmitri's confidence. That meant they were either the size of small elephants themselves or stupidly overconfident.

My guess was the latter. If they wanted a fight, we could give them one.

I reached out to the old ghost sitting in the corner and, with the flick of a mental switch inside my head, borrowed his sight.

There was a flash of pain and a deep roar that swept through my consciousness like a runaway freight train and then I could see again.

I turned my head to look.

All three of them were large muscular men in their midtwenties with that disciplined sense about them that suggested a good deal of training, possibly even military in nature. Their hair was cropped short; they were dressed similarly in jerseys, jeans, and hiking boots; and they fanned out in front of us in an inverted V shape that, if things got ugly, would provide them with the best fields of fire without endangering each other. It was clear from how easily they fell into their roles that they had done this kind of thing before. The confidence in their stance told me that whatever was about to happen, they weren't expecting us to put up much resistance.

We'd see about that.

If it hadn't been for the fact that the one in front had a thick goatee I might not have been able to tell them apart; all three looked like they'd been popped out of the same mold. I found myself wondering if they were brothers or even cousins, maybe.

Through the veil of the ghostsight I could see a bright silver glow flickering around the edge of each of their auras. I'd never seen that particular manifestation before. It made me wonder. Were they human or something else?

I didn't know. That, along with their body language so far, made me a bit nervous.

Goatee looked us over, his gaze settling briefly on me and Dmitri before turning his attention to Clearwater. "The Lord Marshal would like to see you," he said to her.

Now I didn't know who, or what, the Lord Marshal was and

frankly I didn't really care. The way these guys came in, full of confidence and expecting us to follow orders like a bunch of trained dogs, pissed me off.

"That's nice and all, but I don't particularly care what . . ."

I never finished my sentence. Denise laid her hand on my arm, squeezing just hard enough to cut me off before I was through. I looked at her, the question plain on my face.

Into the silence she said, "We'd be happy to accompany you to see the Lord Marshal," she said, "provided you give us your word as his representative that we will not come to any harm, intentional or otherwise, while under his care and hospitality."

Her words had a certain ritual sound to them. I wasn't the only one who noticed, either, for Goatee raised one eyebrow before answering in a similar fashion.

"So swear I," he replied.

Apparently we'd left twenty-first-century America behind in favor of an afternoon romp through the Renaissance. Any minute now I expected them to start spouting "wherefore art thou's" and "by your leave's."

Denise smiled primly in Goatee's direction, and I had the clear impression that the score was Clearwater one, Goatee zero, but that could change pretty quickly. Especially since we didn't have any idea what this was all about.

We paid the check and got our coats. The old fry cook followed me to the door, so I was able to see the Expedition idling at the curb. A second vehicle waited behind it.

I snagged the sleeve of Denise's coat. "Are you sure about this?" I whispered. Agreeing to a meeting was one thing. Letting them take us to that meeting under their control was something else entirely.

Denise shrugged off my concerns.

"They've given their word under oath," she said. "We'll be perfectly safe."

I stared at her. Given their word? Hadn't she ever heard of lying?

Apparently not, it seemed, for she left me standing there alone and marched over to the lead vehicle. I looked over at Dmitri, but he simply stared blankly back at me. Was I the only one who saw a problem with this?

I'm gonna regret this. I know it, I told myself and then followed her into the Expedition, Dmitri at my heels.

The driver was cut from the same mold as the other three. He glanced up in the mirror as the three of us slid into the seat behind him, but he didn't say anything. Goatee climbed into the passenger seat, riding shotgun, while the other two rode in the second vehicle behind us.

No sooner had we buckled up than the driver pulled away from the curb and headed east, toward the Quarter. My connection with the fry cook faded, and I was left in the light, unable to see anything more for the time being.

The ride passed in silence. I was burning with questions, but I didn't want to ask any of them in front of Goatee and his companion for fear of revealing my ignorance. Knowledge is power, they say, and they were already quite a bit ahead of me in that department. No need to give them any more of an edge.

We drove for something in the neighborhood of fifteen, maybe twenty minutes before the Expedition slowed and then pulled to a stop.

"Wait here, please," Goatee said, and then both he and the driver proceeded to get out of the vehicle, leaving the three of us alone.

It seemed a good time to ask Denise what the hell was going on, something I did with more than a bit of fervency.

"Want to fill me in?"

She laughed. "You really are in the dark this time, aren't you?"

"And will continue to be unless you spill what the heck has been going on. We've probably got a minute, maybe two, so stick to the highlight reel, okay?"

She thought for a moment. "Okay. I probably don't have to tell you that cities like this attract all manner of creatures—Gifted and Preternaturals alike. They come for all the same reasons that normal folks do—better jobs, better opportunities, better chances to reach out and seize the American dream for themselves and their families.

"At least, the good ones do. The others have different things in mind, like hunting and feeding off of the one thing they are strictly forbidden to hunt—the Mundanes.

"To help prevent this, a system was set up to keep the overly aggressive species in check, complete with a means of imposing control over those who refused to abide by the rules. Around the turn of the century, a High Council was established in each of the major American cities, a group of elected officials who are in charge of making sure that those who choose to live and hunt and exist within its boundaries keep to the rules without violating them. Are you with me so far?"

I nodded my understanding.

"Each Council appoints someone to act as the Lord Marshal in the area under their control, a kind of mystical equivalent of the local sheriff in the Old West. It is the Marshal's job to maintain order within the city limits, see that the Council's edicts are obeyed, that kind of stuff. He has a team of wardens who carry out his requirements."

Now things were starting to make sense. It was the Marshal's job to vet any newcomers to be certain that they weren't involved in whatever mischief might be going on, hence our "invitation" to pay him a visit. It was the old "I'm the only sheriff in town" routine. He'd sent some of his wardens to collect us, knowing that they could handle any problems that might arise in the process, perhaps even to intimidate a bit if necessary.

Trouble was, I didn't intimidate easily.

As this so-called Marshal was about to find out.

"When we get inside, just let me handle it," Denise said.

Sure, I thought. *Right up until the moment they piss me off again.*

A few minutes later Denise got fed up with waiting. I felt her stir beside me and then the door opened. "Come on, I'm done sitting on my ass. Let's go find the Marshal ourselves."

See why I like her?

Denise took my arm and led me across what I took to be a parking lot and inside a building where it was only a few degrees cooler inside than out; it seemed the Marshal didn't believe in air conditioning. Dmitri followed close behind.

We hadn't gone five steps across the lobby before a voice spoke from a doorway to our right.

"Where the hell do you three think you're going?"

I recognized the voice as Goatee's, and from the sound of it, he was more than a bit pissed that we hadn't done what he'd told us to do.

"To see the Marshal. Isn't that why you brought us here?"

Denise's tone was equally clear: we'll do what we damn well please.

Goatee wasn't done trying to impose order on the situation, however.

"The Marshal is tied up at the moment. You're going to have to wait."

"Oh, no we're not!" she snapped, her anger finally spilling free.

In response, Dmitri moved closer, ready to intervene if it became necessary.

"The Marshal asked to see us and we've honored that request. But my patience has limits, and I'm not waiting around all day until he deigns to entertain us. I've got better things to do. So he can either see us while we're standing here or come find us later when it's more 'convenient.' Either way, I don't really give a shit."

Goatee laughed.

And not just a little chuckle either. From the sound of it, he threw back his head and guffawed at the ceiling like a crazy man.

I thought Denise was going to blow a gasket. She wasn't someone who enjoyed being the butt of anyone's humor, intentionally or otherwise. I waited for the explosion, but she must have pulled an extra helping of patience today because it never came.

Finally, Goatee got himself back under control.

"Aren't you the little spitfire?" he said to Denise.

That did it.

Denise's voice got very soft, something that was never a good sign.

"What did you call me?" she asked, and I felt the air around us stir with her anger.

Goatee began to look a bit nervous, but his ringing cell phone saved the day.

"Yes?" he said into it, then, "We're on our way."

Hanging up, he said, "The Marshal will see you now."

Saved by the bell.

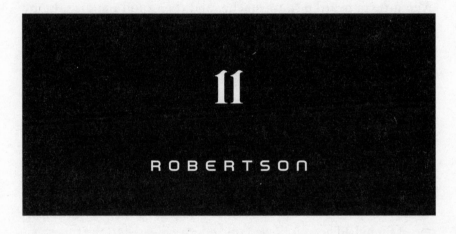

11

ROBERTSON

He's out there.

Somewhere.

Special Agent Dale Robertson stared out the window at the rain-swept Washington streets, his thoughts on Jeremiah Hunt, the man he'd been pursuing for the last several months. Wanted for the murder of a Massachusetts police detective, as well as at least a dozen civilians in just as many states, Hunt was considered a cold-blooded killer, and Robertson had every intention of bringing him to justice.

But he had to find him in order to do that and it was turning out to be more difficult than he'd anticipated.

From his many years in law enforcement, Robertson knew that most fugitives made the same simple mistakes. They'd call home to speak with their spouses or families, never thinking that the lines would be tapped or the calls recorded. They'd buy things with their credit or ATM cards, never realizing that each time they did so they were revealing their general whereabouts to the authorities who were searching for them. They'd dye their hair a different color, maybe even grow a beard or a mustache, and then spoil the disguise by wearing clothes that revealed their tattoos or other body art.

People were creatures of habit, Robertson knew, and it was often those habits that proved to be their downfall when they went on the run.

Hunt, apparently, was different.

In the wake of the events at the old Danvers State Hospital outside of Boston last fall, Hunt had gone to ground. More than fifteen thousand tips and sighting reports had come in to the office of the task force in that time period from various sources. Each and every one of them had been followed up and investigated to the fullest extent possible. None of them had yielded usable leads.

Hunt had been on the run for more than three months, and in all that time he hadn't made a single mistake. He'd disappeared from the radar screen so thoroughly that Robertson was half convinced he'd crawled into a hole somewhere and had then pulled the hole in after him.

Hunt had simply vanished.

But Robertson wasn't yet ready to give up. Not by a long shot.

I know you're out there, you bastard, and I'm going to find you.

There was a knock at his office door behind him.

"Come in," he called.

He turned away from the window to find a younger man standing uncertainly in the office doorway, a file in his hands.

"What is it?" Robertson asked, while doing his best to remember the man's name. *Dalton? Dawson? Something like that . . .*

"Um . . . Agent Doherty, sir. I'm on the task force? On the tip line?"

His voice rose at the end of every sentence, turning his state-ments into questions and betraying his nervousness.

Given Robertson's current mood, he found the man's hesitancy annoying.

"Are you asking or telling me, Agent?" he snapped at him.

Doherty's head pulled back sharply, doing a good imitation of a turtle trying to retreat into his shell. "Sir?"

Robertson shook his head and took a deep breath.

Calm yourself. Don't let that asshole Hunt get to you like this.

"Never mind," he said, extending a hand. "Give it here."

Doherty quickly passed the folder over and then stepped back. Without the documents to hold onto, he didn't know what to do with his hands. He clasped them together in front of his waist, then pulled them apart and let them hang at his sides. His left hand crept up and tugged at his tie, then smoothed his hair.

Robertson glared at him until the other man forced himself to stand still, then turned his attention to the file.

The report was one of thousands just like it that they received every day, a snippet of information that might or might not have anything to do with one of the Bureau's open cases. Each and every one of them needed to be tagged, filed, and assigned to an agent so that it could be followed up on appropriately, regardless of how small or insignificant it sounded. Any qualified investigator knew that a thorough investigation left no stone unturned and Robertson was more aware than most of just how valuable a seemingly unre-lated piece of information could be when it came to solving some-thing. He'd gotten the break he'd needed in the Reaper case last year through a tip that had come in from the phone bank and he'd learned to pay attention to even the most unusual tips. He glanced at the case designation in the upper right-hand corner of the report and his eyebrows rose at what he saw.

BRC-2009-8753.

The Reaper case.

He looked up to find Doherty watching him nervously.

"You have my attention, Agent Doherty."

"Um, right. Okay. Like I said, sir, I'm part of the task force and my current assignment is to monitor the N-DEx."

The National Data Exchange, or N-DEx as it was more routinely called, was a database that collected reports from 200,000 law enforcement agents from around the country at the local, state, and federal levels. Designed as a one-stop shop for criminal justice information and accessing millions of records from databases all across the country, N-DEx had proved to be a valuable resource in the short time it had been operational. An investigator could search the database with just a few clicks of the mouse and rifle through millions of records in minutes.

Robertson had assigned three junior agents to go through the latest N-DEx reports on a daily basis, searching for anything that could be even remotely tied to the Reaper case. He hadn't expected them to find anything of value, but he was too methodical to leave any stone unturned.

"That report," Doherty said, inclining his head toward the file in Robertson's hands, "came in yesterday. My gut tells me it's important, sir."

Robertson glared. "Your gut?" he asked, putting emphasis on the last word, as if the very idea were distasteful.

To his surprise, Doherty stood his ground. "Yes, sir."

Plenty of investigators relied on hunches, or gut instincts, to help them solve a case, so the act itself wasn't all that surprising. That a junior agent would bring a file to the senior agent in charge on just a "hunch" was, however.

Interesting.

He focused on the file. There wasn't much to it, just a single report from a Tennessee state trooper named Hendricks regarding a traffic stop he'd made on Interstate 40.

Robertson skimmed the first part of the report, taking in the background information. Trooper Hendricks had spotted a black Dodge Charger traveling west on I-40 with one of its taillights out. It being a slow month for citations, he'd pulled the vehicle over, intending to hand out a traffic ticket. Upon approach, he'd discovered that the vehicle was carrying three passengers, two males and one female.

He kept reading, still not seeing anything of interest until the phrase "temporary blindness" jumped out at him. He slowed down and focused on that particular section.

The female passenger abruptly began screaming and thrashing about in her seat. Not knowing if her behavior was a result of narcotics or an epileptic fit, I stepped back and reached for my radio, intending to call for help.

It was at that point that the male passenger in the front seat reached out of the vehicle and grabbed my wrist. When he did, I could see a row of intricate tattoos running up his arm. They started at the wrist and disappeared beneath the sleeve of his shirt. While I was focused on his tattoos he must have thrown something in my eyes with his other hand, for a sharp pain filled my head and I suffered some kind of temporary blindness that prevented me from acting further to detain the suspects.

Tattoos.

Hunt had tattoos running up both arms, Robertson knew. He'd seen them when he'd interviewed Hunt while Hunt was being held by the Boston police.

So what? asked a voice in the back of his mind. Thousands of people have tattoos.

And yet . . . and yet there was something here. He could feel it, too. He wasn't sure what it was, maybe the mention of blindness, given Hunt's own familiarity with that state, but something about the report made Robertson feel it was connected to the case.

He looked up to find Doherty watching him closely.

"That's it?" he asked.

Doherty swallowed, but again, held his ground. "Yes, sir. While it isn't in the official report, the officer who was forced to help Hunt escape from police headquarters in Boston said something similar, and I thought the similarity too important to ignore."

Robertson thought about it for a moment and then gave the file back to the junior agent.

"Get your coat, Agent Doherty. You and I are going to Tennessee."

12

CLEARWATER

Goatee led them out of the foyer they'd been standing in and up a broad staircase to the second floor. It was obvious that the building they were in had once been someone's home; Denise had caught sight of a kitchen at the end of the hall on the lower floor, and a quick glance in the two rooms they passed revealed them to be bedrooms. Given the level of dust she'd seen on the windowsills, she guessed that they hadn't been used in a while.

Goatee stopped at the third doorway he came to, opened it, and then ushered them inside with the sweep of one hand. The room had probably once been a bedroom like the others they'd passed but was now set up as an office, with a desk in the center and narrow bookshelves filled with thick texts flanking it on either side.

It was also empty.

"He'll be right with you," Goatee said and left them alone.

Denise was about to go after him when a door she hadn't noticed on the other side of the room opened and another man walked in.

He was medium height and muscular, too, with thick arms and a rough-skinned face. His red hair was cut extremely short in that military style commonly referred to as a flattop, and he walked with a slight limp.

Upon seeing his guests, he stopped short.

Denise could only stare.

"S-Simon?" she gasped out, right about the same time the newcomer was saying her name, and then each of them moved forward and Denise found herself wrapped up in one of her old coven mate's bear hugs.

When he finally let her go, he held her at arm's length and looked at her in amazement.

"Denise!" he exclaimed. "When they told me there was a new Artist in town, I never dreamed it would be you!"

Before she could puzzle through the implications of that statement, Simon turned to her companions.

"Dmitri," he said, to the big man beside her. "It's been a while." He extended his hand in welcome.

For a moment, Denise was afraid Dmitri wasn't going to accept it, the events of the past still standing like a specter between the two men, but then the big Russian grasped his former comrade's hand in his own and gave it a firm shake.

Denise found herself breathing a sigh of relief without even realizing she'd been holding her breath.

Simon extended his hand to Hunt. "And you are . . . ?"

Denise knew Hunt was about to give the fake name he was traveling under, so she answered for him. "Jeremiah, meet Simon Gallagher. Simon, Jeremiah Hunt."

There would be no sense trying to keep a secret from Simon; he was too damn good at ferreting them out, and if they were going to be here for a while it was best if they were clear about who was who right from the start.

Which brought her back to the reason she'd come here in the first place.

"The Lord Marshal asked to see us," she told him, as he let go of Hunt's hand and turned to face her again. "Do you have any idea why?"

Simon smiled. "I should hope I do," he said, with a slight smirk on his face, "particularly since I'm he."

It took her a minute to parse what he was saying.

Simon was Lord Marshal of New Orleans?

Perhaps that, more than anything else so far, made her realize that something was rotten in Denmark.

Just what the hell was going on around here?

Still grinning, Simon said, "Please, sit down," indicating the chairs in front of his desk. When they had, he asked, "Can I get you anything? A drink? Coffee maybe?"

Hunt practically started salivating at the word coffee, but Clearwater declined. Simon picked up the phone and ordered two coffees, black, one for Dmitri and one for Hunt, from whoever answered the phone.

While he did, Denise took a moment to study him. They'd been little more than kids when she'd last seen him; she'd been nineteen, maybe twenty, and he was just a year older. She'd left New Orleans eight years ago, but Simon looked as if he'd aged two decades in the time since. His face had deep lines cut into it, evidence that the years had been neither easy nor kind. The Simon she'd known and loved had laughed a lot; this Simon didn't look like he'd laughed in quite some time.

She wondered how much of that was due to his present position. Being the Lord Marshal of a major city was often a thankless and particularly difficult job.

Just how in Gaia's name did he end up in that position? she wondered.

Most of the Lord Marshals she'd known had been older men, individuals with far more experience than she suspected Simon had. He was a strong practitioner of the Arts, but she wouldn't have imagined he'd be in the running for a position like that, never mind be appointed to the job. It just didn't make sense.

The coffee came, strong and black just the way both men liked it, and they finally got down to business.

"All right, Simon," Denise said. "Tell us what on earth is going on."

"What do you mean?" he asked, feigning confusion, but she wasn't buying it.

"Come on!" she said, letting her annoyance show. "I'm not some fool off the street."

He shook his head. "I never said you were, Denise."

"Then cut the bullshit, Simon! We aren't in town more than fourteen, fifteen hours max and your boys show up, inviting us to have an informal chat with the Lord Marshal? Never mind making it clear that we're going to have that chat whether we really want to or not?"

They stared at each other for a moment, and Denise was gratified when Simon turned away first.

He blew out a long breath and then parked himself on the edge of his desk.

"First, I'm sorry if Spencer came across a bit strong."

He paused, giving her time to respond, but all she did was nod her head. She'd reserve judgment on Spencer for another time.

Seeing he wasn't going to get any more from her, Simon continued. "There's been some trouble lately and everyone is on edge because of it."

For the first time since entering the room, Hunt spoke up. "You mean the illness?"

Denise was shocked to see Simon's eyes narrow in suspicion as he turned to look at Hunt. Safe behind his sunglasses, Hunt didn't seem to notice.

Simon shook himself and then went on. "Yes, the illness. It started a few weeks ago and has been escalating rapidly ever since. As far as we can tell, only the Gifted are being targeted."

Denise thought about how quickly Simon's men had learned of their entrance to the city, the nature of the response that followed, and his use just now of the word *targeted*, adding it all up in her head.

"You think it's deliberate," she said.

Simon nodded. "I do."

They were all quiet, digesting that for a moment. Hunt broke the silence.

"Just what, exactly, are we talking about here?" he asked. "Gene warfare? Magical terrorism? How do they, whoever the hell *they* are, even know who to target, for that matter? It's not like you go around with signs on your heads, right?"

From the glance Simon gave her, Denise knew what he was thinking. She waved her hand in dismissal, as if to say, you can talk freely in front of him.

"That's the problem. We don't have any idea. One day someone is perfectly healthy, the next he's in a coma."

Denise frowned. "What symptoms are they exhibiting before that?"

"Nothing. Nothing at all. It's like," he snapped his fingers, "that. They are healthy and then suddenly, they're not."

Exasperated, Denise asked, "What are the doctors saying?"

Simon got up, moved around his desk, and dropped into his chair with a sour expression. "They're stumped. And lab test after lab test shows nothing unusual. From a scientific standpoint, there's nothing there. These people should not be ill."

That can't be right, she thought. "Obviously you just haven't found the right test yet. What about after the fact? You must have learned something from the autopsies, right?"

But Simon was already shaking his head. "The coroner's office hasn't said anything publicly, but I've got a man inside who's been keeping me in the loop. Apparently they can't even pin down a cause of death. For any of the victims. The autopsies have all shown the same thing: the victims were in good health when they died."

"Oh, this is just getting better and better," Hunt muttered.

Denise didn't blame him; she was starting to feel pretty uncomfortable herself. "Why not interview some of the survivors? Maybe they could tell us more about how they were feeling during the illness, and we can use that to figure out a new angle of attack."

But Simon was already shaking his head, and what he said next scared her more than anything else that had been said so far.

"There aren't any," Simon said, his voice full of weary resignation. "So far, this damn thing has a one hundred percent fatality rate. Which makes it even worse than the freakin' Ebola virus. If you catch it, you die. Period."

13

CLEARWATER

Denise couldn't believe what she was hearing. An illness that targeted only the Gifted and with a 100% fatality rate? It was practically unheard of in nature. If this thing was as deadly as Simon was suggesting, then it had to be man-made magickal or otherwise.

"Would you mind showing me the test results? Maybe let me look at a patient or two?"

Simon looked at her in surprise. "Of course; I can use all the help I can get. But are you sure you want to? If I were you, I'd be making plans to leave town."

This time it was Denise's turn to shake her head. "We're here for a reason and right now it's looking like this might be it. Taking a look at what you've done so far is the least I can do."

As a hedge witch, much of her power came from the natural flow of energies surrounding us all. She could not only see the flow of those energies but could also manipulate them to affect the physical world around her. When someone was sick, the energy within the body was interrupted. Often entire bodily systems would fall out of alignment. A hedge witch's magick was particularly suited to realigning those energies in order to flush the illness out of a person's system. That was why village wise women had been revered for centuries before the advent of modern medical science.

It seemed logical, given what she knew so far, that her premonitions had something to do with this mysterious illness, especially since healing magick was one of a hedge witch's basic disciplines.

But there wasn't much she could do until she saw the patients, she decided, so that was the first order of business. Maybe the fact that she was an outsider would help her see something the others had missed, something that might give them a direction to go in. She said as much to Simon.

"That, at least, we can do." He picked up the phone and told whoever answered that he'd be in the clinic. Then he led them back downstairs, through a connecting corridor, and into the building next door. Denise held Jeremiah's arm, though she wasn't certain if she did so to help guide him or to settle her rapidly fraying nerves.

Perhaps a bit of both, she thought to herself.

When they entered the other building they found themselves in a small lobby that connected to a larger, warehouselike space through a set of double doors. A small break room complete with a rumpled old couch and a Coke machine with a big dent in the center stood off to the left of the doors.

As they headed for the door to the makeshift field hospital, Hunt held back.

"I think I'll stay out here," he said. "No offense, but hospitals, or anything remotely like them, just aren't my thing."

Simon turned to face him, a frown on his face. "You've been

breathing the same air as everyone else for over a day now. If it's airborne, it's likely you've already been exposed," he said reasonably.

But Hunt wasn't swayed. "Maybe, maybe not. But I don't see any reason to risk it just the same. Besides, I'm not a healer. I'd just be in the way."

"All right. Why don't you wait in there?" Simon said, then remembered that Hunt couldn't see where he was pointing. He stood there in confusion for a moment, not sure how to handle the situation, until Dmitri came to his rescue.

"Come on, man," Dmitri said, taking his arm. "I'll keep you company."

As the two men walked into the other room, Simon led Denise into the clinic.

"We've got makeshift clinics like this all over town, with healers and spell-casters doing all they can to slow the pace of the illness. We've even sent some of the sick into regular hospitals, but no one there has any idea how to help them either."

Denise was barely listening though; she was too busy staring in shock at the veritable sea of patients in front of her. The room was filled with row upon row of foldable cots, the kind you can pick up in an Army-Navy surplus store for a few bucks each. She estimated that there had to be forty, maybe fifty of them total, and every single one of them was occupied.

That's when she noticed the silence.

The patients lay in their beds, unmoving. No one spoke. No one coughed or yawned or made any of the hundreds of other sounds you'd expect from a room full of people. There wasn't even a rustle of sheets as someone turned over. A room full of patients in front of her and not a single one of them was making a sound?

She felt the hair on the back of her neck stand up.

"Creepy, isn't it?" Simon asked, apparently realizing what she was thinking. "Every one of them is like that. One minute they're doing okay, talking and laughing, joking with their families, and the next they drop into a comatose state from which they never wake up."

He stepped over to a small table standing off to the left and picked something up, then returned to her side, holding out one of the objects he'd just collected.

It was a necklace, with a large piece of quartz crystal hanging from it like a pendant.

"I fashioned the crystal myself. Charge it with a little energy and it'll throw up a minor ward around you while you wear it. It won't be strong enough to stop anything larger than a small rock, but it will protect you from any stray microbes that might be floating around."

He slipped the second necklace he was holding around his own neck and then motioned for her to do the same with hers.

She followed suit, then directed a little of her own energy into the stone, charging it with arcane energy as Simon had instructed. Almost immediately she felt the whisper of an energy shield slide up over her body, like a second skin. Beside her, Simon did the same with his own pendant.

Satisfied that they were as protected as they could be, they headed toward the patients.

They spent the next two hours examining every patient in the clinic. For each one, it was the same. No external trauma. No visible evidence of bacterial or viral infection; no swollen glands, sore throats, stuffy sinuses. None of them had fevers.

And yet they lay there, eyes open and staring, not seeing anything. Their heartbeats were all steady, but extremely slow. The same was true of their breathing; they took one breath for every four of hers.

At one point during the afternoon Denise thought she saw movement out of the corner of her eye. She turned, hopeful that a patient had taken a turn for the better, but they all remained quiescent and still.

Must have been my imagination, she thought.

When they were finished with the last patient, a young woman about thirty-five with hair like muddy oil, Simon turned to Denise, a questioning look on his face.

"Not a clue," she said. "It's like you said: from a purely physical standpoint, these people shouldn't be sick. I'm not even sure what to do next, to tell you the truth. There are a couple of rituals we can try to see if we can get to the bottom of things, but if those don't work, I'm going to be out of ideas in a hurry."

14

HUNT

I let Dmitri lead me into the break room and find me a seat on the couch. I waited until I heard him settle into a chair nearby and then asked the question that had been hanging on the tip of my tongue for the last fifteen minutes.

"Who the hell is Simon Gallagher?"

To my surprise, it came out a little sharper than I'd expected. This guy set me on edge, like listening to a drill in a dentist's office go on and on and on, and I couldn't quite figure out why. He obviously knew Denise . . .

"Lord Marshal of New Orleans, apparently," Dmitri replied.

I didn't need to see the expression on his face to know he was giving me a hard time. I counted to ten, slowly. Then, "How do the three of you know each other?"

"I met him a few times in the old days, back when Denise and he were coven mates."

"In English, please."

He laughed. "Sorry, sometimes I forget that you're still wet behind the ears when it comes to this stuff."

I bristled for a second, but then relaxed. He was right; I *was* wet behind the ears. Hell, if I'd had a lick of sense or some good information, I never would have listened to the Preacher in the first place, never would have attempted that ritual without knowing more about it or what it was designed to do.

Of course, if I had, I probably never would have gone through with it and would still be wondering what had happened to my little girl, so maybe there's something to be said for jumping in with both feet, regardless of whether your eyes were open or closed.

Dmitri went on. "Mages can operate alone, but most of them like to be part of a Circle, or a gathering of like-minded mages who pledge themselves to support and assist each other. Circles are sometimes called covens, hence the term *coven mates*."

"So they worked together for a while?"

Dmitri shifted in his chair. "It's a little more complex than that. Joining a Circle is a bit like getting married. There's a ceremony, the ritual that ties you all together, and during that ceremony there are promises made, promises to support and protect and defend the other members of the Circle. But unlike marriage vows, which don't have much power beyond the words that are spoken, the promises made in the act of binding a Circle together are backed by an intermingling of arcane power that cannot easily be broken."

I didn't like the sound of that. "So Denise and Gallagher are still tied together in some fashion?"

That's where he surprised me. "No. Denise left the coven several years ago and severed all ties with them in the process."

"What happened?"

"You'll have to ask her. It's not my story to tell."

I badgered him about it for a few minutes, but he wouldn't budge, and he eventually turned on the TV to show the conversation was over. I wasn't sure why it bothered me that they'd known each other before; I just knew that it did.

Something to think on later, I guess.

With my curiosity at least partially satisfied, I leaned back on the couch and tried to relax.

Unfortunately, the dead had other ideas.

Now that I wasn't concentrating on puzzling out the connection between Denise and Simon Gallagher, I felt their presence. They were slipping into the room, not through the door, but through the wall behind me, the one that adjoined the clinic into which Clearwater and Gallagher had disappeared a few moments before. They appeared as vague wisps of light and motion that I saw more out of the corner of my eye than anything else. Hospitals attract ghosts like honey attracts ants, and I guess a clinic full of terminally ill patients would do the same, so I wasn't all that surprised to see them.

Their attitude, however, was not what I was expecting.

Ghosts don't normally pay too much attention to the living, at least not as individuals. It's the emotion we give off that calls to them and not anything related to who we are or what we do. Nine times out of ten they couldn't care less whether you're the butcher, the baker, or the candlestick maker, as long as you're breathing and giving them something to long for by the simple fact that you're on this side of the Curtain and they're on the other.

Normally.

Today was apparently one of those days that was designed to skew the bell curve way out of whack for the rest of us.

These ghosts were angry. Pissed, really. They seeped in from the clinic next door, and the temperature in the room dropped a good ten degrees from one moment to the next. They circled the couch I was sitting on and focused their attention on me so intently that the hair on my forearms stood up straight.

Still, getting glared at never hurt anyone that I know of and most ghosts can't pull enough energy out of the air around them to impact the physical world, so I wasn't too concerned. Angry ghosts are often like angry people; sometimes it's just best to ignore them and hope they go away. So that's what I resolved to do. I closed my eyes and settled in to wait for Denise to finish examining the patients in the next room.

Until the couch skidded three feet across the room.

"Quit screwing around, Hunt," Dmitri said.

"I'd be happy to," I told him, "except I'm not doing anything."

They had my attention now, that was for sure; any ghost strong enough to move a physical object of that size and weight was capable of causing significant harm if it chose to. Since I was already the focus of their attention, it didn't take a rocket scientist to figure out whom they might want to take their destructive tendencies out on, either.

One look with my ghostsight was all it took to confirm that I was in trouble. The ghosts had started to manifest around me, taking physical form. I knew it wouldn't be long before even Dmitri could see them. Because ghosts tend to fade with time, growing fuzzy around the edges at first and then devolving into formless shapes of light and shadow, I knew this group had been around for a while. They no longer retained their features or individual characteristics and appeared more like gleaming negatives of a person rather than the real thing. Their auras, though, were thick and black, the color of anger, and if there is any emotion more suited to channeling power, I don't know what it is.

Even as they swam into view, a wind kicked up, swirling around the room like some kind of miniature cyclone. The chair Dmitri was sitting in began to spin lazily on its axis and the television set in the corner was flung violently across the room to shatter against the opposite wall, all without anyone touching it.

"Do something, Hunt!" I heard Dmitri yell.

I knew it was only going to get worse before it got better; that's how these things always work.

No way was I going to sit still and let them have their fun. Call me heartless, but right then all I cared about was protecting our hides. If what I did sent them on their way sooner than they wanted, well, tough luck.

The tune was already forming in my mind as I pulled my harmonica out of my pocket and put it to my lips. One long discordant note got their attention; they pulled up short and stared at me with their dead eyes.

That's when all hell broke loose.

The couch lifted off the floor a good three feet and slammed down again, sending me sprawling. I held on to my harmonica though, and the minute I hit the ground I was playing for all I was worth, a swirling melody that danced to and fro like the devil on a hot summer night in a glade full of witches.

Okay, not quite that actively, but you get the idea. The ghosts couldn't ignore it either; the music caught them up and sped them along with the melody, until they were swirling around the room in a mad dance, forcing them to use their energy to stay on this plane instead of tossing it about the room like angry little children. Now it was just a question of who would tire first, them or me.

Thankfully they had expended most of their energy in the initial onslaught and so it didn't take long for me to leech the energy from them and stop the manifestations. As they faded away, the charged atmosphere in the room did so as well, until all the anger and misery that they'd called up with them slipped away into nothingness.

Quiet descended.

Into the silence, Dmitri asked, "What did you do to piss them off, Hunt?"

I had no idea.

As it turned out, it really didn't matter.

Angry ghosts were the least of our troubles.

15

HUNT

We did what we could to put the room back to rights and sat around a bit longer, waiting for the others. Eventually Gallagher sent word that their examinations of the patients were going to take much longer than expected and had one of his people show us to our rooms in the building next door. Our luggage had been delivered there earlier by another of Gallagher's men. Dmitri and I shared a pizza for dinner and then called it a night.

The next morning I found Clearwater already up and eating breakfast when I entered the kitchen just after seven. Dmitri was with her, which saved me the trouble of having to track him down as well.

"Good morning," he said, as I pulled out a chair and settled down at the table between them.

"What's so good about it?" I replied.

He laughed. "We're not serving life sentences for homicide yet, for one."

Leave it to Dmitri to get right to the heart of things.

I wasn't in the mood for cheery optimism though, and only grunted back at him in reply. I hadn't yet eaten, but the smell of bacon and eggs was making my stomach churn. I was irritable and more than a bit anxious as a result.

The night had not gone well. I'd awoken several times with my heart pounding and that sense of doom I'd felt as we'd entered the city hanging over me like a cliff about to fall on my head. Even now I could feel that pressure pushing at the edge of my thoughts . . .

Relax, I told myself. *There's still time to get out of here. All you need to do is convince them to go with you. That shouldn't be too hard.*

"I need to talk to you both," I said to them.

"So talk," Denise replied, her fork clicking against her teeth as she took another bite of her omelet.

I shuffled uncomfortably in my chair. I didn't think she was going to like what I had to say next, but it needed to be said. I thought about calling up a ghost in order to borrow its eyesight, just so I could see her face as we talked, and then decided against it. Maybe I was better off staying in the dark for this one.

As she waited expectantly, I debated just how to say what I needed to say. I finally decided that straight out was my best option.

"We need to figure out where we're going and then get back on the road. Being here isn't safe for us."

There was a moment of silence.

Dmitri cleared his throat and started to say something but Denise cut him off.

"You want to . . . leave? Now?"

She didn't sound as angry as I'd expected her to be and so I pressed on, figuring this was my chance to show her the logic behind my decision.

"Yeah, I do. We all should, in fact. Big cities are dangerous for us, you know that. There's too much potential for being seen, for being recognized. We should stick to the smaller towns and communities where there's less of a chance of running into a cop on every street corner."

"What about the people here, Hunt?"

I shrugged. "What about them? They're sick. So are hundreds of thousands of other people across the country."

"And you don't think we should be helping them?"

If I hadn't been so damned eager to have her see my point of view I might have noticed the tightness in her voice, the way she sounded as if she was struggling to hold something back, but I rushed on, heedless, and missed the one clue I had that might have told me what was coming.

"I'd like to, sure," I said, "but that's just it. I can't help them. Neither can Dmitri. Of the three of us, you're the only one who can, but since they've got their own set of healers, I honestly don't see why we should put ourselves in danger by staying."

She wasn't having any of it.

"I'm supposed to be here, Jeremiah."

"Says who?" I countered.

"My vision."

Just how was I supposed to answer that? It's like being asked if you were still beating your wife. No matter what you said, you were screwed. On the one hand, if I told her that I believed in her vision, I was dooming us to remaining here for as long as she felt necessary. If I went the other direction and told her that I didn't believe her vision actually meant anything, I was calling into question her entire belief system, which wouldn't win me any points either.

Still, I gave it a shot.

"That's not true, Denise, and you know it. Your vision showed you a city, that's all."

"A city I recognized as New Orleans."

We needed to leave. I knew that right down to the very core of my being. If we stayed, something bad was going to happen. Why was it so hard for her to understand that our time here was done? Why didn't she get it? I wanted to pound the table in frustration.

I tried to reason with her instead.

"If that's the case, Denise, then where are the flames? Where is the raging fire that you told me about, the one that consumes everything around you?"

She didn't say anything.

To drive home my point, I said, "Your vision showed you a city in flames, not one full of plague victims. These people are sick, Denise, but no one's spontaneously combusting."

Almost casually, Dmitri said, "Fire purifies. You root out an enemy; you burn out an infection. Maybe that's what she saw."

I could have killed him in that moment, but thankfully Denise waved away his comment. "I know what I saw, Hunt."

"I don't doubt it, Denise. I'm not questioning what you saw, simply how you're interpreting it. If we're going to go, we need to do it now, before it's too late."

I shook my head. "Besides, your friend Gallagher seems to have everything under control."

The minute I said it I knew I shouldn't have.

One offhanded remark.

That was all it took to turn the tide against me. The atmosphere in the room instantly changed. When Denise spoke, her voice was full of icy disdain.

"Oh, so that's it?" she asked.

"That's what?" I asked.

"You're jealous."

I recoiled as if bitten.

"I'm what?"

"Jealous. It's got nothing at all to do with those people in there, does it? You just want to get us out of here because you're jealous of my past relationship with Simon."

I couldn't believe what I was hearing. She'd had a relationship with Simon?

"Jealous? What the hell would I be jealous about?"

But she wasn't listening anymore.

I heard her violently shove her chair back and felt her looming over me in anger.

"Feel free to leave, Hunt, but I'm not going anywhere. I'm going to help those people in any way that I can. Not because I'm getting something out of it, but because it's the right thing to do!"

She stalked past me.

On her way out of the room she said over her shoulder, "Don't let the door hit you on the way out, Hunt."

I sat there, at a loss for words.

What the hell had brought that on?

Me? Jealous?

At last, Dmitri spoke. "You can be a complete ass, you know that, Hunt?"

I glared at him. "Shut up and stay out of it."

I heard him stand up.

"You're probably right, Hunt. There probably isn't much she can do for those people in there."

I knew he was pointing over his shoulder toward the warehouse adjacent to Gallagher's apartment.

"But the right thing to do is to try."

He snorted.

"If you had an ounce of brains in that thick head of yours, you'd do the same. Stop being such a self-centered jackass, Hunt, and think about someone else for a change."

He left me sitting there fuming.

16

ROBERTSON

The Bureau kept a number of Learjets in a hangar at Washington National, and it didn't take long for Robertson to arrange to have one of them carry him and Agent Doherty on their fact-finding mission to Tennessee. The flight passed without incident, and it was just after three in the afternoon when they disembarked at the McGhee Tyson Airport in Knoxville, obtained a rental car, and headed for the headquarters of the highway patrol district.

Much to Robertson's surprise, Agent Doherty was not only a good driver but he knew when to keep his mouth shut and didn't pester him with questions during the short trip. That was a good sign; maybe the kid would actually get somewhere inside the Bureau. He made a mental note to keep tabs on Doherty once the Reaper case was over.

They checked in with the desk sergeant, who informed them

that Officer Hendricks was currently on patrol and it would take fifteen to twenty minutes for him to return to the district headquarters where they now were. The sergeant sent a young patrol officer to get them both coffee and then directed them to an interview room where they could wait for Officer Hendricks's arrival.

It was closer to forty minutes by the time Officer Hendricks arrived. He entered the room with his hat in hand, curious why two federal agents had flown out specifically to see him. He was younger than Robertson had expected and there were several fading bruises on his face.

Robertson didn't waste any time in getting down to business.

"Is this your report?" he asked, sliding a copy of it across the table to Hendricks.

The other man looked it over for a moment, then sighed dramatically. "Yeah, that's mine."

The senior agent frowned. "Something wrong, Officer Hendricks?"

The other man looked up and met his gaze, his expression full of resignation.

"I just knew that thing was gonna come back and bite me in the ass, that's all. Shoulda kept my mouth shut."

That attitude wasn't going to help them at all, Robertson knew. He had to get the other man on their side as quickly as possible, and the best way to do that, it seemed, was to tell him the truth.

"On the contrary," he said, "that's the last thing you should have done. We're not here to cause you any trouble, Officer. In fact, we believe you have information that might provide a break in a major investigation."

Hendricks took a moment to digest what Robertson had said, then asked, "What investigation is that?"

Robertson saw no need to mince words. "The Reaper case."

Hendricks's eyes lit up upon hearing the name, but the special agent wasn't finished.

"We believe the man you saw was Jeremiah Hunt, the principal suspect in that case. If it was, you're frankly lucky to be alive, as he's killed more than twenty people in the last ten years, including several police officers. I'm hoping there's more to the incident than what you put in your report. Often it's the little, seemingly insignificant details that make the difference in capturing animals like this guy. Understand?"

Hendricks nodded vigorously. "I'll tell you everything I can remember."

"Take me through it, please."

Hendricks did so in a professional manner, explaining how he'd spotted the Charger headed south with a taillight out and the decision he'd made to pull the car over and issue a traffic citation. There had been three people in the vehicle: two males and a female.

"The driver was wearing sunglasses, if you can believe that."

"Sunglasses?"

"Yeah. Crazy, right? Guy claimed it was because he had some kind of health condition that made his eyes sensitive to the light. I made him take them off anyway."

Robertson leaned forward, suddenly eager. "What color were his eyes?" he asked. He'd seen Hunt without his sunglasses; it was a sight you weren't apt to forget. If the man in the car had been Hunt, there was only one answer that would make sense . . .

"White. Completely white. I'll never forget that as long as I live."

The state trooper actually shivered as he said it, seeming to be as creeped out by the memory of it as he'd been when it happened. Robertson didn't blame him; looking into Hunt's face and having those milky white eyes stare back at you was a downright unpleasant experience.

But it was Hunt. The eyes and the tattoos confirmed it.

"What can you tell me about the woman who was with him?"

Hendricks thought about it for a minute. "To be honest, I didn't get a real good look at her. Dark hair, narrow face, that's about all I can tell you."

Robertson drummed his fingers impatiently against the table-top. That wasn't what he wanted to hear. He had no idea who the woman was and that bothered him. That she was helping Hunt was clear, but Robertson didn't know why. Knowing who she was would go a long way to helping him answer that question, which in turn might lead them to Hunt.

But Officer Hendricks wasn't done.

"If she hadn't started screaming," he said, "he never would have gotten the drop on me."

Robertson's heart rate went up slightly as they got to the heart of the issue. He was close; he could feel it. He decided to pretend he didn't know what the other man was talking about in order to see if he could pull more details out of him.

"I'm sorry. Did you say screaming? About what?"

Hendricks's eyes got wider and Robertson felt his pulse suddenly speed up. There was more to the incident than what Hendricks had included in his report.

"What aren't you telling us?"

Under the close scrutiny of the two federal agents, Hendricks coughed up the rest of what had happened that night. He told them how the female passenger had started screaming and how the driver had thrown something in his eyes, maybe a dust or a powder perhaps, that had allowed them to escape when he was unable to see.

He was clearly embarrassed by it all and kept looking away during his explanation, which told Robertson that even now he wasn't telling the whole truth. There was still something else.

To Robertson's surprise, Agent Doherty decided to speak up at that point.

"Let me get this straight. You pull him over, the chick starts screaming, and in all the confusion he throws pixie dust in your face to disable you? Do I have that right?"

Hendricks mumbled something.

"I'm sorry, I didn't catch that," Doherty said.

"It wasn't pixie dust."

"Then what was it?"

"I don't know."

Doherty laughed, playing the bad cop routine to a T. "Of course you don't. You were only hit in the face with it and presumably had to clean it out of your eyes before you could see again, but you don't have any idea what it was. Does that make any sense to you, Officer?"

Hendricks was starting to bristle. "It wasn't like that. Wasn't like that at all!"

"So tell me what it was like then! And stop lying to me or I'll have your ass in a cell faster than you ever imagined possible!"

Robertson watched the exchange without a word. Doherty had taken Hendricks right to the edge and now it was time to reel him in.

As Hendricks opened his mouth to protest, Robertson leaned forward and said softly, "Where did you get the bruises, Hendricks?"

The question caught the man completely off guard, just as it was intended to. For a second you could see it on his face as he struggled to hold his story together and fit this new element into the overall fabric of the tale, but it was just too much for him and he finally gave up the ghost and sagged in his seat.

"He touched me."

It was barely even a whisper, but it was enough.

"He touched you? What's that supposed to mean?" Doherty

asked, his voice growing harsh, but Robertson waved him off with a quick hand signal. Now was not the time to break out the heavy guns. They needed skill and finesse at this point in the game.

Hendricks looked at Robertson, a pleading look in his eyes. "You guys are going to think I'm nuts."

Robertson shrugged. "Try us."

Hendricks sighed, then shrugged. "The woman in the front seat started screaming and thrashing around, like she was on drugs or something. I didn't know what was going on and so I put my hand on my gun, ready to draw it if necessary. When I was looking at her, the driver reached out and grabbed my wrist."

"And?" Robertson gently prodded.

"And I went blind. One minute I could see, the next I couldn't. Everything went completely dark."

Robertson had conducted hundreds of interviews during his time with the Bureau and had gotten pretty good at picking out the liars from those who were telling the truth. Hendricks wasn't bullshitting him; he really believed that Hunt's touch had done something to his eyesight.

"Then what happened?"

Another sigh. "The son of a bitch hit me. And kept hitting me until I lost consciousness."

That explained the bruises on his face and the delay in reporting the incident, which ultimately had let Hunt and his companions escape.

Robertson sat back and thought for a minute. "Did you feel anything when he touched you? A nick or a sharp little jab, perhaps?" he asked after a time.

Hendricks shook his head, but it was Doherty who picked up on his line of reasoning.

"You think he was drugged," the agent said.

Robertson nodded. "It's possible, certainly. He might have been holding a needle of some kind and jabbed you with it when he grabbed your hand. If he'd coated the tip of the needle with some kind of psychotropic compound, it could account for your sudden inability to see."

For the first time since he'd entered the room, Officer Hendricks seemed to buck up. If he'd been drugged, the fugitive's escape wouldn't have been entirely his fault.

"Would you mind submitting to a few blood tests, Officer?" Robertson asked, and the other man immediately agreed. It had been a few days, and any traces of whatever it was had probably long since fled his system, but it was worth a try nonetheless.

They spent a few more minutes going back through Hendricks's recollection of the events of that evening, but didn't learn anything more. Hendricks hadn't written down the license plate number before he'd been jumped, and the time he'd spent unconscious had wiped it from his mind. *It was too bad, really,* Robertson thought. If they'd had that plate number, they could've identified the car's passenger. That, in turn, might have led to some information on where Hunt was headed next.

When they were certain that they had gotten everything out of Officer Hendricks that they could, they thanked him for his help, suggested he take a few days off to deal with his emotional state, and let him get back to his regular duties. Once he had left the room, Robertson turned to his temporary partner.

"Well done, Agent Doherty. Well done, indeed."

The younger man practically beamed at his boss's praise, but quickly grew sober again.

"But now what?" he asked. "We know he's out there, but we knew that before coming here. How are we supposed to figure out where he went?"

Robertson didn't know.

Or rather, he corrected himself, he didn't know *yet*. But in the ten years he'd been hunting the Reaper, he'd been in this position many times, and something always pointed him in the right direction. This time it would happen as well. He just had to be patient.

17

HUNT

Dismayed at how poorly my conversation with Denise and Dmitri had gone, I kept to myself for most of the day, figuring that a little space would help heal the rift that had developed between us. My nerves were still a wreck, however, so I decided to do the tourist thing to make me forget about it.

I had one of Gallagher's people call a cab for me and asked to be taken into the city. With the lake on one side and the river on the other, New Orleans had always been flavored with the smell of dirty water and rotting vegetation, but since Katrina a stench pervaded everything, soaked deep into the wood and stone, a constant reminder of how close the city had come to drowning. The air was thick with moisture even now, in midwinter, and I wondered how anyone could live in this place year-round and not constantly feel the need to wash the slick film it left behind from their skin.

I did the usual tourist routine—caught a streetcar ride through the Garden District, had a po'boy for lunch in Jackson Square, sat for an hour or two in Preservation Hall listening to some excellent jazz.

By the time the sun went down, I was ready for the French Quarter and Bourbon Street.

Music filled the air: loud, raucous music that spoke to me of life and liberty, of want and excess, and called to me at some deeper, primal level, making me want to lose myself in its rhythms. Horns rang out, in counterpoint to the beat of the drums, and the lonesome wail of a sax rose above them both, drifting over it all from somewhere a few blocks away.

The streets were narrow, the buildings close together, with secret courtyards and hidden gardens scattered throughout the maze so I was never quite sure what I was going to find when I turned a corner. Light spilled from open doorways, punctuated by the gleam and glow of neon signs, but by sticking to the shadows and keeping my sunglasses on, I was able to make my way around pretty well. If I occasionally stumbled when I stepped into a pool of light, well, my actions didn't differ all that much from the antics of many of the street's other travelers and no one paid much attention to me anyway.

I wandered the streets and wherever I went, the dead went with me.

There was no need for me to call them; they came of their own accord, following in my wake like the children who followed the Pied Piper of Hamelin. Just a handful, at first, and then more as we moved through the night, until I had more than a dozen ghosts following me wherever I went.

They didn't try to communicate in any way, they never do, but just trailed along behind me, watching everything I did with an intensity that bordered on obsession. I was used to it and barely noticed, but I could tell their presence was having an effect on those around me. My fellow partygoers gave me far more space than any-one else, as if I were surrounded by a force field that extended out from my body for several feet, and the crowd inevitably started to thin out in any establishment that I stayed in for very long.

Still, I did what I could to enjoy the music and have a good time.

For months I'd been worried about showing my face, convinced that the moment I did someone would recognize me and turn me in to the authorities. I'd gone to ground in a big way, determined not to get caught until I figured out some way of clearing my name. But now, in the wake of the argument with Denise and the general sense of foreboding that had been plaguing me ever since I'd stepped foot in the city, somehow that didn't seem to matter as much. If I was recognized, so be it, I decided. There was more than a hint of fatal-ism to my decision.

The changes I'd made to my appearance would help a little, as did the sunglasses I used to hide my bone white eyes and the long-sleeved jersey that covered my tattoos, but I was still taking a chance by being out in public.

I tried to keep to the outdoor venues, the kind that occupied the courtyards between the buildings, where most of the lighting was focused on the stage or comprised of something like tiki torches, which weren't as invasive to the senses. It didn't take me long to recog-nize the undercurrent of anxiety, desperation even, that ran through the crowds. Everywhere I went the music seemed a little louder, the booze a little heavier, the partygoers a little too intent on tuning it all out. Once in a while I saw someone wearing a paper mask, as if afraid of catching the "mysterious disease" the news kept yammering about, but for the most part it was business as usual.

Later, I found myself wandering a bit farther afield than the tourists usually did. The streets were narrower, the shadows a bit deeper, and the few tourists hurried through as if they didn't belong.

The sound of a saxophone drew me in and I followed it until I found its source. An old black man with hair the color of wet snow sat upon a short stool, his horn to his lips. I even recognized the song, "Lover Man," by the great Charlie Parker. It was the kind of tune that started out slow and languid, a lazy ride on a peaceful river, and then sped up into a rousing melody that took real skill to play.

The old man was good, better than good, really, and it was a pleasure to sit on the curb and listen to him play. He started into another number right after finishing "Lover Man," one I didn't recognize, but that was fine too. His music picked and pulled at me, the way good music will, and I soon found myself with my harmonica in my hand, waiting for the right moment to join in, then riffing off his melody into a substrain all my own that rose and fell alongside his without missing a beat.

The dead began to gather around us in greater numbers, called by the music we were making. I shot a glance at the old man, wondering if he knew they were there, but if he did he paid them no mind and just continued in search of that elusive melody, that perfect refrain.

We played that way for a while, with only the dead for company, and when we were done we thanked each other for the privilege of playing together. Smiling, feeling better than I had in a long time, I pulled a twenty out of my wallet, dropped it into the saxophone case at his feet, and turned to go.

To my surprise, a familiar form stood waiting at the end of the street.

He was a giant of a man, even in death, towering over everything at just a hair above seven feet. His fists were like sledgehammers, his legs as thick as oaks, and he had the disposition of a junkyard bulldog that had been kicked one too many times and now intended to take the leg off the next person who came too close.

His real name was Thomas Matthews, though I'd only discovered that a few months ago, and I'd never called him by that name.

To me, he was simply Scream.

I hadn't seen him since that night in September when he'd helped me put down the shade of a sorcerer named Eldredge. The night Detective Stanton had died. The night the ghosts of two little girls, Matthews's daughter and my own, were finally put to rest.

What was he doing here in New Orleans?

I waved my thanks to the sax player and set off down the street, toward the spot where Scream was waiting. Before I reached it, however, he turned and moved away from me, looking back as he did to be sure that I was following.

All of a sudden the anxiety that had been plaguing me for over a week came back with a vengeance, but I didn't care. I trusted Scream; if there was something he wanted me to see, then I needed to see it.

We moved through the streets for several blocks, until I turned a corner and found myself facing a shallow cul-de-sac. A small wooden church stood across from me. The front doors were open and a faint light like that from candles drifted out from inside.

Scream had disappeared.

Now, I may not always be the sharpest tool in the shed, but even I was able to figure out that whatever it was that Scream wanted me to see had to be inside that church.

Still, I hesitated.

Me and the Almighty weren't really on speaking terms, you see. I'd never been all that religious in the first place and when my daughter disappeared and none of my prayers for her return were answered, I drifted further and further away. Then came the night when I sacrificed my sight and discovered that the world was full of creatures and things with a lot more power and majesty than I'd ever imagined. I saw demons and angels alike, the darkness and the light, and if they existed then I was pretty sure the Big Man Upstairs did as well.

The same Big Man Upstairs I'd cursed eleven ways from Sunday when I'd understood that He was not going to reach down and save my precious Elizabeth.

I hadn't set foot inside a church since long before I knew the truth about the world. I wondered what I would see if I went in now.

When I go in, I silently admonished myself.

Steeling myself for what was to come, I walked across the cul-de-sac, followed the path to the front door of the church, and with my heart in my throat, stepped inside.

No lightning bolt.

That was good, I told myself. Means you're too insignificant to command His attention.

Or He's just waiting until you're not looking for it, a sly voice in the back of my mind whispered.

Telling myself to shut up, I took a good look around.

The interior of the church was small; there weren't any pews, but you couldn't have fit more than a few dozen in the place. At the far end was an altar, a massive wooden crucifix hanging on the wall behind it. Candles lined the altar, throwing off soft light, but most of the rest of the place was shrouded in shadow, allowing me to take a good look around provided I didn't face the altar directly.

Somewhere between fifteen and twenty cots filled the church, arranged in orderly rows, and each of them held a sick man, woman, or child. In the shadows on the far side of the room, a nun sat with one of the patients, her back to me, her voice a low murmur in the otherwise silent room.

I remembered what Denise had told me about the people in

Gallagher's clinic and a shiver ran up my spine. It was downright eerie to see so many people in one place and not have any background noise, not even the sound of anyone's breathing.

What was going on here?

I knew this was what Scream had wanted me to see, so I moved forward, my footsteps on the bare wooden floor sounding uncharacteristically loud inside the small structure. I walked between the first rows of cots, glancing from side to side as I did. In each of them, I saw the same story.

The patients lay on their backs, pillows beneath their heads and their arms resting flat at their sides. The blankets on each cot were tucked in but not so tight as to hold them in place, yet none of them moved as I walked past. Every face was pointed directly upward. Each and every pair of eyes was open and staring, yet seeing nothing. It was as if they all had stopped to look at something above them for a moment and then had frozen there, unable to turn away.

It was creepy as hell.

What made it worse was the fact that none of these people even looked sick. Their breathing was even and steady, their color was good, and there weren't any signs of fevers or lesions or sores that you might associate with a biological agent of some kind.

There had to be something here that I was missing. Scream wouldn't have led me here otherwise. I could feel it nagging at the back of my brain, but whenever I tried to chase it down it just ran away from me.

Remembering the angry ghosts that had emerged from the clinic the other night, I made sure I had a clear path to the door in case I had to escape quickly and then cautiously threw that mental switch deep in my head, the one that activated my ghostsight.

A single glance was all it took.

I literally staggered under the shock of what I was seeing and was forced to grab onto the end of the nearest cot to keep my balance.

With my ghostsight, I see the world's true face. Nothing can hide from me; nothing can defeat the purity of my gaze. I can see through magick and glamours to reveal the real creature underneath as easily as I can see the state of a person's soul.

You've probably heard someone somewhere described as "wearing his heart on his sleeve"? Well that's a pretty good description of how my ghostsight reveals a person's soul; I can see it gleaming about a person, almost as if they are wearing a second skin. Some say that it is this form, this spirit, if you will, that remains behind when a person becomes a ghost, but I'm not so sure that's true. What I do know is that every living person I've encountered since I sacrificed my natural sight had one, and from time to time I've used the appearance of those souls to make a judgment call about who they were or what they were saying. Our souls are the mystical representations of our true selves and reveal us as we actually are, rather than the face that we show the world. We can no more change them than we can the DNA that makes up our chromosomal structure.

Which was all well and good, except for one minor problem.

The souls of every single one of these people appeared to have been violently torn from their bodies. Only the thinnest tattered wisps remained, and even these were fading quickly as I stood there and watched.

Their bodies might still have been breathing, but I knew they couldn't last much longer.

For all practical purposes, every one of those patients was already dead. Their bodies just didn't know it yet.

18

HUNT

I'll be the first to admit that the horror of it was nearly overwhelming. Facing off against angry ghosts and rampaging doppelgangers was one thing, but staring at a room full of people who will never wake up from their comas because their souls have been violently torn away was something else. What the hell could do something like that? I could feel my heart pounding in my chest, and my head hurt from the sudden increase in blood pressure. I knew I had to get out of there or I was going to be in serious trouble.

As I dropped my ghostsight and turned to leave, motion by the front door caught my attention.

Turning, I caught sight of the nun I'd noted earlier. She was moving swiftly toward the front door, her robes swishing around her as she went. I shouted at her to stop.

"Sister! Please wait!"

She ignored me and by the time I managed to thread my way through the maze of unconscious patients and reach the door, the cul-de-sac outside was empty. Whoever she was, she was gone.

No matter. I had no doubt that I'd seen what Scream had brought me to see. Now was the time to figure out just how far this problem extended.

I wandered around for a bit until I made my way back into a more populous section of the Quarter. From there I caught a cab back to Gallagher's.

Walking up to the building, I had to admit that it wasn't much to look at. Certainly not the kind of place I'd expect the city's Lord Marshal to be headquartered in. The clinic itself was a long one-story building that seemed to have more in common with a ware-house than a doctor's office. The walls were cheap stucco over brick, with windows lining the area just under the roofline. Attached by way of a short connecting corridor was the two-story house Galla-gher was using as both home and office. Like the clinic, it had seen better days, though at least it was missing the chest-high water stain that marked so many other structures we'd seen on our drive into the city.

Rather than heading for the house, I turned toward the clinic.

I had to see the patients.

A couple of Gallagher's men were standing guard outside the room, but they'd seen me in their boss's company and didn't prevent me from entering. Once inside, I had a flash of déjà vu as I stared at the rows of cots bearing silent, unmoving forms. If it hadn't been for the lack of the altar, I could have been back in that church at the end of the cul-de-sac.

Then and there, I knew what I would find.

These people were never waking up either.

Still, I had to be sure.

I walked over to the nearest patient, an elderly man with a small patch of hair combed across his skull, and stared down at him for a moment, hoping against hope that I would be wrong, that what I had seen in the church was some kind of weird hallucination, an anomaly that couldn't be explained but that was limited to just that particular group of patients.

Steeling myself, I triggered my ghostsight.

><del><

Fifteen minutes later I knocked loudly on Denise's door. I kept knocking until I heard her get out of bed.

"Who is it?" she asked.

"Hunt."

I heard the lock click and then she was standing there, staring at me in confusion.

"Do you have any idea what time it is?" she asked angrily.

I didn't know and I didn't care. We had more important things to discuss.

"I need you to come to the clinic right now," I told her, "so get dressed and go downstairs. I'm going to wake up Gallagher and Dmitri and we'll meet you there in five minutes."

Even half-asleep she was a quick thinker. "What did you find out?" she asked.

"Five minutes," I said and then turned away, headed for the other bedroom at the end of the hall. Two men stood guard outside Gallagher's door, thanks to his official status as the Lord Marshal of New Orleans. I told them I needed to talk to the Marshal and waited while they woke him up. When he stepped out into the hall, I went through the same spiel. He pressed me for details, but I told him it was easier to show him than to explain and that I would answer any questions he had once we were all in the clinic.

Thankfully, he left it at that.

Dmitri heard the commotion and was already coming down the hallway to join us. I filled him in as quickly as I could.

Less than ten minutes later the four of us were gathered just inside the doors to the clinic.

"All right, Hunt," Gallagher said. "We're all here. Now tell us what you've found out." He spoke in a whisper, as if afraid of waking any of the patients, despite the fact that none of them had moved or otherwise acknowledged anyone's presence since their arrival.

I gestured out at the sleeping multitude.

"They're not sick at all. They've been attacked."

I told them everything that had happened to me that night: how I'd been led through the streets by Scream, how I'd used my ghost-sight to see the patients' true condition while in the church, how I'd come back here to find the exact same thing.

They listened without interrupting me, though I didn't think it had anything to do with my oratorical skills. They were scared; something was feeding on these people, one soul at a time, and if that didn't scare the crap out of you, nothing would.

I turned to face Gallagher. "So what do we do about it?"

To his credit, he'd already thought through the implications and come up with a plan of action. Say what you want about him, he was a better leader than I was.

"We need to confirm just how widespread the situation is before we do anything. Maybe these are isolated cases or there's something different about the patients in these two facilities that we aren't seeing elsewhere."

He turned and looked at Dmitri. "Take Hunt to the clinics on

Jolene, Davidson, Babbage, and Green. Go inside with him and let him get a look at the patients, see if the situation is the same there as it is here. If anyone gives you any trouble, have them call me directly."

He faced me, a sardonic expression on his face. "My people and I have been trying to crack this thing for a month. You go out to play tourist and come back with more information than we've been able to come up with in all of our efforts combined. I don't know whether to hit you or hug you, Hunt, but I can tell you this—you have my thanks."

I was tempted to fire off a wisecrack, but surprised myself by taking his hand when he offered it and shook.

I pretended not to see Denise's smile.

"You've been out half the night. Are you up for this?" he asked, indicating with a wave what he'd just ordered us to do.

"I'm good until the sun comes up. After that, it will get harder for me to see."

"Then you'd best get going; you've only got about an hour."

We borrowed the keys to Denise's Charger and were on the road moments later. The chill I felt as we rolled through the streets had nothing to do with the weather.

We hit the clinic on Jolene first, as that was only a few blocks away. Five minutes was all I needed to confirm what I was beginning to suspect we'd find at all of our destinations: if the patients weren't dead already, they soon would be. A body can only live for so long once the soul has departed.

As it turned out, my suspicions were correct. We found the same thing at the clinics on Davidson and Babbage, and by the time we rolled into the parking lot of the one on Green, there was no doubt what we'd find.

Something was feeding on the souls of the Gifted citizens of New Orleans.

At the rate it was going, there wouldn't be any of them left by month's end.

As the sun came up behind us, we fled home, thoroughly dejected and uncertain what we should do next.

19

HUNT

I was roughly shaken awake by a hand on my shoulder shortly after sundown the next day. When I opened my eyes, I found Dmitri standing over me in the darkness.

"Get dressed," he said. "Something's come up."

It took me only a few minutes to do so, but by the time I emerged from the spare bedroom, Dmitri was gone and Clearwater was waiting for me in the darkened hallway in his place. The look on her face was a mixture of anticipation and concern.

"What's going on?" I asked, sliding my sunglasses on to protect my sight. The lights in the hallway were off, but there was enough ambient light drifting around the corner from the kitchen at the other end to start causing me some problems. It was like looking through a tunnel: I could see just fine looking straight ahead, but my peripheral vision was already lost and the whiteness was starting to creep

132

in from the edges toward the center. The glasses wouldn't help for long, but at least they would make the moment of transition a little easier.

Denise took my arm and led me down the hall. "The daughter of a man Simon knows has fallen ill. From the symptoms, it sounds like she's been the victim of one of these attacks. The trouble is, she's a Mundane."

I stiffened a bit at the way I felt hearing Gallagher's first name roll off Denise's lips and then shrugged it off. Whatever was going on with me lately, I'd deal with that particular bugaboo later.

But I couldn't shrug off the implications of what she'd said so easily. If it was true, if the girl had indeed suffered an attack from whatever had been feeding off the souls of the Gifted here in New Orleans, then that meant things had just escalated to a new level.

Please don't let it be the same, I thought to myself.

As we neared the end of the hall, my vision swiftly narrowed until I was left in a sea of white. I let Denise lead me downstairs and out into the night, where my vision returned.

One of the Lord Marshal's Expeditions sat idling in the driveway with the young guy with the goatee who'd picked us up on that first morning behind the wheel. Goatee's name turned out to be Scott Spencer, which just didn't have the same ring to it, if you asked me. Turns out I'd been right about the military service: he'd served two tours in Iraq before coming home to New Orleans to help his family clean up in the aftermath of the storm.

Gallagher gave him some instructions in a low voice and then we were off, headed through the city streets at a good clip. The revelations of the night before lay heavy on all our hearts, I suspect, but I felt especially bad for Simon. Even if he wasn't the father of that little girl, I knew it had to be hard.

Our destination turned out to be a large home about five miles east. There was a crowd gathered in the yard as we pulled in and parked. As we approached the group, someone at the rear of the pack saw us coming and shouted out in a language I didn't understand. In response there was movement within the crowd and then a pathway opened through its center, toward the house.

Apparently more than a few in the crowd recognized Gallagher. Several of them greeted him by name as we passed and many reached out to touch him, though whether it was a sign of encouragement for him or reassurance for themselves I couldn't tell.

One thing was clear, though.

These people trusted him.

Dmitri, Denise and I received our fair share of looks as we passed through the crowd, but they were of curiosity; no one appeared to mean us any harm. I suspected, though, that if Gallagher hadn't been with us, our reception would have been different.

A gray-haired black man with a worn and weary expression met us on the front porch where the light had been left off, perhaps for my benefit. I put him in his midfifties, probably the father of the family that lived here. He grasped Gallagher's hands with no little show of gratitude.

"Simon, thank you for coming so quickly."

Gallagher waved him off. "You knew I'd come, Pierre. Quickly now, take us to Rebecca."

Pierre nodded, then turned and led us inside the house. No sooner had I passed through the doorway than the interior lights rendered me unable to see, so I was forced to rely on Denise's help to find my way. There were more people gathered in the foyer and the sounds of their discussion quieted as we passed through and then started up again, hushed this time, in our wake. We were led upstairs and down a narrow hallway. I could sense people standing in doorways, clustered together in fear and pain, watching us move past, and my heart went out to them as memories of my own little girl surfaced. I knew what it was like to lose a loved one. I knew all too well what they were going through.

We were led inside a room at the end of the hall. I knew it had to be the little girl's, Rebecca's, room, for the grip Denise had on my forearm suddenly tightened.

"Stay here a minute," Denise said, and let go of my arm.

She moved off and I could hear her and Simon discussing the situation with Pierre, asking about Rebecca's symptoms, medications, the usual kind of briefing before examining a patient.

For the moment, I tuned them out.

As I'd adjusted to my blindness over the years, I'd become adept at knowing who and what was around me at all times. For instance, I knew without having to see him that Dmitri stood about a yard to my right, his presence coming through loud and clear on my mental radar. I knew, too, that Denise, Gallagher, and the girl's father, Pierre, were all standing close to the foot of the girl's bed.

Maybe it was the change in air currents or the way sound bounced off their physical forms; I don't know. All I knew was that I could trust my instincts when it came to this kind of thing.

And right now, my instincts were telling me that we weren't alone in the room.

There was something else in here with us. Even if I couldn't see it, I could sense its presence, something dark and dangerous, like staring into the eyes of a shark at the aquarium and knowing they were looking right back at you.

Goose bumps rose along my arms.

I moved a few feet to one side and reached out with my hand, patting the air until I found Dmitri's shoulder. Leaning forward, I said, "I need to see something."

He shrugged, which I took for permission.

I concentrated a moment, forging the link between us in my mind and then flicking that mental switch the way I'd been taught.

Pain exploded through my head, but I was ready for it and just breathed easy for a moment until it passed. When it had, I opened my eyes and took a look around.

The bedroom was decorated with posters of teen heartthrobs of television programs intermixed with drawings of unicorns, fairies, and, of all things, SpongeBob SquarePants. In other words, it was the room of a girl tentatively reaching out toward her teen years while still holding tightly to the things of childhood. Memories of my daughter, Elizabeth, suddenly filled my head and I had to force them away or I'd end up weeping in the corner.

The furniture in the room was simple enough: a bookshelf, a nightstand, and a bed. Paperback books and a series of porcelain dolls dressed in different period costumes filled the shelves, while a hamster cage stood on the nightstand along with an electric alarm clock. The hamster was curiously still, standing in the wheel inside the cage.

A young girl lay resting in the bed, the thin white sheets pulled up around her face and neck as if she were cold, despite the sweat that clearly stood out on her cheeks and forehead. Her long brown hair fell tangled and damp on the pillow beneath her.

Denise, Gallagher, and Pierre stood in a little cluster a few feet away, talking about the girl and paying Dmitri and me no attention.

The room was otherwise empty.

Yet I still couldn't shake the feeling that we weren't alone. Something was in here with us. I knew I was right. I could feel it, like that tingling feeling you get at the base of your neck when you know someone is watching you even if you can't see them . . .

I dropped my link with Dmitri and triggered my ghostsight instead.

That's when I saw it.

Something was perched on the edge of the headboard, staring down at the girl in the bed below. At first glance it looked like an elderly woman dressed in a chador, those loose black robes that covered the wearer from head to toe, leaving only the face exposed. But when I got a closer look I could spot the differences, starting with the fact that what appeared to be a black robe was actually the creature's flesh. What I had taken to be long, draping sleeves were winglike membranes that stretched from wrist to ankle. Its eyes were as dark as midnight and they stared down at the girl with a sick fascination.

The message those eyes were sending was loud and clear from my perspective.

It was hungry.

"What the hell is that?" I said aloud, pointing at the headboard.

They must not have been able to see it, though, for after a moment Gallagher asked, "What's what?"

Afraid to draw the creature's attention, I kept my voice down but didn't take my eyes off of it. There was no way I was letting it out of my sight. "That . . . *thing*. Right there! Don't you see it?"

"There's nothing there, Hunt."

But there was; I could see it as plain as day. Even as I watched, it stretched out its hands over the sleeping girl. The girl's mouth opened in unconscious mimicry of the creature crouched above her and from it a wispy blue haze began to slip forth. It drifted above her face for a moment, a blind snake searching for its prey, before being pulled steadily toward the open maw of the creature looming over her.

Denise must have sensed it, for I heard her say, "Wait, what's that . . ." though it was more to herself than to the rest of us. I heard her begin muttering the words of a working under her breath.

As I watched, the connection between the girl and the creature squatting above her intensified, the flow from the girl's mouth coming faster and thicker at the same time. As the flow of power increased, the girl's body strained upward in response, like a woman yearning for her lover, and there was something so obscene in that reaction that my stomach churned and it took all my will not to turn away. The girl's body strained upward, until only the top of her head and her toes were touching the mattress. Her body shook violently from one end to the other as twin streams of similar energy began to spill forth from her eyes and follow the other stream upward.

The creature sucked them all up with an obscene kind of enthusiasm, its dark eyes rolling back in its skull as if in ecstasy.

I couldn't let this continue. Heedless of what it might do to me, I rushed forward.

I didn't have a plan, didn't really know what I was going to do, I just knew that I had to protect the girl somehow. As I got closer I reached out and tried to grab it with my hands.

Faster than I thought possible, it lashed out with one arm, striking me in the face and knocking me backward to the ground.

While it seemed to be able to conceal itself from the eyes of my companions, it couldn't mask the fact that it had just knocked me halfway across the room. Nor could it disguise what it was doing to the girl herself. They couldn't see the energy flowing from her, but the others could see how she was arched upward, her body flailing about, lending credence to what I was saying.

As I climbed to my feet, my ghostsight showed me that the trickle of energy had become a raging flood, one the creature was struggling to finish. The more of that energy that the thing consumed, the weaker the aura around the girl became. The shimmering silver light that had surrounded her when I'd first arrived was growing dimmer by the second.

We had to do something and we had to do it quickly. If we

didn't, the girl wasn't going to live through the next few minutes, never mind the rest of the night.

My lack of knowledge was a major handicap here, because I couldn't even explain to the others what it was that I was seeing. By the time I did so the girl might be dead. I needed to let those with more experience with these kinds of things understand what we were facing, and I needed to do it in the next few seconds.

A plan formed in the back of my mind and I grabbed at it in desperation, not seeing any other way to do what had to be done.

Denise was out of reach on the other side of the room, which left me with only one option.

Gallagher.

Even as I turned toward him, I hoped like hell that I would live through the next few seconds.

I didn't bother taking the time to explain; we didn't have seconds to waste. I grabbed him around the upper arm with one hand instead and used the other to point directly at the thing that was killing the girl right before my eyes.

As he started to protest and tried to pull away from my grasp, I shouted, "Look!" and mentally pushed with everything I had.

I'd spent the last several years borrowing the eyes of the dead and had even recently learned how to do the same with the living. But in all that time I'd never once tried to share what I was seeing with someone.

Never mind doing it with a powerful mage who really didn't want me to in the first place.

Lucky for me, he wasn't expecting anything of the sort and I managed to get past his mental barriers and inside his head before he knew what was happening.

In that second I went blind as I forced my sight to override his and the pain exploded inside my skull, worse than anything I'd ever experienced before. Gallagher's innate defenses had sprung into action, snapping into place like mental shields, trying to push me back out of his head. It felt like being struck with sledgehammers from several directions all at once, and I let loose an involuntary cry of pain but refused to relinquish my hold. He needed to see what he was facing and this was the only way I could think of to pull it off.

Thankfully, my gamble worked.

I heard Gallagher gasp at my intrusion and then immediately curse as he got his first good look at what we were up against.

"The girl!" he yelled, his voice ringing in the small room. "Protect the girl!"

By this point I was starting to pay the price for my impulsive act. Pain filled my head, a roaring sensation that threatened to overwhelm my ability to think and to send me spiraling down into my own personal darkness. I found myself on my knees in the middle of that hardwood floor but I had no idea how I had gotten there. What I did know was that I couldn't hold on for much longer.

"Hurry . . ." I muttered, but I don't think anyone else heard me, for the room was full of shouting voices and the shrieking cries of something that should never have been heard by human ears in this world or the next. Or any other, for that matter.

I knew Gallagher would be fighting blind the moment the connection between us was severed, so I fought back against the encroaching darkness and the static building in my head.

The roar of an enraged bear filled the room, letting me know that Dmitri had entered the fight. Whatever was sucking the girl's soul, I hoped the combined might of two mages and a berserker would be enough to deal with it, because I was rapidly reaching my limit.

I clenched my fists in counterpoint to the pressure in my head and tried to hold on, tried so hard for so long that time just seemed to slip away and there was just me and the darkness, fighting for dominion.

The darkness at the edges of my mind crept closer and I felt something burst inside my sinuses, like I'd just taken a baseball to the face. It took me a moment to realize that I'd struck the floor when I fell the rest of the way. Seconds later a warm trickle began leaking from my nose as a harsh buzzing filled my ears, drowning out the sounds of those fighting in the room around me. Eventually, the darkness became too overwhelming and at last I gave up, letting myself be swept away on the tide of oblivion.

20

ROBERTSON

Finally, after months of successfully eluding them, Hunt had made a mistake.

Robertson had known it was going to happen: sooner or later, even the best of them fucked up. Not that Hunt fit into that category, but still, you had to respect the man for managing to stay on the run for so long. Which was why Robertson was so surprised at how this one had gone down. After all, Hunt hadn't seemed like the partying type. Yet that's exactly what proved to be his downfall. He was seen by a retired cop hanging out at a local music hall in the Quarter. That was just the kind of witness Robertson could get behind, a guy who could think on his feet and who was smart enough to let the professionals handle the takedown.

It had been the weirdness surrounding the guy that had caught the retired officer's attention.

"It was like he had this magnetic field around him," he said on the phone with Robertson, "pushing everybody else away from him. It didn't matter where he went, nobody came within five feet of the guy."

At first the witness wasn't positive he'd ID'd him correctly. Hunt had dyed his hair and grown a beard to disguise himself and had even worn a long-sleeved shirt to hide his tattoos, but the witness had seen them when Hunt had pushed his sleeves up for a moment. The ex-cop had the presence of mind to snap a picture with his cell phone and then later match that with the Most Wanted poster on the FBI Web site. Convinced he'd spotted a top ten fugitive, the cop called the local FBI office and reported the sighting. When a copy of that cell phone image arrived in his e-mail in-box, Robertson wasted no time in getting his pilot to turn around and head for New Orleans.

Once there, a team was hastily assembled. It consisted of a mix of local agents and men that Robertson brought with him from Washington. One group was sent to wander the Quarter on the off chance they ran into Hunt again. The other group was deployed in two-man teams and spent forty-eight hours checking the hotels that were a short cab ride from the Quarter, the general consensus being that Hunt, as a fugitive, would have wanted to lose himself among the tourists. When the obvious choices hadn't produced any results, Robertson ordered every hotel in the city to be checked, regardless of how much time or man power it took. He'd settle up with the financial folks later; right now there was no way he was going to let Hunt slip through his fingers again.

To prove just how serious he was about the situation, Robertson partnered with Agent Doherty and took to the streets himself. The two of them were currently working through the list they'd been given for the day, a series of second-rate hotels and flophouses just north of the Mississippi River.

The hotel he currently stood in front of was called the Majestic, but that appellation must have been a holdover from the good old days, for there was nothing majestic about the place now. It was just the kind of rat hole that he could imagine a cop killer like Hunt hiding in, and Robertson felt a short surge of anticipation as he crossed the lobby toward the clerk behind the registration desk.

"Have you seen this man?" Robertson asked him, holding out the photograph so the clerk could see it.

The other man never even looked up from the old black-and-white television he was watching. Didn't even do so much as glance at the photo before shaking his head and saying, "Nope. Never seen him before."

That wouldn't do, Robertson thought, pursing his lips in disapproval. *Wouldn't do at all.*

The clerk was as run-down as the hotel itself, all thin limbs and pasty white skin. Probably hadn't worked out a day in his life, something that Robertson himself pursued with a dedication that bordered on religion.

Without any warning, Robertson reached out, grabbed the other man by his greasy hair, and slammed his head down on the top of the registration desk.

"Oww!" the clerk cried out.

He tried to get up, but Robertson wouldn't let him, holding his head down against the countertop with the strength of one hand. The FBI agent leaned over and got nose to nose with the clerk, staring him directly in the eye.

"Do I have your attention now, you little piece of shit?" he asked in a tone of voice that was scarier for how calm it was.

The clerk nodded vigorously, too worried about what was going to come next to speak.

Robertson produced the photo once more, holding it where the clerk could see it.

"Have you seen this man?"

The clerk took one look and nodded vigorously. "Yeah, I think so. His hair is blond now, though."

Robertson smiled.

Gotcha!

He pulled his hand back, letting the other man straighten up and try to regain some of his dignity. After a moment he said, "You were saying?"

The clerk visibly swallowed, clearly afraid. Robertson's smile grew wider at the sight.

"Um . . . yeah, yeah I've seen him. He stayed for a night and then checked out telephonically the next morning with that other guy and the woman he came in with. Someone picked up their luggage a short time later."

The other guy was probably Dmitri Alexandrov, the man who'd helped Hunt escape from police custody in Boston.

"Did you catch the woman's name?"

The clerk shook his head.

Robertson sighed. "Would have been too easy that way, I guess," he muttered, more to himself than anyone else.

But the clerk heard him and this time it was his turn to smile.

"I didn't remember her name, because I didn't need to. She signed for the room."

He stepped into the back room for a moment. When he returned, he had a registration form in his hand. He handed it to Robertson.

"Denise Clearwater," the clerk said, with one of those eager-beaver expressions that always made Robertson want to puke. "That's her. I'm sure of it."

Robertson hesitated. "How can you be sure this is hers?"

The clerk's eyes practically bugged out. "Hot chicks like that don't come in here very often, man. Trust me, you remember them when they do."

Robertson laughed aloud before turning to Agent Doherty, who had been standing behind him, observing the whole process without saying a word.

"Get me everything you can on a Denise Clearwater," he told the younger agent.

Here I come, Hunt. Here I come.

21

HUNT

I awoke to find myself in bed in a darkened room. My head hurt, and I seemed to have some kind of thick bandage on my nose. At least I was breathing, which was something.

I shifted in the bed and the moment I did so a voice spoke out of the darkness on the other side of the room.

"She didn't make it."

I turned my head and found Dmitri sitting in a chair near the door, watching me. It said something about my mental state that it took me a few minutes to remember that his berserker abilities would probably make it as easy for him to see in the dark as I could. Then what he said finally sank in and I was all but overwhelmed with rage and frustration.

I hadn't even known the girl, but her passing brought back

memories of another time, another place, and that wasn't something I wanted to experience.

After a moment, I asked, "What happened to that *thing?*"

I didn't know what to call it, but I figured he'd know what I was talking about.

He did.

"Dead." The flat way he said it spoke volumes and I breathed a quick sigh of relief. At least it wouldn't be preying on any other children . . .

"Clearwater?" I asked once I had control of myself, and then, after a second's hesitation, "Gallagher?"

Dmitri nodded, as if I'd just confirmed something for him, but he didn't say anything other than to answer my question. "They're fine. Both of them."

Relief swept through me.

He was quiet for a moment, perhaps weighing what it was he intended to say, and then, "Pretty gutsy move, Hunt. Have to say it surprised me, after that shit the other day."

I wasn't too proud of my actions the other morning, but I'd be damned if I let him know that.

"Yeah, well, I'm full of surprises," I said without opening my eyes. The pain in my head was starting to grow worse and I just wanted him to go away. I had a hunch that wasn't going to happen though, so instead I asked, "How long have I been out?"

"A little over sixteen hours."

I stared at him, stunned by his reply. "Tell me you're kidding."

He shook his head.

I'd been unconscious all night and most of the next day? That wasn't good.

"Gallagher is waiting to talk to you, if you're feeling up to it."

Feeling up to it? Hell no. But rather than tell him the truth I simply said, "All right, give me a minute or two."

We sat in silence, until he asked, "You don't like him much, do you?"

Surprised, I actually gave it some thought before answering. Did I like Simon Gallagher? I wasn't sure. I didn't think I knew him well enough to like him or dislike him. But there was something there, something that just seemed off. Like an actor playing a role he wasn't all that familiar with . . .

Rather than answer his question directly, I asked one of my own. "You guys have known each other for a while, huh?"

He was quiet, perhaps thinking about how much to tell me, maybe just drifting through memories of another time and place. I wasn't certain; Dmitri had always been hard for me to read.

"The Simon I knew was younger," he said, "less experienced certainly, but with an attitude to match. He seems to have mellowed a bit since I saw him last."

Dmitri hadn't talked about his past all that often in the time I'd known him, so I was naturally curious. "When was that?"

"Almost a decade ago." His voice turned a bit wistful. "It seems like another lifetime, but I spent a lot of years in this city. I was a Warden for most of them."

Now *that* was surprising. I couldn't picture Dmitri as a bastion of law and order in any city, never mind one like New Orleans.

"Why'd you leave?" I asked.

He snorted. "Why does anyone leave? I'd outstayed my welcome and circumstances demanded it."

And that was all I was going to get on that topic. But he wasn't done talking about Gallagher yet.

"When I knew him, Simon was training as a combat mage. He

had a natural aptitude for it; everyone said he'd be a talent to reckon with if he managed to get his anger under control. It looks like he's managed to do that."

"But?" I could sense the word just hanging there, even if he hadn't said it.

"But Simon was always focused on the end result, rather than the methods and means it took to get there. It's the kind of thing that can be dangerous for a mage. Perhaps even more dangerous for those around him."

Dmitri wasn't worried about what would happen to either of us, that much I could figure out. No, he was warning me for an altogether different reason.

"Is that why she left the city? Because of Gallagher's tendency to let the end justify the means?"

I knew from our earlier conversation that he didn't want to go there, but he surprised me again by answering. "That was part of it. The rest is her story to tell, like I said before. But I know that coming here couldn't have been easy; she hasn't been back since I helped her get settled in Boston."

Keep your eyes on Denise, he was saying. And watch your back.

That I could do.

Apparently that was the end of the conversation, for he suddenly stood up and stretched, making me wonder just how long he'd been sitting there waiting for me to wake up.

"If you're up to it, I think it's time to go see the Lord Marshal," he said.

No, I wasn't up to it, but I had the feeling that Dmitri was going to ignore my answer if I said as much, so rather than going back to sleep the way my body was screaming at me to do, I tossed back the covers and sat up in one smooth motion.

Big mistake.

The room spun around me like a top and I would have fallen if Dmitri hadn't come to my assistance, catching me before I could fall back onto the bed.

"Easy there," he said, as my mind tried to process just how fast he'd crossed the room from where he'd been sitting by the doorway.

I shook him off and then stood on my own. "I'm okay," I told him.

And somehow I was.

For now, at least.

22

HUNT

As it turned out, I'd been recuperating in one of the spare bedrooms on the second floor, just down the hall from Gallagher's office. Dmitri went ahead to let Gallagher and Denise know I was coming, and by the time I made my slow way along the hall to the office where they were waiting, they'd dimmed the lights and put out a few candles. It wasn't something I expected from a hard-ass like Gallagher, so I figured Denise had a hand in it. Either way, I was glad that I was able to see their faces.

I had a hunch this wasn't going to be an easy discussion.

There were three chairs arrayed in front of Gallagher's desk, with Denise occupying the one farthest from the door. I let her help me into the one in the middle. Dmitri decided to remain standing just inside the door.

"How are you doing?" Denise asked, upon seeing the gingerly way I was moving.

I shrugged. What was I going to say? Can't really complain about feeling like you've been hit by a truck when people around you are dying, right?

"Good to see you up and about, Hunt," Gallagher said, but there was an edge to his voice that said otherwise. "Dmitri bring you up to speed?"

I wiggled my hand back and forth. Kinda, it said. "Sorry about Rebecca."

"Me too," he said, his voice filled with pain and regret. For the first time since meeting him, I knew exactly how he felt. In the dim light I could see that he hadn't escaped the battle with the creature unscathed. A bandage was wrapped around his lower left arm and a narrow cut bisected his other cheek. The injuries didn't seem to have slowed him down any, which was more than I could say for myself.

He went on.

"If we're going to make any sense of what happened, I'm going to need you to explain a few things. Starting with what, exactly, you did to me."

I glanced at Denise, who nodded encouragingly. She was one of only three people who knew my secret, so the fact that she approved of letting the cat out of the bag, so to speak, made me feel a bit safer in discussing things.

With her support, I explained to Gallagher about the ritual I'd undergone that had given me not only my ghostsight, but also the ability to borrow the eyes of both the living and the dead for short periods of time. Gallagher made small noises of understanding from time to time, which made me think that Denise must have gone over some of this with him while I'd slept. He'd been immersed in the real world for far longer than I had, so I guess none of it was all that surprising.

With the background clear, I moved on to the events of the night before. "When I realized none of you could see that thing in the room with us, I knew I had to do something. I figured if I could borrow someone else's sight, then maybe I could loan my own in return."

In retrospect it hadn't been the smartest move. If Gallagher had seen my actions as a threat, he could have blasted me into oblivion with the flick of a hand. Thankfully, he'd recognized the real threat and had responded appropriately.

"Once I had control, it wasn't all that hard to pass what I was seeing over to you."

I gave them a moment and then asked, "So what was that thing anyway?"

There was a long pause, then Denise replied, "We don't know."

Huh.

"You don't know, meaning you're not sure or you don't have a clue?"

I was praying it was the former.

She sighed and said, "We don't have a clue."

Not good.

Not good at all.

"So now what?" I asked.

"If you're feeling up to it, I'd like you to use your sight and take a look at the body, see if you can tell us anything further about it," Gallagher replied.

Having a close encounter of the dead kind with that thing was not something I was really interested in doing, but I couldn't see a way out of it, and so before I knew it we were all trooping downstairs, heading for the clinic next door where they had apparently stored the creature's body for safekeeping.

Despite my long rest, I was still a bit weak, so I used the fact that I couldn't see anything with all the lights on as cover for my need to lean on Denise as we made our way next door.

As we crossed the clinic floor, I kept my ghostsight in check and did my best to avoid looking at any of the patients. I didn't want to see the fluttering remains of their souls or think about what it must have felt like to have them ripped out while they were still alive. Two nights ago it had been a bit abstract, but now, having seen the process in action, there wasn't any way to distance myself from it. These people had died horrible deaths at the hands of a creature most of them probably couldn't have ever imagined. The sheer terror they'd probably felt during it all set my pulse to beating in my ears.

I was glad this thing was dead, for all of a sudden I wanted to kill it all over again.

We crossed the length of the clinic and passed through a set of double doors. The smell of cooking lingered in the air, and I knew we were in the kitchen. I assumed we were just passing through, maybe on our way outside to another location, but after a few more steps we stopped.

A door opened in front of me with a slight sucking sound and cold air wafted over my skin.

The walk-in freezer?

You have got to be kidding me!

Gallagher said, "The three of us examined the body earlier and didn't find anything unusual. But that doesn't mean you won't. Before we consider this a dead end, I'd like you to take a look."

"You're going to need this," Dmitri said, pushing a heavy jacket into my hands. "It's cold in there."

I slipped it on and then followed the cold into the depths of the freezer.

Denise called out one last piece of advice as the door was closing behind me.

"Whatever you do, don't touch the bedpost."

Bedpost?

But then I heard the door close behind me and was too busy fighting down a sharp spike of panic as the realization that I was sealed in the dark with a dead thing threatened to overwhelm me. I took a couple of deep breaths, got my heart rate under control, and turned to the task at hand. My eyesight quickly adjusted to the darkness and the place swam into view around me.

The shelves lining the walls were full of the stuff you'd expect to find in a freezer: meat and vegetables and various dairy products, all in industrial-size packages. But it was the body on the folding table in the middle of the space that drew my attention.

I stepped up and gave it a long look.

The creature, whatever it was, looked smaller in death than it had in life, a phenomenon I'd noticed before in my days of working with the Boston PD as an unofficial consultant. The dead always look smaller, as if the departing soul took something else along with it, reducing what was left behind.

What it didn't look was any less deadly, however.

It was humanoid in shape, with two arms, two legs, and its head all extending from a central torso. Its black, leathery skin hung loosely on its frame and it was easy to see how I could have mistaken it for being a woman dressed in some kind of robe, particularly at night from across the room. But that's where the resemblance ended.

There was no mistaking the circular maw that served as a mouth, nor the fact that the interior was lined with multiple rows of teeth, all bent inward at a slight angle, designed, I guessed, to pull its prey into its mouth one bite at a time. Its eyes, open and staring at the ceiling above, were pupil-less black orbs that jutted out a good inch from the narrow skull like a fish. Probably had incredible peripheral vision, making it tough as hell to sneak up on.

The winglike membranes that I'd glimpsed the night before were thinner than I'd expected, calling into question my earlier hunch that they allowed the creature to take to the air like some kind of giant bat. They seemed more vestigial than anything else, something that hadn't evolved at the same speed as the rest of it.

The body was laced here and there with parallel slashes, evidence that Dmitri had gotten in a few good blows with those claws of his, and the business end of a two-foot stake made from a broken bedpost was embedded in the left side of its chest, right about where you'd expect the heart to be if the thing followed any semblance to human physiology.

The bedpost had obviously delivered the killing blow, but it made me wonder why they had needed it in the first place. Couldn't they have just blasted it into oblivion with their magick?

I made a mental note to remember to ask them that very thing.

Steeling myself, I reached out a hand and poked the creature with my index finger, half expecting it to lash out in response.

Nothing happened.

"Of course not, you idiot," I muttered, "it's dead."

Satisfied it wasn't going to suddenly sit up on me, I lifted each of its arms and examined its hands one at a time. The fingers were long and narrow, with one extra knuckle on each, and were tipped with thick talons that reminded me of those on a hawk or other bird of prey. An image of the thing perched on the frame of Rebecca's bed swam through my mind and I knew the comparison wasn't that far off.

I spent another fifteen minutes examining the creature as thoroughly as I could but didn't find anything that I would label "unusual."

I mean, yes, the whole damn thing was unusual, I'll give you that, but that hadn't been what I'd understood Gallagher to mean when he'd said it, and aside from the fact that the creature existed at all, I didn't see anything else of particular interest.

I even tried using my ghostsight, to no avail.

If there had been anything of interest here to find, it was beyond my limited abilities to ferret out.

23

HUNT

Back in Gallagher's office, with a hot cup of coffee in my hands and my body beginning to warm up, I relayed to the others what I'd found, which was essentially nothing. They weren't surprised; after all, they hadn't found anything either.

Unable to contain my curiosity any longer, I asked Gallagher the question that had been bugging me ever since I'd seen that bedpost jutting out of the creature's chest.

"What's up with that stake? Why not just blast the thing with your Art?"

He stopped his pacing for a moment to answer me. "The room was too small," he said, with more than a trace of frustration. "If I'd cut loose I would have run the risk of hurting one of you or possibly even one of the family members watching from the hallway."

"Never mind the fact that using our Art in front of witnesses is generally frowned upon," Denise added, for my benefit.

I still didn't see how they'd gone from hammering it with a magickal lightning bolt to stabbing it in the heart with a bedpost, of all things. "What did you do, grab the nearest thing to hand? What if it hadn't worked?"

"Then we probably wouldn't be here talking about it, Hunt," Gallagher snapped.

Yeah, no shit, Sherlock, I wanted to say. That was precisely my point. We'd gone into the situation totally unprepared and had apparently barely escaped with our lives. I wasn't all that impressed with how things were going.

Which brought me to my other question.

I turned toward Denise and asked, "What would have happened if I'd removed the stake?"

There was a certain undercurrent of amusement in her voice when she answered. "I don't know, but there are enough creatures out there with the ability to regenerate and heal their wounds that I thought it best to leave well enough alone. Removing it might have started the healing process. I didn't think you'd want it waking up in the middle of your examination."

She had that right. Having that thing suddenly sit up? No, that wouldn't have gone over well with me at all.

"Well, at least we can all rest easy now," I said, trying to look at the bright side.

Gallagher grunted. "How's that?"

I gave him a quizzical look; it seemed obvious to me, but if he needed me to explain it . . . "We saw that thing stealing the soul right out of the little girl. Seems obvious that we've got our killer. Things should start getting back to normal."

Silence greeted my statement.

"Right?" I insisted, getting a bit nervous given their continued silence.

After another long moment, there was a discreet cough from the other side of the room. Dmitri.

"Sorry to be the bearer of bad news, Hunt, but there were two more cases reported this morning. Both in different parts of town. And both happened long after we'd killed the one you examined," he said.

Now I understood the general feeling of doom and gloom. If it had been that hard to take down one of them working alone, then dealing with several at once was going to be a real pain in the ass, to say the least. Never mind the fact that we didn't have any idea where to find these things . . .

"Okay, now what?" I asked.

Denise spoke up. "We take what we've got to the High Council. They've got the resources to figure out what these things are, so let them come up with an appropriate solution, I say."

More silence.

Even I knew that wasn't a good sign.

"What?" Denise asked.

"We can't go to the High Council with this. It . . ."

Denise cut him off. "Of course we can, Simon! This is exactly the kind of situation the Council was created for in the first place. You're the Lord Marshal, for Gaia's sake, they have to listen to you."

A sense of inevitability had crept into the room when I wasn't paying attention and now it hung in the air around us. My gut ached in that way it does when you know something terrible is about to happen, even if you don't know exactly what. I was struck with the sudden urge to tell Denise to shut up before it was too late, before the other shoe dropped.

I wasn't quick enough.

Gallagher waited patiently until Denise finished her little tirade and now, in a softer voice than I would have expected, said, "We can't go to the Council, Denise."

"Why not?"

"Because they're dead."

The thud I heard was the proverbial other shoe dropping.

"What happened?" I asked, when I realized that Denise had been shocked into silence.

Gallagher sighed. "What did you expect? They got sick and died, just like everybody else. Or that's what we thought, at least. Did you think I'd been elected to this post?"

"Um, actually, yeah, I did."

He laughed, but it was a hollow, bitter laugh, full of pain and darkness. "Four weeks ago I was just one of the Marshal's lieutenants. Then people start getting ill, dying, and suddenly everyone is looking to me to take charge because I was the most senior staff member still alive. Trust me, being Lord Marshal was the last thing I wanted."

"So you're saying we're on our own?"

"Pretty much. There are a few major players left in town who didn't take off after the news of the High Council's death got out, but not many. I've been in touch with each of them, trying to coordinate a response to all of this, but it hasn't been easy. Until now, we didn't know what we were facing."

We still don't, I thought.

I had to give the guy credit. Whether he'd wanted to be Lord Marshal or not, he'd stepped up when necessary and done what he could to help people. My own initial reaction, by comparison, was downright embarrassing.

"So my question still stands. Now what?"

The attacks this morning clearly showed there were at least two of the creatures still out there, but beyond that we really didn't have any idea what we were facing. The whole city might be infested for all we knew.

I thought about the nun I'd seen in the church the night before. It was clear to me now that it hadn't been a nun at all, but rather one of these creatures. I'd thought the "nun" had been praying with the patient, when, in fact, the creature had probably been feeding on the poor person's soul while I was right there in the room.

I physically shivered when I realized how much danger I'd been in without even knowing it.

If I'd caught up to it there at the end . . .

I hadn't, though, and that was all that mattered.

That and stopping these things before the situation grew any worse.

"We need to figure out what these things are if we're to have any hope of stopping them," Gallagher said. "The Council would have been our best resource, but they certainly aren't the only one."

Denise laughed, but it was a bitter, tired laugh. "The Council was the best and brightest of us, Simon. That's why they *were* the Council, for Gaia's sake. Without them, we've got nothing."

I'd never heard her sound so defeated.

But Gallagher didn't agree.

"We can ask Blackburn," he said.

From the shouting that erupted after Gallagher made his suggestion, I got the sense that consulting this Blackburn character was the last thing on earth Denise and Dmitri wanted to do.

Trouble was, I was starting to get the feeling that it didn't matter what we wanted. Things were moving too fast for that.

24

HUNT

Six hours later, just before midnight, I found myself sitting against the gunwale of a decrepit old skiff as it made its way slowly through the bayou toward Blackburn's, its puttering engine sounding like it was going to give out at any minute and leave us stranded in alligator country. Gallagher didn't seem concerned, though, so I tried to keep my nerves to myself and hoped that he knew what he was doing.

It wasn't easy. It was made more difficult by the fact that both Denise and Dmitri had flatly refused to accompany us.

After the initial argument in Gallagher's office had died down, we'd decided that before going to Blackburn we would first see if we could find any information in the High Council's library about the creatures.

That seemed like a good idea to me. At least until we'd set foot in the place.

Despite the fact that I couldn't see anything, it was clear just from the way our voices were echoing that the room we were standing in inside the Chief Councilor's mansion was enormous. It was supposed to hold all the knowledge that the seven mages who made up the Senior Council had accumulated during their long years as practitioners of the Arts. With their deaths, control of the place had passed to Gallagher.

We were armed with photographs of the creature and a determination to search the library for any hint of what we were facing.

How the hell we were going to do that given the size of the place, I had no idea.

As it turned out, neither did the others.

They guided me to a chair and left me there as they began to search the floor-to-ceiling bookshelves, looking for anything that might prove helpful. They brought stack after stack of books and parchments back to the study area in the center of the room and spent hours paging through them, to no avail. Conversation went from hopeful and enthusiastic to practically nonexistent as the scope of the task became evident. We could spend days in there without knowing if we were even getting close.

Hell, for all we knew, they'd already skipped past what we were looking for without even knowing it.

Finally, after hours of hunting for what was the equivalent of a needle in an entire county of haystacks, Gallagher again brought up the idea of consulting Blackburn.

Another argument ensued, but this time Gallagher had his mind made up.

"Ignoring a resource as powerful as Blackburn is stupid!" he finally shouted, silencing the others. "You can stay here if you want, but I'm going."

"Then go!" Denise snarled in return. "But you'll be going alone. There's no way in hell I'm getting near that thing!"

Dmitri hadn't said anything himself, but given the animosity that was pouring off him in waves, it didn't take a genius to figure out that he supported Denise's decision.

The fact that Denise used the word "thing" to describe Blackburn didn't escape me.

Which made what I did next surprising, even to myself. I'm still not sure what perverse need for self-inflicted suffering made me speak up at that moment.

"I'll go with you," I said.

Which was how I now found myself being ferried through the bayou in the dead of night with only Gallagher and an old Creole fisherman for company.

The cypress trees, their branches hanging down almost to the water's edge like mourners with their heads bowed, cast odd shadows across the water in the bright moonlight. Our guide steered us along without trouble, as if he'd been doing this very thing for untold years.

For all I knew, he had.

To my surprise, the swamp was alive with sound, even at this hour of the night. The frogs had a chorus all their own, from the guttural belching of the bulls to the chirps of the smaller tree frogs. They were joined by the incessant buzz of the insects that swarmed around us and the occasional hoot of a far-off owl.

From time to time a loud splash could be heard, and each time it happened, I tensed. I watched the water, wary of gators, but other than an occasional glimpse of something moving off in the distance, I didn't see anything.

"So you think this Blackburn guy will help us?" I asked, if for no other reason than to keep my mind off the alligators I knew had to be out there in the swamp watching us and thinking about their next meal.

He took his time answering. "He might."

My, that was reassuring. "What do you mean, might? I thought that's why we came out here in the first place."

"It's not that easy, Hunt. Blackburn can be . . . difficult."

I wasn't going to let him off that easily. "How so?" I asked.

His silence was longer this time, and I found myself wondering what he was afraid of. Blackburn couldn't be that bad.

"A long time ago, Blackburn was one of our best and brightest. They say that he could have risen to head the High Council, if he'd wanted. But somewhere along the way he fell off the path, so to speak, and something happened to him."

Around us, the night fell quiet, as if even the denizens of the swamp waited to hear what Gallagher had to say.

"Blackburn encountered something out there, in the darkness where man was not meant to go, and it changed him. Made him . . . different. Both more and less human, if that makes any sense."

Oddly enough, it did. I'd once encountered a being like that myself and the experience had changed me as well. I knew more than one person who would say it wasn't for the better, either.

Gallagher went on. "Blackburn bought himself an old estate on the edge of the bayou and retreated there over a decade ago, cutting himself off from the rest of the practitioners in the city, unable or maybe just unwilling to interact with them any longer. Frankly, I'm not sure he's even still alive."

I wasn't sure who was the bigger fool, him for thinking Blackburn would have any interest in helping us or me for blindly following along.

Gallagher fell silent at that point and wouldn't say anything further. I sat there, staring out into the swamp around us, and wondered what would possess a man to retreat into a place like this. And what might make another man seek him out knowing what he already knew. It revealed a side to Gallagher that I hadn't suspected and I wondered if it had anything to do with Denise's departure from both the Circle and the city.

Eventually our guide said something in a language I didn't understand and Gallagher answered him in the same tongue. A few moments later he pointed out across the water.

"There. Pointe du Lac in all its glory."

I stared at the decaying structure and wondered just what the hell I was doing here.

Once, long ago, the mansion might been the height of southern elegance, but those days were long gone. Now it was a crumbling hulk, half smothered beneath vegetation. Rot showed through where the paint had been worn away by the passage of time and the moisture of the swamp, and I had a sudden image of the whole place falling down around our ears the minute we stepped inside.

"You have got to be kidding me," I said.

Gallagher said nothing.

The boatman guided our craft over to a dock hidden beneath the draping branches of a cypress grove. Unlike the house, the dock was well kept and probably no older than a few years. It told me right away that there was more here than met the eye.

After tying up at the dock, Gallagher and I disembarked and made our way across the overgrown lawn to the house proper, picking our way across the rotting porch to the front door.

Gallagher reached for the door handle, but I stopped him before he could open it.

"Don't you think we should knock or something?"

"What for?" Gallagher asked. "He already knows we're here."

I was still trying to digest the implications of that statement when he pushed the door open and strode inside. With nothing else to do, and nowhere else to go, I followed.

25

HUNT

Gallagher led me through a series of darkened rooms full of cloth-covered furniture and the occasional lighted candle. Despite the dim light, he moved with purpose. It was immediately clear that he was familiar with the layout of the house.

I wondered if that was because he had been here recently or because nothing about the place ever changed.

We emerged from a long hallway to find ourselves in what must once have been a drawing room. An old crumbling piano stood to the left, the dust and cobwebs that covered it clear evidence that it had been a long time since music had filled this room. More cloth-covered furniture was scattered here and there about the place, with no real rhyme or reason to the layout that I could see. Directly across the room was a large fireplace and a few red coals still burned in its grate.

Clearly, someone had been in the room, and not too long ago, either.

To the right of the fireplace was a set of French doors. Both of them were open to the night just beyond.

Gallagher held up a hand, indicating we should stop where we were. From inside his coat he removed the photographs of the creature's corpse that he had brought with him to show to our host.

As we stood there, I became aware of a thick stench that was slowly seeping into the air. It was like the smell of carrion on the highway under the hot summer sun mixed with the smell of rotting vegetables and the taste of sour milk on the tongue.

I wanted to gag, to force the smell out of my system, but I held back when I noticed movement near the open French doors.

Our host kept to the shadows just beyond the doors, a tactic that I assumed was designed to keep us from seeing him too clearly, from seeing what he had become. But darkness hides no secrets from me, and I had a moment to see just what it was we were dealing with. After getting a good look, I can honestly say that I wish I hadn't.

Nothing living should ever look like that.

Blackburn appeared as if he'd begun to rot from the inside out. His skin was deathly pale, with that waxy look common to a corpse two days past its prime, and his veins showed through it as a twisting lattice of black lines that pulsed at odd intervals.

Long stringy hair framed a narrow face that was terrible to behold. His eyes were oversized and red, and his ears had lengthened and came to a point at the tips. When he turned his head to look in my direction, I could see that his nose was nothing but a seeping hole in the center of his face.

His voice, when he spoke, was like the drone of a thousand hungry insects. My skin crawled at the sound of it.

"You know my price?" he asked.

Gallagher nodded. "I do and I accept it fully."

He turned to face me, and in the darkness I could see the tension pouring through his frame. "No matter what you see, don't move," he told me earnestly. "He'll kill us both if you interfere."

"What's he going to do?" I asked, not caring that Blackburn could hear.

"It doesn't matter," Gallagher said. "Just don't do anything."

He turned away and held up the photographs in his hand. "We need to know what . . ."

That's as far as he got.

One minute Blackburn was standing just outside the French doors, watching us, and the next he was standing on the other side of Gallagher, so close that he could have kissed his cheek had he wanted to. Something long and wet, like the tongue of a frog, emerged from Blackburn's mouth and plunged deep inside Gallagher's ear. Blackburn's eyes fixed on mine and I realized with a sudden shock that he knew I could see quite well in the dark, that he could have done all this without my seeing any of it, that he'd chosen to show me what he was doing so I would know the extent of what it took to barter with him should I ever return on my own.

I fought the urge to vomit as Gallagher stumbled and would have fallen had I not reached out and steadied him. By the time I had done so, Blackburn was again on the other side of the room, standing in the shadows near the French doors.

The photographs Gallagher had held in his hand were nowhere in sight.

"Jesus Christ, Gallagher, are you all right?"

He shook his head, like a swimmer trying to clear water from his ear, and his voice had a faraway sound to it as he said, "Will be . . . just give a moment . . ."

He shook himself again, this time his entire body, like a dog shaking off water, and then stood tall on his own. His voice was steady once more.

"I've paid your price," he said to our host.

"Yesssss," Blackburn said and his voice dripped with the lazy sounds of satisfaction. "Ask your question."

"The creature in the images," Gallagher said, pointing to the photos that I now saw Blackburn was holding in his hands, "what is it?"

Blackburn barely even glanced at them. "The streets of the city are full of Sorrows."

I felt my anger rise. We'd come here for information and we'd paid his price. Now the son of a bitch was going to dick us around? Not a chance. I opened my mouth to challenge him, but before I could Gallagher's hand thumped me heavily on my chest.

"Don't," he warned. "He answered our question. Anything more will require that you pay the same price that I did. Is that what you want?"

Blackburn lifted his head, his eyes gleaming at the prospect of another bargain.

The sight of his eagerness made my guts churn.

"Not a chance in hell," I replied.

Blackburn licked the thin, narrow edges that served as his lips. "What is a single memory against the answer to your most precious question?" he asked. "It's really just a small price to pay. Surely you can spare a single memory?"

I stared, my revulsion growing. Without taking my eyes off of Blackburn, I asked Gallagher, "Is that true? Is that the price of his knowledge? A memory?"

"Yes," the mage replied and the pain in his voice made it plain it wasn't as easy as Blackburn made it out to be.

We'd gotten what we'd come for; it was time to get the hell out of there, I decided.

Gallagher didn't say another word, just began backing out of the room.

I followed suit, not looking away from where Blackburn watched us with hungry eyes until we'd left the room behind.

Our guide was waiting for us and we made short work of casting off and getting underway.

Back in the boat, I couldn't help but ask.

"What was it?" I asked.

"What was what?"

"The memory. What memory did he take?"

Gallagher was silent for a long moment, so long that I thought he wasn't going to answer. But he did, eventually, and when he did his voice sounded as if he had aged twenty years.

"I don't remember," he said.

26

HUNT

The sun was starting to rise as we made our way back into the city, and by the time we returned to the High Council's library, I was left unable to see. Gallagher led me inside, where we found the others asleep at the table, open books and parchments piled up around them.

After guiding me to a chair, he shook the others awake.

"Sorrows," he told them. "According to Blackburn, we're dealing with a pack of Sorrows."

That generated another round of arguing until I couldn't take it anymore.

"Quiet!" I hollered and to my surprise, they stopped.

Into the silence I asked, "Would someone please tell me what a Sorrow is?"

"It's a myth. A legend. Nothing more," Denise replied, and I could practically hear her glaring at Gallagher as she did.

"Blackburn believes differently," he shot back.

"Blackburn's brain rotted away a long time ago and so will yours if you keep it up! How could you let that thing do that to you?"

I didn't want to listen to their spat. Or rather, I did want to listen, would probably have enjoyed it immensely in fact, but now wasn't the time, so I quickly threw out a suggestion.

"If there's any information available about Sorrows, real or imaginary, this would be the best place to find it, right? Particularly since we now know what we are looking for?"

Grudgingly, they agreed.

This time it didn't take long.

"I think I've got something," Dmitri called out, waking me from the catnap I'd been enjoying while the others were digging through the shelves. He waited for the others to join us and then explained, "The manuscript isn't in the best of shape, and it's written in a mix of Latin and Greek, but I think I can read most of it."

He scanned the page in front of him, translating as he read it aloud.

"It's the journal of an eleventh-century practitioner who was creating a kind of bestiary, information on various supernatural creatures that he'd pulled together from other sources," Dmitri explained. "Here's what he has to say about the Sorrows."

Unearthly in nature, Sorrows were once harbingers of the dead, tasked with guiding the souls of the dead on their journey into the afterlife. But the Sundering infected them with

madness and they forgot the purpose for which they had been
created. They became corrupt, preying on the souls of the liv-
ing like a pack of rabid dogs.

"The Sundering?" I wondered aloud, but no one knew what it meant. For all we knew it could have been anything from a minor spell to a major cataclysm. We could look it up, I supposed, but that would take additional time we really didn't have.

Dmitri went on. "There is a paragraph or two that is illegible and then it picks up again. 'From a distance they resemble a woman wrapped in a cloak and can thus be easily overlooked, but upon close examination they cannot be mistaken for aught but what they truly are: abominations against man and nature.'"

I thought about the Sorrow I'd seen in the church the other night, the one I'd mistaken for a nun. How was it that I'd seen it without difficulty, yet the one in Rebecca's bedroom had managed to remain hidden until I'd used my ghostsight?

I put the question to the others.

"Perhaps it's something it can turn on or off at will," Gallagher suggested. "An offensive mechanism of some kind?"

"Not offensive, defensive," Denise replied. "When it's feeding, its attention is elsewhere, making it more vulnerable. Hiding itself from view, like a chameleon changing its color, would offer it some measure of protection."

We had Dmitri check the text to see if it said anything on the issue, but it did not. Nor did it give any idea of the Sorrows' strengths or weaknesses; we were just going to have to figure that part out on our own.

It did, however, give us hope that they could be defeated. The writer had wrapped up his entry with one final statement,

After many months, the Temple Knights located the last of the Sorrows' nests and put the rest of the unholy creatures to the sword, ridding our world once and for all of the evil that they had wrought.

"Guess they missed a few," Denise said. She'd gone for light-hearted, but the comment came out flat, reminding us that we were going to have to do considerably better.

Something about the wording was bothering me and it took a moment to puzzle it out. "It says nests. What's that about?" I asked.

Simon grunted with distaste. "Sorrows always find a secure location within their hunting grounds to act as a kind of lair. Somewhere along the way someone started calling those locations nests and the name stuck."

Lovely. At least we had one thing going for us now though: we knew what we were up against.

With that information in hand, we got back in touch with our various allies throughout the city, asking them to keep watch for anything that even remotely resembled a Sorrow.

Finding the Sorrows was the first step in solving our problem.

27

ROBERTSON

After getting Clearwater's name from the clerk at the Majestic, Robertson put his people to work trying to track her down. Canvassing the neighborhood led to a sighting at a two-bit diner down the street from the hotel a few days earlier. Upon questioning the waitress, Robertson learned that Clearwater and her companions, whom he knew to be Hunt and Alexandrov, met with three other men before leaving together in a pair of SUVs. Soldier types, the waitress had called them, but that didn't really give Robertson anything to go on. There'd been military personnel, from the regular army to the National Guard, in New Orleans since the hurricane; unless they'd been in uniform, there was no way to tell them apart.

The vehicles had been black, Yukons or Suburbans, something like that, according to the waitress, and no, she hadn't thought to take down the license plates. Why should she? They weren't of any interest to her.

It looked like the diner was a dead end.

That didn't mean they were without recourse, however. Robertson assigned several local agents the task of digging into her background. Who was she? Where was she from? Did she have a record of past convictions? How about outstanding warrants?

While it certainly seemed like she was willingly aiding and abetting a fugitive, which itself was a federal crime, he told himself not to jump to conclusions. Perhaps she'd been taken captive by the other two. Given all the depraved things that Hunt had done over the years, kidnapping certainly wouldn't be a surprise.

He'd know soon enough.

In less than an hour he had a decent-sized file on his desk detailing the life and times of one Denise Clearwater. It made for rather boring reading, actually.

Born and raised in San Diego, California to a middle-class family. Father and mother were both killed in an auto accident when she was sixteen. She attended the University of California for a year before moving to New Orleans and transferring to LSU. Moved to Massachusetts in 2003, or at least that's when a driver's license was issued to her at an address in Brookline.

No serious run-ins with the law, though she did have a penchant for speeding: four tickets in the last three years. She'd accepted responsibility on all of them and had paid the fines on time without argument.

Her credit report was limited, which was a little unusual. She had accounts in two major banks, one of which held a small nest egg that looked like she'd built it slowly over time, but no credit card history to speak of. It looked like she paid cash for most everything. She'd inherited the house in Brookline from a distant aunt, which probably explained the sudden move east, and with the mortgage paid off there was no real need for a credit history.

In other words, she appeared to be your average American, though one with less debt than most.

Not the kind of individual he'd expected to be found in the company of Alexandrov, a black marketer, never mind a confirmed killer like Hunt.

His unwilling accomplice theory was looking more likely.

At that point he split his people into two squads and put them on different tracks. The first group would delve further into Clearwater's life, looking for any connection between her and Hunt or Alexandrov. The various timelines would be compared and any common circumstances would be examined in more detail. If they'd interacted with each other for any reason at any time in the past, Robertson wanted to know about it. At the same time, the second group, comprised mainly of local police officers, would work their contacts and the streets, trying to determine where the trio had gone after departing from the diner.

Surprisingly, it was the second group that hit the jackpot first.

Clearwater had been seen in the company of two adult males at the home of a family named Lafitte the night before last, according to a beat cop who, in turn, had gotten the tip from one of her local snitches. She'd passed along the address, as well as the fact that the family wouldn't be in this afternoon; they were attending the funeral of their daughter, who'd recently passed away after an illness.

Years ago Robertson might have been troubled by the need to intercept a man at his own daughter's funeral, but he was well past that point now. Justice waits for no man, and catching the witness at an emotional moment might make him or her reveal something he or she would otherwise not want revealed.

"Doherty!"

His new protégé stuck his head in the open office door. "Yes, sir?"

"Grab your jacket, we've got a funeral to go to."

They arrived just as the casket was being carried into the mausoleum. They waited until the line of mourners had paid their respects to the father, a gray-haired man in his midforties who went by the name Pierre Lafitte, and then approached, flashing their badges.

"Mr. Lafitte?" Robertson asked.

"Yes, that's me."

"We need to speak to you for a few minutes, if that would be all right . . ." Robertson indicated the car they'd parked beneath the shade of a nearby tree.

Lafitte clearly wanted to be left alone in his grief, but it wasn't often the FBI showed up, and like most honest people he wanted to be helpful.

Reluctantly, he followed the others over to the car.

Doherty got behind the wheel while Robertson and Lafitte sat opposite each other in the back. The senior agent wasted no time in getting to the point.

"I'm very sorry to intrude, Mr. Lafitte. You have the Bureau's condolences."

No harm in being nice, he thought, *at least, not at first.* He could always pull out the hammer if he needed it.

"Do you recognize this woman?"

He passed him the photograph from Clearwater's file, the one from her driver's license.

Robertson was watching carefully. He saw Lafitte's eyes widen slightly before the mask clamped down upon his face.

"I don't think so," he replied.

Robertson smiled. "I know this must be a difficult time, Mr. Lafitte, but please, think carefully."

The other man fidgeted in his seat. Rather than answering directly, he tried to stall. "What did she do?" he wanted to know.

Thinking to play on the man's sympathy, Robertson said, "We believe she's being held against her will by this man," and handed him the mug shot from Hunt's arrest earlier that year.

Again there was that flicker of recognition, but this time Lafitte's face went hard.

"I haven't seen either of them. Are we finished here?"

That did it. Robertson was done playing Mr. Nice Guy. It was clear that Lafitte had seen both Clearwater and Hunt and that the informant's information had been correct. It was time for the hammer.

"Doherty?"

The younger agent passed a folder over the back of the front seat. Robertson took it and began leafing through it while Lafitte looked on.

"Again, I'm sorry about your loss. You have an older child too, don't you? A son, I think?"

The older man nodded cautiously. "Yes," he replied.

"William, right?"

Again the nod, but this time with a bit more force. "What's that have to do with this woman you're looking for?" Lafitte asked, anger leaking into his tone.

Robertson smiled again. "I see that William is out on bail, awaiting trial for that possession charge."

"Now you just wait a minute!" Lafitte stormed. "My son has nothing to do with this Clearwater woman! You leave him out of it!"

Robertson's gaze hardened as he said, "It would be a shame if something happened to revoke that bail, wouldn't it? So let's stop fucking around. Tell me what I want to know, and I'll forget I ever heard of William Lafitte."

Lafitte finally got it. His anger withered away like a balloon leaking air. He sat back in his seat and looked away, out the window across the cemetery to where the workers were sealing the doors to his daughter's mausoleum.

"What do you want to know?" he said wearily.

Ten minutes later the conversation was finished. Lafitte climbed out of the car and walked away across the grass, never looking back.

That was fine with Robertson; he'd already forgotten the broken old man. He'd gotten what he'd needed from him: the name and address of the man with whom Clearwater, and presumably Hunt, were staying, and Lafitte's promise not to mention their conversation to anyone.

28

HUNT

By midafternoon the next day the calls began flooding in. Strange, dark-robed creatures were being glimpsed here and there throughout the city, never for long and never all that closely. There had been other sightings before this, people now realized, but where they'd previously been dismissed as tricks of the eye or simple tiredness on the part of the viewer, now they were taken more seriously. Unsurprisingly, there were more sightings in the areas were the Gifted congregated than elsewhere in the city.

One thing was certain. The sheer number of reports and the distance between them made it clear we were dealing with more than just a single pack.

We had our work cut out for us.

Nor did it take a rocket scientist to figure out that the work was going to be bloody. If we wanted the attacks to stop, we were going to have to hunt down the Sorrows that had infested the city, just as our predecessors had done so many years before.

First, though, we had to find them.

Adding the wardens to our number gave us fourteen able-bodied individuals. That wasn't enough to search a city the size of New Orleans, so we needed to be smart about what we were doing. Gallagher suggested that we split into pairs of two and have each pair concentrate on an area where there had been a higher incidence of sightings.

"Wait a minute," I said. "Why can't Denise just scry out their location for us?"

"I can try, but I don't think we'll have much luck," she said. "Scrying works best when you have something that belonged to the target to use as a focus: an item of clothing, a piece of hair, a dab of blood. Because objects like that are tied to the target in metaphysical ways, the practitioner can use them to trace the link back to the source."

Remembering the way she'd used the charms from my daughter's favorite bracelet as a focus during her scrying efforts the previous summer, I nodded in understanding.

Denise went on. "Unfortunately, I don't have anything like that to use."

"Can't you, I don't know, use the blood from the body in the freezer or something?" I asked.

Denise laughed. "Sure, if I wanted to be sure the corpse hadn't gotten up and left the freezer. The focus has to be specific to the target in question. I can't use the blood from one Sorrow to track other Sorrows. It will simply ground me back to the original source."

"So we can't track them that way?" Dmitri asked.

"With enough power and Art, anything's possible. I think it's a long shot, but I'm willing to give it a try."

"Scrying isn't my forte, but I can add my power to your own. Maybe that will be enough," Gallagher told her.

So the decision was made. I'd pair up with Dmitri while the wardens would split into five teams of two, leaving our two mages to see if they could pinpoint the Sorrows' locations as best they could.

Word also went out to all of the Gifted still in the city, identifying the Sorrows as the real threat behind the attacks and urging them to take whatever precautions they thought necessary to protect themselves.

No one really had any idea if wards would work against the Sorrows, but that didn't stop Simon and Denise from throwing some up around the clinic just in case.

When they were finished, Gallagher gathered his people in the courtyard for a briefing. As the meeting got underway, I pulled Dmitri aside.

"What can you tell me about them?" I asked, waving a hand in the general direction of the group gathered around Gallagher.

"What do you want to know?"

"Are they all combat mages like Gallagher?"

"I don't know any of them personally—they're all long after my time—but if Gallagher stayed true to form when assembling his team, I'd guess that at least half of them are. The others will probably be a mix of healers, illusionists, and the like."

"Think they're any good?"

"From what I've seen so far, which admittedly isn't much, I'd give them a solid B. They look like they've been through a few scrapes before and do a decent job of following orders."

"I sense a *but* in there somewhere."

He grunted in acknowledgement. "I've had a chance to talk to a few of them. A handful have some experience with this kind of thing: Spencer and Mitchell did a couple of tours in Iraq with the

National Guard and Kramer is a former cop, but the rest have never dealt with anything this dangerous. It's hard to know who will break and who won't when the shit hits the fan, ya know?"

It wasn't the biggest vote of confidence I'd ever heard, but it wasn't the worst either. There wasn't anything we could do about it anyway; they were all we had.

A memory from our first day in New Orleans jumped up suddenly, prompting another question.

"If they're all Gifted in some way, why can't I see that with my ghostsight?"

"They're wearing charms specifically designed to block abilities like yours. Wardens have to face all kinds, and keeping the enemy from knowing exactly what they're up against can sometimes make the difference between a peaceful resolution and a violent one."

That explained the faint shimmering aura I'd seen in the diner that day. I can't say it made me happy to hear it though; I'd thought my ghostsight couldn't be fooled.

Seems I still had a lot to learn.

I tuned in to what Gallagher was saying.

". . . stick to the areas you've been given. If you spot one of them, don't do anything overt. There are only two of you per team and that's nowhere near the level of force that will be needed to overcome one of these things, never mind a group of them. Try to follow them if you can and determine the location of the nest, then call it in. We'll figure out a proper response from there. Everyone clear?"

There were nods all around.

"All right. Spencer, you're with Daniels. You've got sector one. Gomez, I want you with . . ."

It wasn't the best plan I'd ever heard, for there were far too many variables that we didn't have control over, but it was going to have to be good enough.

Dmitri and I were assigned to the French Quarter, something neither of us was all that thrilled about. We did, however, understand the logic behind Gallagher's choice. I was a stranger to the city and it had been years since Dmitri had been here, which in a way made us both a bit of a liability.

My partner spent several minutes grumbling about the assignment, until I reminded him that it was one of the few areas in which there'd been a confirmed Sorrow sighting. With his spirits improved, we set out on patrol.

The next few hours went by *very* slowly. We took a cab to the Quarter and then made our way through the crowds on foot, searching every back alley and dark corner for a sign that might lead us to a Sorrow nest. We found nothing.

It was close to eight o'clock when we got the call from Spencer's team down in the Ninth Ward that changed everything.

29

HUNT

Gallagher was already there when we arrived and the three of us were quickly brought up to speed. Spencer and his partner were preparing to search a high school that had been condemned in the wake of Hurricane Katrina but had yet to be torn down, when they spotted something coming down the street toward them. They'd quickly taken cover and watched in amazement as a group of Sorrows swarmed into the school before them.

The pair had waited ten minutes, making certain the Sorrows weren't simply going to emerge again, and then retreated a short distance down the street before calling it in.

The Lower Ninth Ward was one of the areas hit hardest by the destructive power of Hurricane Katrina and very little of it was left standing, so it wasn't a huge surprise that the Sorrows had decided to set up a nest there. Very little traffic, human or otherwise, passed through. This area, formerly home to many poor and working-class black folks, had largely been abandoned and those who remained behind weren't exactly the type of people to make a public outcry over anything anyone else was doing.

I'd heard stories about the devastation, but seeing it with my own eyes was something else entirely. House after house had either been knocked flat by the storm or bulldozed into rubble later when it became apparent that there was no way to salvage them. There were entire city blocks where nothing was left but piles of debris. Years later the place was still a disaster zone.

The school was at the end of the block about forty yards from where the five of us huddled behind another abandoned building.

Spencer went on. "While we waited for you guys to arrive, I ducked in for a quick look around."

He ducked in for a quick look around? This guy had major cojones apparently . . .

"The Sorrows have taken over the annex at the rear of the building and have turned the empty swimming pool into some sort of nest."

He shuddered when he said *nest*, which told me all I needed to know about how much fun this was going to be.

A tactical discussion followed, with Dmitri and Gallagher quizzing Spencer for information about the approach angles and sight vectors and a hundred other things that made very little sense to me but were apparently vital for our response to the threat before us. I tended to favor the more direct approach: wait until the monsters were all asleep and blast them into oblivion.

If the things even slept, that is.

A van arrived while the others were still hashing out the plan and the rest of the wardens poured out of it, dressed in dark clothing with night-vision goggles around their necks. A few of them were armed with some sort of short stocky machine gun, but they were the exceptions. The majority of them intended to fight fire with fire, so to speak. Bracers and amulets seemed to be the latest fashion accessories, and I could only guess that they helped focus their magick in some way. The threat was supernatural in nature, so they were going to use their Art to remove the threat before it could do any more harm.

Thankfully one of them had brought a weapon for me and I received a quick thirty-second course on how to use it. It didn't seem all that tough: point and shoot, basically. A lever near the trigger guard released the empty magazine, and all I had to do was slap a fresh one into place and I'd be ready to rock 'n' roll again.

I was keyed up, far more than I expected. My heart was racing and my breathing sounded labored even to my ears. I didn't know what was wrong with me; I'd done this kind of thing once before and hadn't felt this uncomfortable, but then again, I'd had my fear for Denise's life to drive me onward then. This time around, I was risking my neck for people I really didn't even know.

What's that old expression? God protects heroes and fools alike? Right now I was having a hard time figuring out which one I was.

Spencer led us around the side of the building to where he'd left a door propped open after his earlier recon. Pulling a red-lensed flashlight out of the pocket of his fatigue pants, he flicked it on and disappeared inside with us on his heels.

The place stank of lake water and rot, the smell so heavy that for the first few minutes it was difficult even to breathe, but then it gradually faded as my nose got used to the stench. The floor beneath our feet was covered with a thick layer of silt that helped to deaden the sound of our boots as we moved deeper into the building. Those of us who could see better tried to help the others avoid the worst of the debris that had been left scattered about the corridor when the lake waters had receded.

Spencer led us down a series of interconnected corridors, across the gymnasium, and through the women's locker room. On the far side of the showers, a short corridor ended in a set of double doors that hung loosely on their frames, with just enough room between them to allow a man to slip through.

As soon as the doors were in sight, Spencer brought up his hand in a signal to halt and settled into a crouch. The rest of us followed his lead.

"The pool's just on the other side of those doors," Spencer told us. "You've only got about ten feet of tile before you reach the edge, so watch yourself when we get inside. The Sorrows are clustered in the deep end of the pool on the far side of the room."

Gallagher pointed to Dmitri and me. "I want the two of you to take the right-hand side of the pool. Spencer and his team will take the left, while I'll cover the shallow end to keep any of them from trying to get out."

"What's the play?" Dmitri asked, and Gallagher's response was eloquent in its simplicity.

"Kill them before they kill you."

Right.

I held my gun a little tighter, took a deep breath, and motioned to Dmitri to lead on. Time was a wastin'.

We crept forward until we reached the doors and then slowly eased through the opening one at a time.

A row of windows ran along the opposite wall just below ceiling height, but since it was long past sunset the little bit of ambient light that was seeping through the dirty glass wasn't enough to cause me any difficulty with my sight. I glanced around the room, taking in the scattered lounge chairs along the edge of the pool and the tangled pile of lane ropes off in one corner but knew we could get around both obstacles without difficulty.

I glanced at Dmitri, got a short nod in return, and, summoning my courage, took a few steps forward.

The pool stretched out before us in a long rectangle, but we still weren't close enough yet to see into its depths. My hands were slick with sweat where they were clamped tight around the stock of my gun, and I could hear my heart pounding in my ears. I walked with extra care, afraid the slightest sound would give us away. If we could get the drop on them, we had a far better chance of coming out of this alive . . .

I caught motion to my left and a glance showed me Spencer and his men moving into position on the opposite side of the pool. I wasted a second wondering what the place would look like through the night-vision goggles they all wore and then pushed the thought aside, knowing I had better concentrate if I didn't want to end up another soulless victim.

As we moved forward the last few feet, the bottom of the pool finally came into view.

It was a snake pit.

The Sorrows lay together in a huddled mass at the lowest section of the deep end, twisted and curled about one another so it was hard to see where one ended and another began. They were moving, the dark flesh of one sliding over or against another's, and I was reminded of a shark's need to keep moving through the waters of the ocean lest it suffocate and die; their motion had the same frenzied yet purposeful sense to it.

Not one of them noticed our approach; none of them so much as looked up as the eight of us got into position. Ahead of me, Dmitri braced himself with one foot against the lip of the pool and pointed his weapon downward at the creatures moving below him, ready to cut loose as soon as the signal was given. Along the other side, Spencer and his men were waiting for Gallagher's signal and readying their own power.

That's when everything went to hell.

30

HUNT

Gallagher had been gathering his power since we'd first entered the building and he raised his hands, getting ready to send a blistering wave of mystical energy down at the mass of Sorrows at the bottom of the pool.

Spencer and his men followed suit.

I turned my face away and squeezed my eyes shut, not wanting the sudden light to hinder my vision.

I'd seen Denise unleash her power in our confrontation with the doppelganger, but she'd be the first to admit that her abilities didn't run in an offensive vein. Gallagher's certainly did, and, even without seeing it, I could feel the intensity of the blast that was poured into that pool from the mages surrounding it. The backs of my eyelids lit up like a Fourth of July fireworks show, and for a moment I couldn't see anything, anything at all.

When I opened my eyes I stared down into the depths of the pool, expecting to see nothing but the charred remains of the Sorrows we'd targeted.

I couldn't have been more mistaken.

The Sorrows were swarming up the sides of the pool in every direction, the magick having washed over them without any obvious effect!

My mind froze at the sight.

We had a minute, maybe less, before they'd be upon us.

How the hell did they survive that?

I might have stood there and stared, waiting like a sheep to be disemboweled by slashing claws, if one of the wardens hadn't pulled the trigger on his weapon.

Bullets flew and the sound of the shots filled the room, echoing in the enclosed space, snapping me from my reverie.

As the first of the Sorrows raced up the side of the pool in front of me, I raised the barrel of my weapon, prayed like hell that I'd hit something, and squeezed the trigger.

The gun jerked in my hands. My aim must have been true, for I saw the Sorrow for just a split second as it was flung over backward. That was all I saw, however, for the brilliant flare of the muzzle flash pushed back the darkness and stole my sight.

I stumbled backward, unable to see anything for several seconds except the whiteout in my head. Gunfire erupted on all sides, the sound echoing in the enclosed space, hammering at my ears and destroying my usual means of orienting myself, leaving me to stumble about, afraid that I'd either fall victim to one of the Sorrows or stumble into someone's line of fire and get killed by our own people.

Interspersed with the gunfire I could hear the shrieking of the Sorrows and the roar of an enraged bear, which told me that Dmitri had gotten into the fight.

Something grabbed my ankle and yanked me off my feet. Unable to see, I hit the ground hard, smacking my head against the deck surrounding the pool. Claws dug into my calf and began to drag me backward.

Shaking my head to clear it, I activated my ghostsight.

The white fog I'd been enveloped in fell away, revealing the snarling face of the Sorrow that had hold of my leg and was hauling me back toward the edge of the swimming pool.

I'd retained hold of the gun in my hand and I didn't hesitate to make use of it. A quick burst struck the Sorrow square in the chest.

It jittered with the impact of the bullets, shrieking in rage, and dropped out of sight.

In the brief reprieve, I looked around. Given that just about every living thing in the room was supernatural in nature, I could see them all with my ghostsight. Dmitri had shifted and he stood a few feet away from me, driving back wave after wave of Sorrows as they threatened to overwhelm us. Across the pool, Spencer and his men were fighting hand to hand with the creatures and losing. Two men were down, surrounded by Sorrows, their life force being stolen even as I watched. Gallagher was still on his feet, blood trailing from a wound on the side of his head and a trio of Sorrows trying to corner him against one wall where they could all come at him at once.

Clearly, we were losing.

I scrambled to my feet just in time to see the Sorrow I'd shot start scaling the side of the pool for a second time. It wasn't that I'd missed; I hadn't. The bullets just weren't effective against the Sorrows. The kinetic energy in the strikes was knocking them down, but it wasn't killing them. Not even close.

Apparently I wasn't the only one to realize that we were in trouble, for just at that moment Gallagher started yelling, "Fall back! Fall back!"

I didn't need to be told twice. I turned and headed back in the direction we'd come, stumbling along with the others, keeping my gaze on the aura of the man in front of me so that I'd have a means of finding my way out.

The Sorrows harassed us through the halls but fell back as we neared the exit, letting us escape into the night air without further confrontation.

We stumbled to the vehicles, practically fell inside them, and got out of there as quickly as we could.

The raid had been a complete bust and, when the butcher's bill was taken, cost us two good men.

31

HUNT

It took time to recover mentally from the failed attack. In the aftermath, we struggled to keep despair from overwhelming us. No one could have anticipated that the Sorrows would be resistant to magick, never mind modern firearms, and given what we'd faced as a result, we'd done well to escape with the loss of only two men.

But it was still a failure, a miserable failure at that, and we were hard-pressed not to succumb to the feeling that we were not only outnumbered but outmatched as well. It wasn't just what we knew that could get us killed; it was what we didn't know.

Those who'd made it out alive were all sporting injuries of varying degrees of seriousness. Denise and the rest of the medical volunteers had their hands full getting us back into fighting shape and even with the accelerated healing Denise could deliver through her Art, we still needed rest.

Forty-eight hours later, Dmitri, Denise, Gallagher, and I gathered together in the kitchen to consider our next move.

"We've got three problems facing us," Gallagher said, by way of opening the meeting. "One, locate the other nests. Two, figure out a way to counter their ability to hide from sight, and three, come up with a way to hurt these things."

There wasn't any disagreement; Gallagher had hit the nail on the head.

He went on. "In the wake of our failure, I've had people searching round the clock through the books in the Council library, searching for additional references to the Sorrows. About an hour ago, we got lucky.

"It was a tiny reference, but it suggested that Sorrows have the same weakness that many other enchanted creatures do, and that's iron."

He paused, debating what he was going to say, it seemed, and then went on. "I have to apologize. Another half hour of searching might have brought this to our attention and we could have avoided the fiasco of the other night."

Denise reassured him that he'd done the best he could and he seemed satisfied with that. I, on the other hand, wasn't as inclined to let him off so easily.

"So how do we know that there isn't more information over there? Shouldn't we wait to act before we've gone through it all?"

I knew he was shaking his head even as he said, "That would take too long. The number of attacks is growing daily and if we wait too long they will surpass our ability to respond to them. I've still got people looking, but we're going to have to act now with what we've got."

I was tempted to remind him that doing so was what had gotten us all nearly killed, but in the end I held my tongue. He didn't need me to remind him of his failure. I'm sure he'd be hearing the screams of his men for the rest of his life.

Now was not the time for divisiveness.

Denise spoke up. "Why don't we each take an issue? I'll continue with my scrying efforts. Simon, why don't you see if you can do anything about the visual problem, and Jeremiah and Dmitri can handle the weapons issue?"

With that, the meeting broke up.

Quite frankly, I didn't have any idea where to begin with the task we'd been given, but not Dmitri. No sooner had we received our marching orders than he was headed for the front door, tugging me along in his wake.

I waited until we were in the truck and on our way before asking the obvious question. "Where are we going?"

"Garden District."

I might not have been all that familiar with the Big Easy, but that, at least, was a name I recognized. It conjured up images of what I'd seen on my earlier wanderings: antebellum homes surrounded by beautifully landscaped gardens, where old and new money intermingled in full view of the tourists staring with longing through the windows of the historic streetcar running down the middle of St. Charles Avenue.

"Why, might I ask?"

"Why what?"

"Why are we going to the Garden District?"

He laughed.

"Cuz that's where the armory is," he said.

32

HUNT

Dmitri explained that the previous Lord Marshal, the man he'd personally worked for before leaving the city, Charles Winston, had lived deep in the heart of the Garden District. The original mansion had been built in the late 1860s, but after assuming control of the estate, Winston had torn out the wine cellar and replaced it with a custom-built armory. According to Dmitri, it was stuffed to the rafters with the latest and greatest in modern weaponry.

Even better, Dmitri knew where to find the spare key.

It didn't take us long to cross the city and arrive at the Winston estate. Dmitri explained that the former Lord Marshal had lived alone, so we weren't worried about running into anyone and having to explain our presence; as representatives of the current Lord Marshal, we had every right to be there.

Since he could see in the dark nearly as well as I could, Dmitri left the lights off once we were inside, allowing me to move around without his help or the use of my cane. There wasn't time for sightseeing though; he moved through the ground floor like man on a mission, leading me into the kitchen and then down a flight of stairs to the lower level.

The door to the armory was a massive vaultlike contraption that required a digital combination to open. Dmitri strode confidently over to the keypad located to the right of the door and punched in an eight-digit code. There was a loud beep and then the door clicked open.

I'm not a gun freak, not by any stretch of the imagination, but even I was impressed when I got my first look at what was in that room. Racks lined three of the four walls, holding more firearms than I had ever seen in one place. Everywhere I looked the cold sheen of burnished steel winked back at me. There were pistols, shotguns, automatic rifles, even one of those monster machine guns you see in action movies. Ammunition for each weapon was carefully laid out on shelves beneath each rack, the colored boxes looking like soldiers lined up in rows.

Dmitri was like a kid in a candy shop: his eyes opened wide as he wandered down one side of the vault, his hands occasionally reaching up to caress the blackened muzzle of a weapon.

It was an impressive collection.

But it wouldn't do us a damn bit of good.

"While I can appreciate your need to wallow in the equivalent of gun porn, we seem to be forgetting something important."

He barely looked at me. "Yeah? What's that?"

"Firearms don't work against Sorrows."

Reluctantly, he turned away from the guns and pointed toward the back wall. "Yeah, I know. But the guns aren't what we came here for. That is."

Instead of firearms, the rear wall was devoted to melee weapons of every shape and size: swords, axes, maces, flails, and a hundred other weapons I'd never seen before and couldn't name if my life depended on it.

I watched as Dmitri reached up, pulled a broadsword down from its mount, and gave it a few experimental swings through the air in front of him.

"You know how to use that thing?" I asked.

He shrugged. "Of course," he said, as if it was as common as pumping gas or changing a tire. He'd been a warden, after all.

I, on the other hand, had absolutely no experience with a weapon like that.

Trying to put a brave face on it, I said, "Right. How hard can it be?" and stepped over to give him a hand.

We found two big carrying cases in one corner of the room and began to load as many of the weapons as we could into them. Dmitri concentrated on the edged weapons, while I filled my case with those you'd use to bludgeon someone to death. It was cheery work, trust me.

Once we had a good assortment, we carefully sealed the cases and began carrying them out to the truck for transport back to the clinic.

As we moved through the house with our burdens, I happened to glance through an open door to one side. Winston had been in the process of renovating when he'd been struck down: the floor of the room was covered with dust cloths, and a set of hand tools was lying in a neat pile off to one side, just waiting for the work to begin again.

I stopped, staring at the tools. A tiny germ of an idea began to form in the back of my mind, and I did what I could to nudge it along.

Something about the tools . . .

Inspiration struck.

Son of a bitch, I thought, stunned at the idea that was unfolding in my head.

It might actually work . . .

Dmitri was already outside and I hurried to catch up, calling his name as I did so.

He was sliding the case of weapons he was carrying into the rear of the Expedition when I emerged from the house. He finished what he was doing and then turned to face me.

"What now?" he asked.

"I think I've just solved our problem."

He gestured to the weapons we'd already loaded into the truck. "I thought that was what we were doing here."

"I've got something better."

"Like what?"

"Take me to Home Depot and I'll show you."

33

HUNT

When we returned to the clinic, Denise and Gallagher were waiting for us.

Gallagher sounded more tired than usual. I suspected he'd pushed himself a bit too hard. It had apparently been worth it, however, for he passed each of us a small jar, saying, "It's not perfect but it will do in the short term. Just use it sparingly; we don't have that much."

I could hear the others unscrewing the lids to their jars. A horrible stench burst forth the minute they were opened.

"Ugh! What that hell is this?"

"A salve for your eyes. It's a fairy ointment derivative. Rub a little of it on your lids and you'll be able to see through the Curtain that separates this world from the next. If it works as well as I expect it to, the Sorrows will light up like neon signs."

I could hear Dmitri sniffing loudly next to me. "What's in it?" he asked.

"You probably don't want to know."

I knew I didn't. I was also thankful that I didn't need to use the stuff; my ghostsight allowed me to see the Sorrows without any assistance, even in the light of day.

That was a good thing, as there was no way in hell that I was putting anything that smelled like that near my face.

Next it was Denise's turn.

"I have good news and bad news," she said. "The scrying worked, but perhaps too well." There was a rustling sound, like that of newspaper pages being turned. Denise said, "I've marked the hits I got on this map."

There was a moment of silence while the others took a look.

"*Chyort voz'mi!*" Dmitri said sharply and I didn't need a translator to know he wasn't happy with what he saw.

"Somebody want to fill me in?"

Denise sighed. "I got a hit on forty-seven different locations."

Forty-seven? There couldn't be that many, could there?

"How the hell are we going to manage forty-seven packs of these things?" Gallagher asked. The tiredness in his voice had turned to disgust. It sounded like we were outgunned from the start.

But Denise wasn't finished. "It's not as bad as all that."

"It's not?" Sure as shit looked bad to me.

"No," she said emphatically, "it's not. Without a proper focus to zero in upon, the scrying can't be targeted properly. As a result, we end up with a forty-eight-hour window of possibilities."

I thought that one through for a minute. "So, the circles mark locations were the Sorrows are now or where they have been during the last twenty-four hours?"

"Or where they will be by this time tomorrow," Gallagher said. "How do we separate one from the other, then?"

Dmitri spoke up. "Correlate the sighting reports with the markings on the map. If a Sorrow was spotted in that area during the past twenty-four hours, we eliminate it from the list. It won't be perfect, but it will at least start limiting the playing field."

It wasn't a bad idea, and Gallagher said he'd get someone right on it. In the meantime, we still needed to come up with a way to deal with the Sorrows when we confronted them.

Thankfully, my partner and I had already solved that problem. "Dmitri?"

By way of answering, he reached into the large duffle bag he had brought with him into the meeting and lifted out one of the cordless pneumatic nail guns we'd bought at Home Depot the night before. He pointed it at Gallagher's desk and pulled the trigger. The short hiss of the escaping gas was lost in the loud thunk that followed as the projectile sank deep in its target.

I wish I could have seen the expression on Gallagher's face as he stared at the three-inch carpenter's nail that was now three quarters embedded in the side of his desk.

"Sweet Gaia. That's brilliant."

I thought so, too. The nail guns were the cordless variety designed to handle the framing tasks at any modern construction site. They weighed less than seven pounds, could be managed with one hand if necessary, and held roughly four thousand nails at a time. We'd bought fifteen of them, all that the store had in stock, as well as enough boxes of nails to keep us in business for several weeks. The iron content in the nails would be dangerous to the Sorrows and the portability of the nail guns themselves would make it easy for everyone to carry them wherever they were needed.

Along with the nail guns, we'd sorted through the two cases of melee weapons we'd taken from the Marshal's armory and picked out ten or twelve that we thought would be useable, from KA-BAR combat knives to small hand axes. If the Sorrows got in close, at least we would have something in hand to defend ourselves with.

Or so we hoped.

As it turned out, Dmitri was right. It took us almost an hour to match the reports against the locations Denise had identified, but by the time we were finished we had eliminated seventeen locations from our list, bringing the new total to thirty. While it was still a lot, it was at least beginning to reach manageable levels.

With that it was time to bring in the rest of the troops.

Gallagher gathered them together in the backyard and went through what we had learned since our earlier defeat. He walked them through the use of the nail guns they'd been issued and urged them to take one of the handheld melee weapons he and I had retrieved from the armory.

When he was finished, Denise took over, identifying the potential locations and giving instructions on what to do should they encounter anything. Jars full of the eye salve Gallagher had created were distributed to each team leader, and they were given a few minutes to apply it and get used to the effect it had on their vision. They'd all seen Dmitri transform in the midst of battle the other night, but it was still kind of funny to watch them recoil when they turned and looked in his direction. I'd forgotten how unnerving a good-sized polar bear was to behold up close, regardless of the fact that he was on your side.

Numbers were important at this point, so rather than sending us out in pairs, Gallagher reshuffled things a bit and arranged us into two separate teams. The four of us, plus two of the wardens, would return to the high school and face the nest there. The other team would head to the first location on Denise's list to begin hunting for another nest.

For the second time that week, we went on the offensive.

34

CLEARWATER

Hunt had been a liability on the last mission; he knew it and so it didn't take much for Simon to convince him to play a different role. He would still accompany them, but this time he'd remain with the vehicles and be ready to help provide whatever assistance they needed when they came back out again.

Which left five of them to handle the pack of Sorrows. Denise just hoped it would be enough.

The last attack had shown that the Sorrows were highly resistant to magick, but that didn't mean that magick was no longer useful as a weapon in the attack. Quite the contrary, in fact. It just meant that she and Simon were going to have to be more indirect in their use of it, attacking the space and surfaces around the Sorrows, rather than the Sorrows themselves.

They arrived in the same fashion and even parked in the same location. The warden who'd been watching the site for the last twenty-four hours emerged from cover and confirmed that the Sorrows were still inside.

In eerie mimicry of the previous visit, Spencer led the way. Nothing seemed to have changed: there were no sentries and the Sorrows were in the same location as they had been before.

Simon nodded in her direction, indicating it was time for her to do her thing. Denise took a moment to gather her concentration and then called up her Art, using her affinity with all things natural to reach out and alter the gravity of the area at the bottom of the swimming pool, making everything in it weigh considerably more than it had the moment before.

As if summoned by the touch of her magick, the Sorrows awoke as one and then multiple pairs of eyes stared up at them out of the darkness.

"Now!" Simon shouted.

The team opened fire. The nail guns made a short sharp noise— *thunk, thunk, thunk thunk thunk*—and in the confined and tiled space it echoed five times louder than it normally would have. Trapped by the increased gravity and wounded by the iron content in the nails, the Sorrows shrieked with rage and fear.

In seconds, the room was complete chaos. Shouts and screams from both sides filled the air, and the cacophony was punctuated again and again by the sharp sound of the guns as they spat their deadly little missiles at the creatures. The nails didn't stop the Sorrows, but they sure as hell hurt, if the screams the creatures were making was any indication.

Maintaining her gravity well required both power and concentration, and it wasn't long before Denise felt it begin to slip away from her. A Sorrow near the edge of the effect broke free and rushed her, racing up the side of the pool and leaping into midair in front of her. She was knocked to the ground by a backhand sweep from the creature's arm, only to watch as the creature was torn apart before her eyes by the rampaging polar bear.

Around her she could see several of Spencer's people were tossing aside their makeshift firearms, the hoppers of the nail guns now empty of ammunition, and pulling their weapons from their belts to wade in and engage the Sorrows in hand-to-hand combat.

The battle was just as short and bloody as the first time they'd entered these grounds, but the outcome was entirely different. As the old scroll had suggested, the Sorrows were deathly allergic to the iron in their blades and what wouldn't have proved to be a mortal wound against a human being was deadly to the creatures they faced. In the end, they triumphed. All of them had a minor injury or two, but none was life-threatening. Simon ordered Spencer and his men to round up the bodies of the Sorrows and burn them, using the cans of gasoline brought along for just that purpose.

>+++<

Over the next two days they located and destroyed three more nests. The first two were handled without incident, but they lost another man while taking down the third because by then the Sorrows had begun anticipating their movements and had been ready and waiting for them when they arrived. For creatures that were supposedly of limited intelligence, it was an unsettling display of adaptability and initiative.

Denise and Jeremiah were discussing the latest developments with Simon when his cell phone rang. He glanced at the number, excused himself from the conversation, and answered the call.

When he hung up a few minutes later, his face was flushed red with excitement.

"Come on," he said, as he snatched his coat off the back of his chair. "We've got to get over to the Garden District."

"Why?" Denise asked, even as she jumped to her feet and reached for her own jacket.

"Dmitri's waiting for us at the Sidhe enclave over on St. Mark's."

"What's he doing there?"

"He says they've caught a live one."

It took her a minute to realize he was talking about a Sorrow.

The Sidhe had captured a Sorrow!

The SUVs were all in use so they took her car and Simon played navigator as she drove through the empty streets. Hunt spent most of it staring out the window at the darkened city. Just a few days ago the streets had been full of revelers, but now their numbers had dwindled. It was almost as if they'd caught wind of what was going on, some survival instinct in the back of their minds telling them that now was not a good time to be out and about on the streets of New Orleans. She couldn't say she blamed them.

They pulled up in front of another gleaming estate, this one of white marble, and parked in the circular drive. Seconds later they were clustered together on the front steps as Simon rang the bell.

35

HUNT

The Sidhe met us at the door with their glamour firmly in place, doing their best to pass as ordinary humans. Their magick was no match for my ghostsight, however; it stripped the illusion away and let me see them as they truly were. To my surprise, they didn't look all that different from you and me, provided you could ignore their snow white hair, violet eyes, and skin the color of a Minnesotan in midwinter. The pointed ears were a bit of a giveaway as well.

Gallagher had called them Sidhe, but it would have been easier if he'd just said elves. For that was exactly what they looked like to me, Elrond with an attitude.

No sooner had we stepped inside the door than Gallagher and Denise began a heated discussion with our hosts in a language I didn't understand, leaving me to fend for myself for a few minutes. Unfortunately, the house we were in, an old plantation home built in the late 1700s, was lit so well that all I could see was an ocean of white. Even my ghostsight wasn't very helpful; I could see the Sidhe, sure, but nothing beyond that.

Which, when I thought about it for a moment, didn't make any sense.

Where were all the ghosts?

An old place like this should've had at least one or two resident spirits hanging around in the background. Usually they would be popping out of the woodwork right about now, as if my very presence had summoned them to take a look, like they'd done that first day outside the clinic.

But there wasn't a ghost in sight.

Come to think of it, I'd seen very few on the ride over as well. That realization was vaguely disquieting; when we'd arrived in New Orleans a few days ago, they had been practically everywhere. You couldn't turn your head without seeing a ghost hanging on a street corner or watching from behind the window glass. Suddenly they'd all disappeared?

Gallagher's negotiation was still going strong and I was bored standing around in the light, so I decided a little experimentation was in order.

I took out my harmonica and played a short tune, looking to borrow someone else's eyes for a while in order to see what was happening around me.

For the first time since I'd been actively summoning ghosts, nothing happened.

Frowning, I brought the harmonica back to my lips and tried again, this time playing with a bit more force, letting my sense of the city around me affect the tune. What came out was a bit harsher, a bit more demanding, than the previous attempt had been. I played for almost five minutes. Long enough that I could feel the others' attention on me, wondering what the hell I was doing, I'm sure. At that point, unable to summon even a single spirit, I gave up.

Maybe the Sidhe had done something to keep them out of the house—wards at the door, that kind of thing. Or maybe there was something else going on here that I hadn't considered.

I heard footsteps approaching and turned toward them.

"Put that thing away," Gallagher told me as he got closer. "You're making our hosts uncomfortable."

I obliged, sliding my harmonica in my pocket while at the same time making a mental note to try again once I was outside the boundaries of the Sidhe's property.

"From what I've been told, the Sidhe awoke in the middle of the night to find the Sorrow trying to reap the soul from one of their comrades," Gallagher explained. "They eventually managed to overpower it and decided that a living Sorrow might help us solve this thing faster than a dead one. They've got it locked up in a shed out back. Dmitri and one of the Sidhe are standing guard."

I knew how tough the Sorrows were, knew what it took to kill them, so hearing that our hosts had actually captured one alive gave me new respect for their abilities.

It also made me wonder why they weren't in charge of tracking these things down and containing them. I put the question to my companion.

"The Sidhe are an . . . ancient race," he said. "They live among us but don't normally get involved in what they consider 'human' issues."

"Human issues? But they've been attacked too!"

He sighed. "Yes, and in their view they dealt with the threat just as they will do again if necessary. The only reason they called us at all was because of a debt they owe the Council and, as Marshal of the city, I'm the Council's most accessible representative."

Sounded pretty damned selfish, if you asked me.

Gallagher went on. "When we get out there, I'd like you to use that unique perspective of yours and let me know if you see anything unusual. Denise and I will be doing the same."

I was standing in a fairy enclave, taking orders from a mage and getting ready to look at a soul-sucking beast through the eyes of a ghost. And he wanted me to point out the unusual?

Denise slid her arm through mine. "Ready?" she asked.

I kept the irony of my thoughts to myself. "Lead on, woman, lead on."

She did so, using a low voice to narrate what she was seeing as we moved through the house so that I wouldn't be left out of the loop. The Sidhe took us through the sitting room, into the kitchen, out the rear door and across the lawn to a shed as big as a three-car garage.

Once outside, the whiteout faded as my eyes adjusted to the darkness and I could see again. Dmitri was waiting for us by the shed door. When he saw us coming, he took a key from his pocket and turned to the door behind him, unlocking the thick chain that held it secure. Another of the fairy folk stood at his side, a modern compound bow in hand. As Dmitri unlocked the door, the Sidhe fitted an iron-tipped arrow into his bow and drew it back into the ready position.

Seems they weren't taking any chances.

Denise pulled a jar of that foul-smelling salve out of her pocket and smeared some around her eyes before passing it to Gallagher, who did the same.

Dmitri opened the shed door and ushered us inside the space.

The smell of engine oil and gasoline was still hanging in the air, but whatever had once filled the space had been moved elsewhere. In its place was a massive wooden table that looked like it would take several men to move.

A good thing, too, for the captured Sorrow was secured right to the top of it.

Beside me, Denise let out a gasp, and I decided that this would be a good time to have a look for myself. I activated my ghostsight.

The Sorrow swam into view in front of me.

Thick iron chains crossed the creature's chest at several intervals, pinning its arms to its sides, and several more secured its legs at thigh, knee, and ankle. A wide leather strap held its head against the tabletop in an upright position, a thick steel buckle dead center in the middle of the Sorrow's forehead.

For a moment it lay there unmoving, almost as if it couldn't sense that we were there, but then its eyes flew open and it snapped its jaws at us repeatedly.

I made sure to keep my distance; after seeing how quickly they could rend one's soul to tattered slivers, I wasn't going to take any chances. But my companions didn't share my reservations, and after watching them work for a few minutes I got over my hesitation, trusting that whoever strapped it down knew what they were doing.

This Sorrow didn't look much different than the last one I had examined. The same wrinkled gray flesh. The same buzz saw–like mouth. The same strange odor, like a wet dog crossed with an angry skunk.

But there was nothing else.

Nothing new.

My shoulders slumped in resignation.

Gallagher must have seen my reaction, for he said, "We're not done yet, Hunt."

He stepped up to the foot of the table, just a few inches beyond the creature's reach, and took a moment to prepare himself. Or at least that's what I think he was doing, as he stood there with his head hanging down and his arms extended out to either side, palms up and open. I'd seen Denise in a similar posture a couple of times, usually when she was about to try a minor working, and figured that Gallagher was getting ready to do the same.

Aware that the Sorrow probably wasn't going to like what he was about to do all that much, I made sure I was well out of reach.

Gallagher brought his hands up in front of him and cupped them together as if he were making a snowball. Closing his eyes, he began chanting softly, repeating something in Latin several times until a light began to blossom between his hands. As he spread his hands apart, the ball grew, until it was several feet in diameter. When it was big enough, he turned his hands outward, palms toward the head of the table, and gave a little push.

The sphere of light drifted forward, washing over the Sorrow's feet and sliding slowly toward the other end of the table.

As it passed over the Sorrow's form, it revealed what we couldn't see with our own eyes. Thankfully, since it was arcane in origin, I was also able to see it with just my ghostsight.

Where the flesh of the other Sorrows I'd seen had all been unmarked, the skin of this one was covered in crisscrossing bands of black energy, as if it had been wrapped in strand after strand of arcane razor wire. Each strand cut deeply into its skin, and in several places it actually disappeared down into it like a burrowing worm before reemerging from some other spot on its body several inches away. The bands pulsed with a life of their own, constricting and releasing in an odd, complicated rhythm that must have been agony to the creature as they cut again and again into its flesh.

"Holy shit!" Dmitri said and I had to agree with him.

Holy shit, indeed.

There was no way the Sorrow had done that to itself.

Which left only one explanation.

Someone was using magick to control the Sorrows' activities!

36

CLEARWATER

Denise stared back at the others, astounded by what they'd just un-covered. Up until this point, they'd been operating on the general sense that the Sorrows were just obeying instinct; they'd evolved into predators, and predators, as a rule, fed on their prey.

But now the game had changed.

Someone else had been orchestrating this whole thing.

But who? Or what?

As she turned back to the Sorrow, an idea began to form in the back of her mind. It was a long shot, she knew, but they didn't have much more to go on at this point and it just might work. If it did, they'd be a lot closer to putting an end to this.

With nothing to lose, she threw it out to the others.

"We have to let it go," she said.

Hunt visibly started. "Are you nuts? If we let it go, it will just end up feeding on someone else."

He was right: they would be taking that chance. But there were more pressing concerns right now. "And if we don't," she replied, "then we lose our only chance of tracking down whoever is behind all this!"

Simon frowned. "What do you mean?"

"The first scrying didn't work as well as we wanted because we didn't have a focus to tie us directly to our target," she explained. "Now we do."

She knew her old coven mate was no slouch; he got it right away. "We use blood from the Sorrow as a focus and then follow it right back to its lair!"

"And hopefully to whoever is controlling it as well." It was that last part that was questionable. The scrying might simply show them another Sorrow nest, like those they had dealt with over the last few days, but even that would be useful as it would allow them to eliminate another of the creatures' strongholds.

Simon thought it over, looking for holes in her logic. "We're going to have to work fast, though. The blood will only be good as long as it is still in its liquid state. If it dries and hardens, it will be useless to us."

That meant they were going to have to do the ritual from right here in the Sidhe's enclave, rather than back at the clinic, but she could work with that. She'd have to replace her usual tools, but the Sidhe were sure to have substitutes lying around the house, given how mixed up in magick they were as a race.

It wasn't the sanest plan, she knew. For it to work, they had to release the Sorrow back into the city, thereby giving it the chance to take another life, maybe more. But even if there was a one in ten chance of it leading them back to the chief architect, she thought it was worth the risk.

Unfortunately, the Sidhe didn't think so. In fact, they almost threw her and the rest of the group out when Denise explained what they wanted to do. The only good Sorrow was a dead Sorrow, the Sidhe claimed, and they told Simon they wouldn't even consider turning the creature over to him and his people if that was what they intended to do.

But Simon didn't give up. He argued with them for more than an hour, personally pledging to dispatch the Sorrow himself if the scrying didn't work, and in the end they finally gave in, though not without some trepidation.

Denise didn't blame them; she was worried it wouldn't work, too, and she was the one who came up with the idea. But even with her doubts, she still thought it was the best option.

Extracting the blood sample turned out to be a piece of cake; a quick swipe with a knife along the creature's exposed leg, a carefully placed bowl, and she had what she needed. She didn't even bother bandaging the wound because she knew that the Sorrow's accelerated healing ability would seal it up again in no time.

Instead, they retreated to the safety of the mansion itself, leaving Dmitri and the Sidhe to deal with the difficult job of releasing the Sorrow. While they dealt with that issue, the rest of them made sure they did everything possible to allow the scrying to succeed. They were only going to have one shot at this.

Denise sent Simon and Jeremiah into a side room to prepare the site while she and a Sidhe named Evening collected the materials she would need for the working. In the kitchen she found a wide-mouthed stone basin, which would work well as a scrying vessel, and salt, which would fill the lines of the protective circle. A wooden ladle would allow her to transfer the blood from the bowl to the basin when the time was right; a pair of candles from the mantelpiece would provide the proper environment for the entire event.

Back in the sitting room she found that the boys had cleared away the furniture and rolled back the carpet, revealing the wooden floor beneath. Using the salt she carried, Denise sketched out a protective circle, sealing it around herself as she worked. The circle was designed to serve two distinct purposes. Since she would be vulnerable during parts of the ceremony, the circle would protect her from any outside influences. At the same time, it would serve to keep anything inside the circle from getting out.

Just as she was finishing with the circle, Dmitri entered the room. The fact that he was there let her know that the Sorrow had been successfully released. It was time to get started.

She began as she always did, invoking the four guardian elements, one at each of the cardinal points of the compass.

Turning to the east, she said, "O Guardian of the East, Ancient One of the Air, I call you to attend us this night. I do summon, stir, and charge you to witness our rites and guard this Circle. Send your messenger among us, so that we might know that we have your blessing, and protect us with your holy might."

A light breeze stirred her hair, despite the fact that all of the room's windows were closed.

A quarter turn brought her to the south. "O Guardian of the South, Ancient One of the Fire, I call you to attend us this night. I do summon, stir, and charge you to witness our rites and guard this Circle. Send your messenger among us, so that we might know that we have your blessing, and protect us with your holy might."

She suddenly felt warm, as if she'd caught a fever. It only lasted a moment, just enough to let her know that the spirit had heard her. Sweat dripped down her neck as the feeling passed.

The west was the home of the element of water, while the north belonged to earth. She moved through them both, until she stood facing east once more. The air around her now felt charged with energy, and she knew that the protective circle was active.

Picking up the ladle, she dipped it into the bowl of the Sorrow's blood and then poured what she'd collected into the stone basin. Rather than sinking into the water as it normally would have done, the blood spread across the surface instead, creating a crimson slick that filled the bowl from edge to edge. She gave it a moment to settle and then moved to the next part of the scrying.

She took a deep breath, pulling power out of the air around her as she did so, and then blew it back out across the surface of the bloody slick, charging it with energy and activating the scrying.

Within seconds an image formed inside the basin, an image that corresponded exactly with what the Sorrow was seeing as it made its way through the dark city streets. For all practical purposes, Denise was looking out at the world through the Sorrow's eyes: what it saw, she saw. She hoped that she'd be able to recognize enough landmarks to retrace the creature's route.

But it only took a few moments for her to realize that her intentions were too ambitious. The creature stayed in the shadows and kept its head down for the most part, so there was little for her to see but the street passing beneath her feet. The Sorrow only glanced up occasionally, and even then there was little to see. The Sorrow seemed to be responding to some inner guidance system rather than using external landmarks to gauge its position, and Denise knew that she would not be able to make heads or tails of where it was going.

Something more drastic was needed.

She was in the midst of trying to figure out just what to do when something large loomed out of the darkness.

As the Sorrow drew closer to the object, Denise recognized what she was looking at, though she never would have expected to find one here, in the midst of dry land.

It was a Mississippi riverboat, tossed up on its side in the middle of the empty street. Dried river mud still clung to its sides, but the weeds that grew around it said that it had been here for months, maybe even years, and the gaping holes in its hull made it clear that it would never float again.

Denise expected the Sorrow to go around the boat, so she was surprised when it headed right for it. As the Sorrow closed in on the boat, something began interfering with her spell. She could feel the link between her and the Sorrow starting to fade and something told her that she had to act fast if she wanted to continue tracking the creature.

Whatever it was that was interfering with her link was too strong for her to overcome; another few seconds and her scrying spell would dissipate altogether.

Without any real options, she did the one thing she could think of.

She plunged her hand into the middle of the stone basin, sending a pulse of power flooding down her arm at the same time. When that energy met the blood and water in which her hand rested, there was a resounding crack of power that hammered the air inside her protective circle, nearly knocking her over. She held her ground through sheer force of will and was relieved to feel the corresponding surge flow back out of the bowl and up her arm just before the link between her and the Sorrow faded.

Her last effort was not in vain; the visual link was transformed into a physical one. For a short time she would be able to sense the Sorrow's location like a presence in the back of her mind and would be able to make her way toward it just as if she were following a set of directions simply by gauging how each direction "felt" to her.

A wave of dizziness washed over her, the backlash from using so much power in so short a time, but she knew the effort was worth it. She shook her head to clear it and then reached out with one hand to break the circle of salt that surrounded her.

Simon and Jeremiah were at her side the moment the barrier faded.

"I know where it is," she told them. "But we'll have to hurry."

37

HUNT

Denise was worn out from the ritual she'd performed, but as she explained, we didn't have time to waste. The link she created between herself and the Sorrow had a limited life span, so we got out of there as quickly as we could. Leaving Dmitri behind to deal with the Sidhe's apprehension over letting the Sorrow loose, Gallagher, Denise, and I piled into the Charger and took off into the night.

Gallagher drove, allowing Denise to concentrate on following the link she'd created. Unfortunately, we soon found out her directions were a bit problematic: she was connected to the Sorrow as the crow flies, while we were forced to deal with one-way streets and multiple turns to keep us headed in the right direction. Conversation in the car was kept to a minimum; neither Gallagher nor I wanted to disturb her concentration.

We left the Garden District behind and headed toward the river, passing through several less-than-desirable neighborhoods that had been left to crumble and decay in the wake of the government's foot-dragging after Katrina. Eventually we found ourselves in an abandoned industrial park along the bank of the Mississippi.

Denise slowed the car to a crawl and cautiously made her way through the empty streets, carefully noting each building we passed as if looking for a particular one. Apparently she found it, too, for it wasn't long after that she pulled the car to the curb and turned off the engine.

I glanced around.

No riverboat in sight.

Anticipating my question, Denise said, "The boat's half a block down, just beyond the last building in this row. I don't know how good a Sorrow's hearing is, so I didn't want to take any chances."

Getting out of the car, we followed her down the street and around the side of the last building in the row. Peeking around the corner, we saw our destination.

The boat had been washed up out of the river, probably during the floods that accompanied Hurricane Katrina, and had come to rest in the middle of the street that led down to the loading docks a few hundred yards away. It had fetched up against a huge pile of debris—dirt and trees and other assorted detritus—so that its decks were canted at a slight angle.

Moving around inside was therefore going to be difficult.

We stood there and watched for several long minutes, but nothing moved.

"What do you think?" Denise asked.

"I think it's time we take a look," Gallagher replied and moved to head in that direction, but I reached out and grabbed his arm.

"Wait a minute! We shouldn't go in there alone. What if something goes wrong? We should call in the others for backup."

Gallagher scoffed. "We don't have time to wait for the others, Hunt. We need to see what's in there now; we can't afford to miss this opportunity."

Denise didn't say anything, so I took that as tacit agreement with his stance.

"We should at least have some weapons with us," I insisted.

Gallagher grinned. "You forget, Hunt, we," indicating himself and Denise, "are weapons." He shook himself free and moved off.

I reluctantly followed.

We didn't want to enter the derelict through the same route the Sorrow had taken, for stumbling on a nest of those things in the dark was not anyone's idea of fun, so instead we pulled ourselves up onto a nearby pile of debris and slipped in through a hole on the deck above.

It was dark inside, dark and hot, and it felt like we were crawling into the gullet of some massive beast ready to devour us at the slightest misstep. I didn't have any trouble seeing, given my unique means of sight, but I knew the others were going to need some kind of light if they were going to keep up with me. As a result, we decided I would scout out ahead while they followed behind. That would keep them from ruining my sight while at the same time giving them ample warning if they needed to douse the light quickly.

"You're sure it's still here?" Gallagher asked and Denise nodded.

"Can't you feel it?"

Now that she'd mentioned it, I realized that I could too. There was the same electric tension in the air that we'd felt at the sites of the other Sorrow nests. One thing was certain: there were Sorrows somewhere inside the hulk of this old boat.

As Denise conjured up a small ball of light to hold in her hand and light their way, I set out toward the bow of the ship. My plan was simply to make my way forward and hope I found what I was looking for.

Since I didn't really know what that was, I wasn't all that confident in my eventual success, however.

It didn't take long to realize that the old riverboat had been converted into a floating casino. Signs throughout the deck halls pointed the way toward the casino floor, and I steered our group in that direction, figuring that would probably be the biggest area within the ship itself and the obvious place to find the nest.

With the signs to lead me, it didn't take me long to reach the midpoint of the vessel. The hallway we were following suddenly opened up, splitting in two and continuing around either side of the vessel, while directly in front of us you could look over the railing and see down into the center of the vessel, which, I assumed, held the casino floor.

I could hear a rustling sound, as well as smell a familiar odor, coming from the deck below us. I settled into a crouch and waited until the others had drawn close enough to see my signal to wait.

Denise doused the light as planned, and I gave my eyes a moment to readjust before I crab-walked the rest of the way forward until I was directly behind the railing that guarded the rather steep drop on the other side.

Cautiously, I raised my head until I could see over the railing and down to the casino floor on the deck below.

I immediately wished I hadn't.

Like the pool back at the high school, the floor beneath us was a writhing mass of Sorrows. There had to be fifty, maybe more, of the creatures, all intertwined amidst the ruins of craps tables and slot machines.

Standing in the Sorrows' midst was a tall figure dressed in a sweeping cloak of a dark, shimmering material and tall leather boots. Its back was to us, so I couldn't tell if it was male or female, and the few wisps of long white hair that I could see falling beneath the wide-brimmed hat it wore didn't help me decide one way or the other.

The figure was chanting something in a language I didn't understand while drawing strange symbols in the air with its left hand. In its right, it held a long-handled sickle, the edge of the blade gleaming with a pale blue light that seemed to emanate from deep within the metal from which it was formed. The figure's hands themselves, at least what I could see of them, looked skeletal, with the yellow tint of ancient bone visible even from that distance.

As the figure's left hand flexed and moved, the churning pit of Sorrows at its feet responded in kind.

It was creepy as hell, and I knew I'd be seeing the scene in my mind's eye for a long time to come.

Apparently I wasn't the only one who thought so. As Denise reached my side and took a look for herself, I felt a shudder run through her frame.

"What is that?" her look said when she turned to face me, but I didn't know and could only shrug my shoulders in reply.

I waved my hand into the darkness behind us, the signal for Gallagher to move up, and a few seconds later he emerged from the shadows to crouch at my other side.

I cocked my head in the direction of the railing and he slowly drew himself up a few inches to peer over it as we had done.

"Go mbeire an diabhal leis thú!" he swore and quickly dropped back down behind the edge of the railing.

I stared at him in shock.

The language he'd just spoken in was damned similar to the one used by that thing below us!

He pulled me and Denise close and said, in English this time, "We need to get out of here. Right now!"

The look on his face said it all. He was absolutely terrified!

Gallagher turned to head back the way we had come, Denise at his heels, but I couldn't resist one more look over the railing.

The figure had stopped its chanting and now stood stock still, its head cocked slightly to one side as if listening. The Sorrows at its feet were still as well, their heads raised out of the mass of bodies in an eerie replica of the pose held by their master.

It must have heard Gallagher's outburst, for even as I watched, it turned its head to look in my direction.

I don't know what scared me more, the strange visage that stared up at me from the deck below or the fact that it had turned its head around one hundred and eighty degrees without turning its body. Its skin was stretched as tight as a drum over the bones of its face, and its eyes stared out at me like gleaming pools of malevolence. I was frozen in place, unable to move a muscle. My mind was screaming at me to run and all I could do was stand there and stare dumbly back at the dark eyes that stared at me.

If I'd been alone, it would have ended right then and there.

Thankfully, I wasn't. Realizing I wasn't with them, Gallagher came back to find me. He must have recognized something was wrong, for the next thing I knew he slammed me bodily to the floor, breaking the strange connection between me and the grim reaper below us. The instant my gaze fell below the level of the railing I could move again, as if I'd been released from some kind of spell.

For all I knew, that was exactly what did happen.

A howling cry rose up from the deck below us, and I didn't need to look to know that the Sorrows had just been released to pursue of us.

Gallagher hauled me to my feet and sent me stumbling down the corridor after Denise, who was already a dozen or so yards ahead.

"Go, go, go!" Gallagher screamed behind me, and, trust me, I went.

We raced back through the ship at a dead run, plowing through any obstacles that got in our way because we didn't have time to go around. Twice Gallagher was forced to discourage the Sorrows from getting too close by tossing a humming, spitting ball of energy back the way we'd come, knocking those in the front ranks to the ground and slowing those coming up from behind.

While it didn't stop them, it did give us a chance to widen our lead slightly and that was good thing.

We burst out of the hole we'd used to gain entrance, scrambled down the debris pile, and ran like hell for the car parked on the other side of the building just as the Sorrows emerged from the wreck behind us.

Ahead of me, Denise skidded to a stop, turned to face back the way we had come, and raised both hands above her head.

"Gravitas!" she cried, flinging her hands forward as she did so.

Something invisible shot past my ear, and I glanced back just in time to see the pile of debris holding the ship up explode upward as if someone had set off fifty pounds of TNT in its midst. Dirt, trees, and Sorrows went flying in all directions.

Even with the slight delay she'd taken to blast the Sorrows, Denise still beat us to the car. By the time I slid into the backseat, just a second or so behind Gallagher's arrival, she had the car started and was smoking the tires as she spun it around in preparation for getting the hell out of there.

The Sorrows might be fast, but there was no way they were going to outrun a car powered by a 6.1-liter Hemi V-8 engine and driven by a woman who loved speed more than your average NASCAR fan.

By the time we roared out of the industrial park, we'd left the Sorrows eating our dust and unable to follow.

38

ROBERTSON

Robertson sent Doherty and another agent to stake out the location Lafitte had given to them while he put the necessary elements in place.

Clearwater was apparently staying with a man named Simon Gallagher, a well-respected local resident who ran a halfway house and clinic for the less fortunate, which, in Robertson's view, meant roughly half the city. Busting into the place could have unexpected consequences if the press got wind of it. He could imagine the headlines already, some garbage about police brutality and government displeasure with social programs—all of it shouted from the rooftops.

Never mind the fact that he'd need to get a local judge to issue the search warrant on nothing more than the comments made by Lafitte, which probably wouldn't happen. Even if it did, it would likely take three or four days; nothing in the Big Easy happened at the pace he was used to back in Washington.

No, he needed to come at this from a different direction.

That's when the idea to stage a phony health inspection came to him. All he needed was a cop or two and a couple of city vans. The rest he could handle himself.

It took the rest of the afternoon and early evening to coordinate the raid, but he decided that would actually be to his benefit. The health department was normally a nine-to-five operation, so there wouldn't be anyone there if Gallagher chose to call it in and confirm his credentials.

Shortly after eight, Robertson pulled over to the curb two blocks from the clinic. Doherty opened the door and slipped inside.

"Anything?"

Doherty shook his head. "No sign of Hunt, Clearwater, or Alexandrov. There was a shift change about two hours ago, but that was all."

Robertson considered the situation. If he went in and Hunt wasn't there, he'd be taking the risk of alerting Hunt to his presence. On the other hand, if he could deprive Hunt of a location that he felt was safe, that might push him into making an error.

And errors, as Robertson knew, were the bane of a fugitive's existence.

The chance to catch Hunt unaware overrode his caution. They were going in.

He gave the signal to the officer waiting patiently in the squad car behind him. Blue and red lights lit the night as the officer pulled around him and led the small caravan the rest of the way to the clinic parking lot.

Robertson sent Doherty to handle anyone who might be in the three-story house next door and then walked toward the clinic. By the time he reached the door, the officer, Lewis was his name, was waiting for him and the rest of his men, six in all, who were coming up behind them.

With a nod from Robertson, Lewis went into action.

He pounded on the door with the butt of his flashlight. "Police!" he shouted. "Open up!"

Moments later the door was opened by a tall Hispanic man dressed in doctor's scrubs.

"Can I help you?"

Robertson flashed his badge, knowing in the dim light that the other man wouldn't be able to see it clearly, and said, "Health inspection. Step out of the way, please."

Without waiting for a response, he pushed past the other man and entered the building.

He gestured to the others, telling them to spread out and search the place. The facility wasn't all that big and it didn't take long for them to relay the fact that none of the people they were looking for were present.

Which meant he had to turn to option B. Put Hunt back on the street to throw him off balance.

The man who'd opened the door finally broke away from the cop who'd been instructed to detain him as long as possible and he marched over to Robertson.

"What the hell is going on here? And who are you? A health inspector you said?"

Rather than answer the man's questions, Robertson went on the offensive.

"I'm going to need to see your permits and all of your hazardous-waste paperwork. Then I'm going to need to examine randomly selected patient records, to ensure that proper HIPAA procedures are being followed."

"Permits? Waste paperwork? What the hell are you talking about?"

Robertson whirled on the man.

"Your name?"

"Ferrara. Charles Ferrara."

"Well, Charles, say hello to your worst nightmare. You thought the IRS was a pain in the ass?" Robertson laughed. "Not even close!"

He pointed at the double doors in front of him. "Is this the clinic itself?" he asked, and then, without waiting for an answer, stepped inside.

The room was full of makeshift hospital beds; there had to be twenty, maybe thirty, in all, and every single one of them held a patient.

But what brought him to an abrupt halt three or four steps inside the room was the fact that none of the patients was moving. They lay on their backs, with their arms at their sides and their eyes staring upward. It was like they were mannequins rather than living, breathing people.

"What's wrong with them?" he asked softly, suddenly afraid to wake any of them up.

Ferrara answered dismissively. "It's complicated; you wouldn't understand."

Just like that, Robertson knew he was lying. He had heard enough liars in his day to know when someone was being untruthful, especially about something as major as this.

They don't know what it is.

The thought leapt into his mind from out of nowhere, but the minute it had he knew it was true.

They had a room full of people who looked like they were in some kind of a coma and didn't know how it had happened or what was going to happen next . . .

It was a frightening thought.

These people belonged in a hospital, preferably one with a containment unit, rather than in some street-side clinic. Just keeping them here was not only endangering their lives, but endangering the lives of others in the city. If this thing was infectious in any way, they could have a full-scale disaster on their hands.

It might even be too late.

Despite his growing concern, Robertson wanted to jump for joy at the opportunity in front of him. He no longer needed to manufacture a reason to shut the place down, even if only temporarily; one had just been handed to him on a silver platter.

With Ferrara already forgotten behind him, Robertson pulled out his cell phone and made the first of a series of calls. By the time he finished some twenty minutes later, the first of the units dispatched to transfer the patients to a full-scale medical facility was already arriving.

If that didn't bring Gallagher running, nothing would.

And once he had Gallagher, Robertson was sure he could track down Hunt.

39

HUNT

As we raced down the street, Gallagher's phone rang. He answered it, listened for a few minutes, and then said, "Okay, gather whoever you can and meet me at the house on Nineteenth."

Hanging up, he turned to the two of us and said, "Local authorities just ordered our people to shut down the clinic. They want the sick to be transferred to the nearest hospital, and they hauled in some of my people for questioning. We've got another house we maintain for emergencies, so we're going to have to operate from there for now."

After that, he refused to talk while in the car about what we'd seen, insisting that we wait until we were all safely ensconced behind the protective wards surrounding our new location.

I held on to my temper and waited.

Our new location was a three-story, multifamily home in a fringy neighborhood. Gallagher pulled around to the extended drive in back, preventing the Charger from being seen from the street, and then led us inside.

Once there, I didn't waste any time confronting him for some answers.

"What the hell is going on?" I asked. "You knew that thing back there?"

It was more an accusation than a question.

"I recognized it, yes," he said, his tone grimmer than usual.

"Want to fill us in?" Denise asked. She hadn't gotten as good a look as I had, but I could tell by the sarcasm in her voice that she too was wondering what was up.

We were seated in the kitchen with the lights on, which meant I was back to being blind again. For once, that was actually fine with me, as I wanted to listen for what Gallagher wasn't saying, more than what he was, and I didn't want any visual distractions. Dmitri had been right: Gallagher had led us into danger, more interested in the end result than what could happen if we encountered trouble, and we'd almost paid the price for it.

I wondered what he knew that he wasn't sharing with us.

"In Wales, he's the Angeu, the King of the Dead," Gallagher began. "Other cultures have other names—the Bretons of southern France call him Ankou. To most of us here in North America, he's the Grim Reaper. Different names, same being."

You have got to be shitting me . . .

"Death? Are you telling me that thing we just saw was Death himself?"

I couldn't keep the shock out of my voice. Having just run away from Death was a bit too weird even for me, regardless of how strange things had gotten over the last few years. Mages, doppel-gangers, and berserkers, okay. Heck, I could even deal with fairies. But Death himself?

Give me a freakin' break.

Unfortunately, that's exactly what Gallagher was telling us.

"Not Death per se, or at least not as you are suggesting, but a personification of him just the same. Some say the Angeu was the first child of Adam and Eve, cursed when his parents abandoned him in the Garden. Others claim he is the last to die in any given year, forced to collect the souls of the dead until his replacement ar-rives. I don't really know; all I do know is that once the Angeu sets his sights on you, it's as good as over. He's got the power of any num-ber of Old World demigods put together."

Demigods?

"What the hell is a Welsh . . . um, demigod, doing in New Or-leans?" I asked, amazed I could even get the question, crazy as it was, out of my mouth.

"Stealing souls, obviously. But for what purpose, I don't know."

Neither did Denise.

At that point Dmitri joined us, having finally returned from the Sidhe enclave. He handed something to Gallagher, though I couldn't see what it was, and then sat down at the table with us. He listened closely as we brought him up to speed.

As usual, Dmitri focused on the practical aspects and didn't care too much about the reasons behind it all. "It doesn't matter why he's doing it," he said. "I couldn't care less, in fact. All that matters is that we put an end to it."

In one sense he was right: stopping the Angeu was what was im-portant, when you got right down to it. But understanding the how and why behind it all could very well provide us with the means to do that very thing. Without it, we were just shooting in the dark. We were having a hard enough time dealing with the Sorrows, never mind an entity that could control dozens of them at once.

And if it was really the personification of Death . . .

"How do you kill Death, for heaven's sake?" I wanted to know.

"You don't," said Gallagher, "or rather, you can't. Not really. But you *can* send him back where he belongs. According to legend, the Angeu isn't native to this plane but resides in Annwyfn, the Welsh underworld, in a great fortress of glass known as Caer Wydyr. He comes here only to collect the souls of the dead and must return when he has done so."

I laughed, but there was no humor in it. "Apparently, no one bothered to tell him that."

"Thankfully, there is a way to force him back."

A moment later the sound of thick, heavy pages turning filled the air. "I asked Dmitri to stop by the council chambers on his way over and pick this up for me. I know they're in here somewhere . . . ," Gallagher said, the second half more to himself than us. Eventually, he found whatever it was.

"Ah. Here we go. The Knives of Findias."

"The who of what?"

I couldn't see it, but I knew I was getting one of those looks, the ones that say, "Don't be an idiot, Hunt."

"The Knives of Findias, crafted by the druid Uicias in the city of the same name deep in the heart of Tir na nOg."

Uh huh. So much clearer now, thanks.

Denise came to my rescue. "How will the knives help us against the Angeu?"

"Well, alone they're no different than any other pair of ceremonial daggers: a bit of steel with a point and a sharp edge. But when they are used together, they have the power to return a soul to its rightful place.

"Which for the Angeu . . ."

". . . is back in Caer Wydyr," Denise finished for him.

I have to say that I wasn't all that thrilled with the plan.

"So let me get this straight," I said to them. "You're suggesting that we hunt down a pair of knives that may or may not even exist, fight our way through that horde of Sorrows we saw at the boat, and get close enough to the King of the Dead to stab him with two cere-monial daggers without getting blasted to oblivion in the process? That's your plan?"

Gallagher grunted. "Do you have a better one?"

Well, yeah, I did. Getting the hell out of town sounded like a great plan to me, but I knew it wasn't going to go over very well with the rest of them, so I just kept my mouth shut, much as it galled me to do so.

Ever the practical one, Dmitri asked, "Where are they? The knives, that is?"

To my surprise, Gallagher had an answer for him.

"Chicago," he said.

"For the last months they've been on display at the Field Mu-seum, actually."

40

CLEARWATER

They needed the soul knives if they were going to have any chance of defeating the Angeu, which meant someone had to go to Chicago and get them. With Jeremiah wanted by the FBI and Simon insisting that he continue to coordinate the wardens' activities, Denise became the logical choice. Dmitri volunteered to go with her, confident that Denise could bail him out with a little judicious use of her Art if his fake ID didn't stand up to airport security.

Which left only the question of how they were to obtain the knives once they arrived.

"Is there anyone we know who can pull some strings with the curator?" Denise asked. "We wouldn't need them for long, maybe a week at most."

The three men stared at her without saying anything.

Thinking they were upset with the time frame, she said, "Okay, let's say two weeks to be safe, then."

Simon cleared his throat, a habit he'd had from the old days when he wanted to say something uncomfortable to her. She picked up on it right away.

"What?" she asked, starting to get a bit irritated. *Did they think it was going to take them three weeks?*

But that wasn't it at all.

"They aren't going to loan us the knives, Denise," he said.

She frowned. "Well then how do you expect . . . Oh. I see."

And she did.

They expected her to steal the knives right out of the museum!

"No way," she said. "Not a chance!"

This time it was Hunt who answered her. "There isn't any other way, Denise. They certainly aren't going to give us the knives."

She didn't like it. Didn't like it at all. She told the others as much.

"I understand your reticence," Simon said, "and if there was any other way to do this, I wouldn't ask. But with the Council dead we don't have the luxury of taking that route, and doing so would take too long anyway."

In the end, they managed to persuade her, but only by agreeing that the knives would be returned to their rightful place and an anonymous donation made to the museum to cover the cost of repairing any damage done.

The last flight to Chicago had already left for the evening, so they reserved their tickets online, checked in through the automated system, and then caught a decent night's sleep.

First thing the next morning, they headed for the airport.

Denise was a little apprehensive as they approached the security checkpoint, but things went without a hitch and before she knew it, she and Dmitri were sitting in the gate area, waiting for their flight.

>+—+<

The purchase of two tickets using a credit card issued to Denise Clearwater hadn't gone unnoticed by the FBI watchdogs, who notified Robertson, who in turn sent Doherty out to the airport with orders to secure a seat on the same flight and follow them to their destination.

Doherty did as he was told. When the two targets boarded flight 937, bound for Chicago, the special agent was seated three rows behind them on the opposite side of the aircraft.

Wherever they were going after arriving in the Windy City, he intended to be there too.

>+—+<

Because they were planning on staying only one night, they had a single carry-on bag each and didn't have to wait for luggage after deplaning. They caught a taxi in front of the terminal and had it drop them off at their hotel, which was only a few blocks from their true destination, the Field Museum.

They checked in with the front desk and were given adjoining rooms. They ordered lunch from Denise's room and while they ate they used a tourist map that had been kindly provided by the concierge to go over their plan step-by-step.

The museum had been built back in 1893 to house the biological and anthropological collections from the World's Columbian Exposition of the same year. It was renamed the Field Museum of Natural

History about ten years later in honor of its first major benefactor, Marshall Field, and today occupied a stretch of parkland that also housed the Shedd Aquarium and the Adler Planetarium, making it one of the most visited locations in the city of Chicago.

That meant there would be a lot of people roaming around inside the place, which made things a little bit riskier for them than Denise would have preferred. Still, she couldn't come up with a better idea to accomplish what they needed to accomplish.

Dmitri was a quick study and didn't need more than a short review of what they'd discussed the night before, which reassured her that he'd done this kind of thing before. Rather than making her uncomfortable, the knowledge that an experienced hand was there only helped to steady her nerves. After all, she mused, she usually didn't spend her days robbing a national museum.

Getting in was going to be easy. They'd simply buy two tickets at the front door and waltz on in. But getting out again, with the soul knives in hand? That was going to be the hard part.

Simon had told them that the knives were part of the exhibition of European treasures currently housed in the special exhibition gallery on the second floor. Unfortunately, the map they were looking at made it clear that there were actually four such galleries on that floor—one at either end of the main hall, as well as one each to the left and right of the two-story central gallery that split the building in half. It looked like they were going to have to figure out which was which and then finalize the details of their escape once inside. It was a detour, yes, but only a minor one and she didn't think it would cause them too much trouble.

At least, she hoped it wouldn't.

With lunch over, and the plan firmly in mind, the two of them set out to do what they had come to do.

They bought tickets like the hundreds of other tourists visiting the museum that day and walked in through the front door. The gallery they wanted turned out to be the first one they entered on the second floor. The large rectangular space was filled with artifacts from several different early European cultures, from the Vikings to the Welsh. The knives were laid out on a bed of black velvet in a glass case about halfway through the exhibit and Denise had no trouble locating them thanks to the shimmer of arcane energy they gave off.

They were wicked looking things: the blades as dark as midnight, their handles wrapped in bits of worn leather. They weren't very long, the blades probably six or seven inches at most.

Now all they had to do was get them out of the case and then out of the museum.

In order to do that, they had to wait until the museum shut down for the day. And since they needed to still be inside the building when that happened, to avoid having to break in as well as break out, they set out to find a place to hide during the changeover.

A utility closet at the far end of the gallery turned out to be just what they needed. Once they knew where it was, they wandered around the rest of the museum, basically wasting time until an announcement over the intercom let the guests know that the museum would be closing in fifteen minutes.

Hearing it, they made their way back to the second floor, waited until they were certain no one was looking in their direction, and then slipped inside the closet. In order to keep the cleaning crew from walking in on them, Denise cast an obfuscation spell on the door, effectively masking it from the crew's memory and sight. If the cleaning crew needed supplies, they'd wander down to the closet on the first floor instead, without giving the closet on the second floor even a passing thought. The spell would wear off in a few hours, but that was long enough for their purposes. The cleaning crew should be long gone by then. Denise and Dmitri settled in to wait.

>++<

Doherty had been reporting back to Robertson on an hourly basis. This time, when he got his superior on the phone, he thought he knew what was going on.

"They're going to rob the museum," he said.

Robertson, as expected, was incredulous. "You can't be serious," he replied.

But Doherty was. He explained how Clearwater and Alexandrov had been casing the place for the last hour and how they'd just done what they could to secret themselves in a utility closet. What else could they be doing?

"I don't know," Robertson said and Doherty could hear the concern in the other man's voice. It was the unusual and the unexpected that got him every time.

"Stay with them," his boss told him. "If they commit a crime, stop them, but otherwise, just continue to tail them for now."

"Roger that," Doherty replied and settled in to wait and see what Clearwater and Alexandrov would do.

>++<

The moment they left their hiding place behind, Denise used her Art to circumvent the alarm system, keeping the motion sensors from registering their presence as they moved across the gallery floor.

When they reached the exhibit, Dmitri waited until Denise had sent a surge of electricity through the sensors protecting the glass, burning them from the inside out, and then lifted one of his heavily booted feet and sent it smashing through the front of the glass case.

Denise scooped up the knives and turned to leave.

A man's shout rang out across the gallery.

"FBI! No one move!"

Where in Gaia's name did he come from? Denise wondered.

The newcomer was in his midthirties with dark hair and a nervous expression on his face. He was dressed casually, in jeans and light jacket, but the badge on a lanyard around his neck and the pistol he was pointing at them made it hard to take him for anything but an officer of the law.

"Hands up where I can see them!"

Denise glanced at Dmitri, expecting him to make a move, but he simply shrugged and put his hands up.

Knowing he must have a good reason, Denise did the same.

The FBI agent crossed the gallery and stopped several feet away from them. The gun in his hand pointed first at Dmitri, then at her, and then back again at Dmitri, as if he couldn't decide who was a bigger threat.

"Put the knives down, slowly, and then kick them over here," the agent told her.

Any time now, Dmitri, she thought.

Wanting to appear cooperative, she lowered herself into a squat and put the knives on the floor, one next to each foot. She stood back up again, slowly, just like she'd been told, and then used her right foot to slide the first one in his direction.

The agent kept his eyes on her and didn't even look at the knife.

Come on, come on.

She repeated the action, this time with her left foot.

This time, his gaze slipped downward, focusing on the knife for just a second, maybe two.

It was enough.

Without warning, Dmitri changed.

One moment he was human, and in the next he wasn't. In his

place was an eleven-hundred-pound polar bear with an attitude to match.

Shocked into immobility, the FBI agent didn't stand a chance. To give him credit, he tried, he really did. He was in the midst of turning toward Dmitri, his gun arm swinging away from Denise and in the direction of the threat, when Dmitri clubbed him to the floor with one massive paw.

That was it.

Lights out.

Denise let out a breath she didn't realize she was holding and bent to check on the officer. He was unconscious and probably would be for some time. Blood was flowing freely from several scratches across his scalp, but none of them was deep enough to be life-threatening and his pulse was strong.

From behind her there was a grunt of pain as Dmitri shifted back. While he dragged the agent over to the same utility closet they had hidden in earlier and left him inside, out of sight, she picked up the soul knives and stashed them in the satchel she'd brought along for just that purpose.

They left the building through the same door they had entered through earlier that afternoon and set off down the street at a steady, but unhurried pace.

They were two blocks away when they heard the first of the sirens. Several squad cars roared past moments later, responding to the alarms they'd set off at the museum. They kept their heads down, just another couple out for a walk, and managed to hail a cab a few blocks later.

Denise was concerned about getting the soul knives through airport security, but in the end, that too proved to be much easier than she had expected.

Rather than trying to plant a suggestion in the minds of half a dozen different TSA agents, Denise decided it would be easier to alter the image on the X-ray machine while simultaneously jamming the flashing light that signaled an alarm. She waited until her bag was about to go through, then said a few words beneath her breath and directed her will at the monitor.

That was all it took. Twenty minutes later they were boarding their flight back to New Orleans, the weapons they needed to banish the Angeu back to where it belonged stuffed unceremoniously in the small duffle bag Denise carried in one hand.

HUNT

With Denise and Dmitri gone, and Gallagher coordinating the activity of the seven wardens and the handful of medical volunteers who'd joined us at the new safe house while at the same time trying to determine what the Angeu could be up to, I was left to fend for myself for the day. The scarcity of the ghosts at the Sidhe enclave still troubled me. Was it an isolated incident, perhaps due to the presence of the Sidhe themselves, or was it more widespread and we just hadn't noticed?

I intended to find out.

I convinced Gomez to drive me around the city for a few hours and used that time to observe the city's spectral population.

Or rather the lack thereof.

On the day we'd arrived in New Orleans the dead had been

everywhere. I couldn't turn my head without seeing half a dozen or more. And now they were nowhere to be seen.

There were still a few haunts hanging around, those spectral presences that were so old as to be little more than whispers in the dark, and more than a handful of apparitions, which were nothing more than memories of a life caught in an endless loop. But the true ghosts, those spectral presences that still retained their human form as well as the ability to interact with the world around them as independent creatures, were few and far between.

I caught sight of a few in the heart of the Quarter, but they slipped away before I could shanghai them with a tune from my harmonica. The usual summoning songs didn't work either; while on Bourbon Street I had my driver pull over and wait for me by the side of the road, but after almost half an hour of playing, I was forced to give up without having called a single ghost to my side.

I did, however, earn $9.50 from tourists slipping me their change.

I was certain that the Angeu had something to do with the missing ghosts but couldn't put two and two together to make four.

Part of the problem was the fact that I didn't really see the lack of ghosts as a negative. I never understood what role they played in the grand scheme of things, and being followed around by them on a regular basis could be downright irritating.

I headed back to the safe house more confused than when I had set out earlier.

The afternoon passed slowly and when I had a chance to discuss the issue with Gallagher, he was as much at a loss as I. Unfortunately, his optimism kept him from recognizing the true depth of my concern.

"Don't worry, Hunt," he told me. "Once Denise returns with the soul knives, we'll be able to set everything right again."

I seriously doubted that. He was putting all his eggs in one bas-ket, and if there was anything I'd learned over the last few years it was that desperate plays often don't turn out as well as you hope they will. But after my demoralizing day, I didn't have the energy to argue the point with him. Instead, I wandered off to bed a good hour earlier than usual, figuring catching up on my sleep might not be a bad idea.

Unfortunately, my body had other ideas.

I lay there, wide awake, for quite a while before giving up and getting out of bed. The window in my room looked out over the front of the property, letting me see up and down the road in either direction, and I sat there awhile, just watching.

Looking for some reassurance.

Hoping that I'd see a ghost or two if I sat there long enough.

Where were all the ghosts?

The question was haunting me.

At the time I had no idea that my inability to sleep was going to save my life.

But that's exactly what happened.

The sound of an approaching engine caught my ear and it wasn't long before a dark-colored Hummer appeared at the top of the street.

Except it wasn't.

A Hummer, that is.

Not unless Hummers now came draped in the spectral image of a rickety old cart pulled by a team of horses as a standard feature.

The horses were an odd pair: one young and vibrant and full of vigor and the other old and decrepit and more than likely blind in at least one eye, given the way it stumbled forward. But the worst thing that my sight showed me was the hunched figure I could see in the driver's seat, a figure dressed in a dark cloak and wide-brimmed hat.

I didn't need to see that skeletal face to know just who it was that I was looking at.

As I was trying to process the fact that the Angeu had reversed the cards on us and tracked us to our base of operations just as we'd done to him earlier, he raised his hand and used one long bony finger to point in my direction.

As if on cue, a group of Sorrows swarmed over the sides of the cart and rushed toward the compound.

I had just seconds to get the word out or we were going to be overrun by a dozen or more of the soul-sucking creatures.

I did the only thing I could think of.

I stepped into the hall and yelled my head off.

Ridiculous or not, it saved lives. My own included.

The wardens had been prepped for just such an emergency; with this many of the Gifted clustered in one location, we'd always been a prime target for the Sorrows and plans had been made to deal with an attack should one happen. By the time I hit the ground floor, Gallagher's people were pouring into the hallway from the rooms on either side, armed with both handguns and melee weapons, and lights were going on all around the compound.

As a result, I found myself in the midst of the conflict, blinded by the light, and unable to see much of anything.

It wasn't the safest place to be.

Shouts rose, mingling with the howling cry of the Sorrows, and then everything was a chaotic mess, with men and women facing off against the Sorrows as the creatures tried to force their way inside the house. Thanks to their unearthly nature, the Sorrows glowed with a shimmering silver aura and so stood out slightly against the whiteout I currently was seeing, but my human allies did not. Unable to see them, I didn't dare try and make my way out of the fighting, so there was nothing to do but back into the nearest corner and hope I could defend myself if the Sorrows broke through.

When a momentary lull fell over the fighting, Gomez took pity on me, pulling me out of my corner and shoving me inside a nearby room, out of the main action.

Seconds after he did, I heard him give a painful shout in the corridor outside the door and wondered if the distraction had proved to be his undoing. I fervently hoped not.

In the dark room my eyes adjusted and I could see again.

I was in a small storeroom, if the boxes of goods lining the walls were any indication. A single window looked out over the side yard, which led around to the rear of the property.

Out in the hallway, someone, Spencer maybe, was shouting for Gallagher's men to fall back, and hearing it I knew that I couldn't stay here much longer. There was no way I could take on the Sorrows myself. If they caught me, I was as good as dead.

I hustled over to the window, shoved it open, and climbed through. Once outside I made my way around to the back of the house, heading straight for the fence along the rear of the property. Decatur Street ran past the house on the other side of that fence. In the event of an emergency, Gallagher's people had been instructed to regroup several blocks away from the clinic, and Decatur Street could take me there just as well as any other.

With a last look back toward the beleaguered men and women fighting inside the house, I slipped over the fence and headed off down the street, feeling about as useless as a priest in a whorehouse.

42

HUNT

The rendezvous point was an empty warehouse several blocks to the south and I headed in that direction as soon as I was clear of the compound. If we were going to have packs of Sorrows hunting us through the streets, I wanted to put a few more bodies between them and me without delay, and there was definitely a certain safety in numbers.

I moved through the night without difficulty, thankful for my ability to see in the darkness. Not only did it keep me from crashing into what would otherwise have been unseen obstacles, but it let me see what was coming my way, preventing the Sorrows from sneaking up on me from the shadows.

Rather than heading directly for the warehouse, I took a circuitous route, making random left and right turns for the first few blocks in order to confuse the trail. The Sorrows might not have the ability to reason things out, but the Angeu certainly did. I stopped at an intersection and turned around, staring back the way I had come, searching for anything moving amidst the parked cars and recessed doorways.

I glanced at the street sign above my head, made some mental calculations, and then set off down the narrow street to my left, intent on reaching the rendezvous before too much more time had passed.

Half a block later a figure stepped out of the shadows ahead of me, blocking my way. From his height and the width of his shoulders, I knew it was a man, but that was all; the light behind him kept him in silhouette, hiding him in shadows that even I couldn't pierce. There was something about him that seemed familiar, something about the way he stood or carried himself that set that old alarm bell in my gut ringing in warning. I'd met him before; I was sure of it.

I slowed and looked back over my shoulder, just in time to see two men emerge from one of the cars I'd run right past a few seconds before and step up behind me, cutting off my retreat.

I was boxed in from the front and the back.

Not only that, but the trap had been sprung with such elegant precision that even I had to admit that they knew what they were doing, whoever they were. I was starting to suspect that I might be in a little bit of trouble.

"Never let them see you sweat" was my motto, so I slowed my walk, casually glancing to either side as I did, hunting for a way out of the mess I'd suddenly found myself in.

That's when the one in front decided to speak up.

"Hello, Hunt. Remember me?"

Unfortunately, I did. It was hard to forget a man who'd told you straight up that he intended to see you hang for what you'd done. Especially if you knew that you were innocent of the very thing he'd been accusing you of. The man in front of me was my own private bogeyman, the one I'd been waiting to catch up with me for more than three months, and I recognized him the moment he opened his mouth.

Dale Robertson.

Special Agent, Federal Bureau of Investigation.

Where in heaven's name had he come from?

Forget what I said about a little bit of trouble. With Robertson here, I was in a whole LOT of trouble.

My shock must have been readily apparent, for Robertson actually had the audacity to chuckle. "What's the matter, Hunt? Cat got your tongue?"

He shouldn't have laughed. If he hadn't, I probably would have simply stood there in open-mouthed shock as his men closed in from behind and arrested me. But that laugh galvanized me into action. Although a moment before I'd been all but frozen where I stood, his obvious delight at surprising me burned away my indecision like fog in the morning sunlight. I knew that if I let them take me, I'd never see anything but the inside of a jail cell for the rest of my life. I had to act and I had to do it now.

"Nah," I said, glancing around casually as I did. "I'm just looking for words that are small enough for you to understand."

A white Cadillac was parked against the curb, blocking my access to the street, but I knew without having to think about it too much that going in that direction was suicide. If I got past the car I'd be in the open street, a clear target if they decided to shoot first and ask questions later.

To my right was a long stretch of brick wall that extended all the way to the end of the block, where Robertson was currently standing. An alley bisected it, most likely to allow delivery trucks to make deliveries to the rear of the building next to me, but its entrance was blocked by a wrought iron gate and secured with a thick chain and padlock.

It looked like I didn't have anywhere to go, and I knew that this particular spot had been chosen exactly for that reason. The trouble with a plan you throw together at the last second, though, is that you often miss simple little details like the one staring me in the face right now.

The gate to the alley was locked, yes, but there was a gap at the top large enough to allow a man to slip through if he was willing to deal with a bit of a bump and tumble on the other side. Not wanting to telegraph my move before I made it, all I had time for was one quick glance, but it looked like I could fit.

It was either that or take my chances out in the street.

My silence must have stretched for too long, because Robertson took a couple of steps forward, his hand going to the gun I was sure was inside the dark suit jacket he was wearing.

"Aren't you the joker, Hunt? Enough of this bullshit," he said. "Face the wall and put your hands over your head. You're under arrest for the murder of Detective Miles Stanton and Hector Morales."

I didn't bother with a response. I knew that I hadn't killed either of them, that they'd actually been killed by a doppelganger masquerading as me during the height of the events in Boston several months ago, but there was no way I would ever be able to prove that to Robertson. I'd look certifiably insane just trying to do so, and a life sentence in a facility for the criminally insane was just as bad as one in a federal penitentiary. Perhaps worse. No way was I going to let them take me in.

I feinted left, toward the open street, and then threw myself in the other direction, my hands grabbing the iron bars of the fence and hauling myself upward, my feet scrambling for purchase against the painted iron.

Shouts filled the air, but I wasn't listening; I'd heard all I wanted to hear from that smug-faced bastard already. If I stopped to hear what he had to say, I would be lost while the night was still young.

Reaching the top of the gate, I scrambled part of the way over it and then let gravity take over, falling in a heap on the other side.

So far, so good.

I didn't have time to gloat, however, since I could hear running footsteps approaching the gate from the other side. I surged to my feet and took off down the alley, headed for the opening at the other end. If I could reach it before they thought to send anyone around the block, I'd have a chance to lose them in the warren of side streets.

Before I could do that, though, I had to avoid getting shot in the back. The alley was narrow and unfortunately empty of anything large enough to provide cover. Even though it was pitch black, I would be in serious trouble if they decided to start shooting, since there was nowhere for me to go until I reached the other end. If they opened fire, it would be like shooting a pig in a barrel. They couldn't miss. I hunched over, trying to present a smaller target, and kept running.

To my surprise, no one shot at me.

I burst out of the alley, cut between two parked cars, and dashed across the street in a diagonal line to my left, headed in the direction I'd originally been traveling. Going the other direction might have taken me farther away from Robertson and his men, but it also led back to where I had come from, and for all I knew the Sorrows were still back there, waiting like spiders in their web.

I'd rather take my chances with the goon squad from the FBI any day of the week.

At the next intersection I turned right again, but not before shooting a look up the street to my left. Just as I feared, Robertson was racing toward me, his gun held high in his right hand. He was less than a block away. He must have doubled back in an effort to try to cut me off, leaving his two accomplices to chase after me down the alleyway, like a hunter uses his hounds, forcing the fox out ahead of the pack where it was more vulnerable.

Damned if it wasn't working, too.

I didn't think he'd seen me yet, the streets being heavily shadowed, with the streetlamps few and far between, and for a moment I considered simply dropping to the ground and rolling under one of the cars parked nearby, hoping he'd miss me in the darkness. I dismissed the idea as quickly as it had come, however, knowing that if he had seen me I would then be a sitting duck, unable to extricate myself from beneath the vehicle with any speed or dexterity.

Running was still my best option.

No sooner had I made the decision than a shout sounded from over my shoulder and a bullet spanged off the car next to me, ricocheting into the darkness. Apparently the two men who'd followed me down the alley had just caught up. I didn't bother to turn and look; they were back there somewhere, that's all I needed to know. I took off at full speed down the street in front of me, trying to increase the distance between myself and my pursuers.

I hadn't gone another ten steps before I began to feel it. My heart was hammering madly away, my breath was coming in short, sharp gasps, and my chest felt like it was on fire. My efforts over the last few days had worn me out and now I was paying the price.

Knowing I needed to increase the distance between myself and my pursuers, I took a chance and ducked down a narrow alley that suddenly came up on my right. If I could reach the other end before they got to the one I'd just entered, I could effectively lose them in the tangle of streets beyond.

I raced forward, dodging bags of trash and discarded debris, my gaze set firmly on the other end and the sanctuary it represented.

Twenty yards became ten.

Ten became five.

Almost there . . .

Something punched me in the back and knocked me sprawling, just as the sound of a shot echoed in my ears. My face collided with the pavement and I slid forward, propelled by a combination of my own momentum and the force of the shot.

For a moment, I didn't feel anything, didn't feel anything at all, and then the pain exploded through me—intense, agonizing pain that started in my shoulder and spread throughout my body, nearly overwhelming in its searing fire. My head was spinning and darkness loomed at the edges of my sight, but I fought back against it with everything I had. If I passed out now, it was all over.

Get up! my mind screamed at me. *Get up now!*

If I didn't, I was dead. I knew that much and yet the simple act of pushing myself up onto my knees was nearly impossible. It felt like it took forever. The voice in my head kept screaming at me the whole while, urging me to get to my feet and get out of there, before it was too late. All I wanted to do was lie down and rest, to take a break for a little bit, but that voice got me going, and before I knew it I staggered to my feet and stumbled off down the road.

I glanced over to see the left front of my shirt soaked with blood and looked away, afraid to know any more. *Deal with it later,* the voice soothed, *first you need to get away.*

Who was I to argue with that logic?

The problem was that my feet didn't want to cooperate with me any more. It was like they suddenly had a mind of their own; they felt heavier with every step and my fine motor control was slipping, causing me to weave and stumble erratically.

I wasn't going to get much farther: that was obvious. My only hope of survival was to find a hole and pull it in after me long enough that they stopped looking.

In the meantime, I'd just have to keep from bleeding to death.

I staggered out of the alley and turned, though at that point I couldn't have told you which direction I was heading. All I knew was that I was now out of sight and momentarily safe from any more gunfire. I made it a short way farther down the street before falling again, the pain in my side pounding out a rhythm with my beating heart. I could hear shouts coming from the alley behind me, and knew I had just moments left to figure something out.

That's when the sound of gurgling water reached my ears. Not two feet away, one of the city's many canals ran parallel to the street. Having seen them previously, I knew they were filled with muddy water the color of milk chocolate. What that water would do to my shoulder wound didn't bear thinking about, but right now that didn't matter as much as getting out of sight as quickly as possible. I'd worry about sepsis if I survived the next five minutes.

On hands and knees I stumbled to the edge of the street and toppled down the short embankment into the slick water below.

I thought the water would hide me for a few moments. What I hadn't counted on was the current. It was much stronger than I ever would have imagined, seizing me in its grip and shoving me ten feet downstream before I even came up for air. When my head eventually did break the surface, I had just enough time to suck in a mouthful of air before it dragged me under again.

My weakened state left me at the mercy of the canal, which tossed me end over end so often that I no longer knew which way was up. My lungs were burning, my chest ached, and all I wanted to do was let go and rest, just let my body drift with the current. That wouldn't be so bad, would it? Just let the canal take me where it would? All I had to do was let go of the breath I was holding in my lungs and relax . . .

I slammed bodily into something jutting out into the water and instinctively grabbed at it, latching on with hands that felt like claws. My lizard brain took over at that point, pure survival instinct, and I found myself scrambling upward against whatever I was holding onto until my face broke the surface of the water and I could grab another lungful of air.

One breath became two, then three, pushing back the fear and panic until I was clearheaded.

I discovered I was clinging to the end of a drainage pipe that jutted out into the canal by just a few inches. Half a foot farther from shore and I would have washed right on past, never even knowing it was there.

That was the third time I'd cheated death tonight. Eventually, he was going to catch up.

No sooner had the thought occurred to me than I heard shouts from the road nearby.

"Anything?" a voice called, and I nearly lost my grip when the reply came from just a few feet away atop the embankment to my left.

"Hang on. I'm not there yet."

A chill that had nothing to do with my injury went through me as I realized that I hadn't lost my pursuers after all. They must have seen me go into the canal and followed it downstream, hoping to catch a glimpse of me in the water. If they looked over the edge of the embankment I was going to be as obvious as an elephant in a bird bath.

I glanced frantically around, searching for something to hide behind.

My gaze fell on the end of the drainage pipe I was clinging to.

It looked just large enough . . .

Trying to make as little noise as possible, I held on with my hands and tried to lower my body around the outer edge. If I lost my grip, the current would sweep me right back underwater. I knew I couldn't survive another battle with the canal, but at the same time remaining where I was wouldn't be healthy either.

I heard footsteps crunching through gravel right above my hiding place at the same moment my feet caught the lip of the pipe.

It was now or never.

I managed to pull myself up and into the pipe just as a beam of light flashed across the exact spot where I'd been moments before. I didn't stop there but quietly worked my way deeper into the pipe, wanting to get deep enough so that they wouldn't see me if they decided to look inside. After a minute or two I couldn't go any deeper and just sat there in the slow trickle of water moving beneath me, staring at the light outside the pipe and wishing for it to go away.

A few minutes later, it did.

I was wet, cold, and exhausted, never mind bleeding from a gunshot wound to my chest.

But I was alive.

That alone was enough.

I slumped against the side of the pipe, suddenly bereft of whatever energy had sustained me until now. My limbs felt like lead and I could barely find the will to sit up.

I just need some rest, I told myself. *Just a few minutes of rest.*

And with that passing thought, I slipped into unconsciousness, my head slumped against the concrete and my blood mixing slowly with the water that ran past me from somewhere deeper in the pipe's darkness.

43

CLEARWATER

As they came down the street and saw the activity in front of the clinic, Denise knew that something had gone horribly wrong. Police cars lined either side of the curb, and there were two white City of New Orleans vans in the small parking lot. A uniformed officer stood watch by the front door while several men and women in civilian clothing went in and out, carrying cases of equipment in each hand.

"Don't stop!" she said to Dmitri, and he did as he was asked, gliding past their former base of operations without slowing. Farther down the street, he pulled over to the side of the road and parked in such a way as to allow them to watch what was happening back at the clinic through the rearview mirrors.

"They must have been watching us the whole time," Dmitri said and Denise figured he was right. How else would that FBI agent have been there right at the moment they were stealing a national treasure? The question was not were they being watched, but rather how much did they know? And more importantly, did they already have Hunt?

Just then she spotted a familiar face among the crowd of onlookers. Rolling down her window, she waved him over.

It was Gomez, one of Gallagher's people.

He caught her eye, nodded, and then casually made his way over to the vehicle. Without waiting for an invitation he slipped into the backseat.

"Go," he said and Dmitri did so, ignoring the honking horn from the driver of the Nissan he'd just cut off with his larger SUV.

"What happened?" Denise asked.

Gomez's disgust was palpable. "Health inspection. Can you believe that shit? We had to relocate to a new safe house."

Denise frowned. "Why didn't Simon just call to let us know?"

This time Gomez wouldn't look at her. "We were attacked by the Sorrows last night, shortly after getting set up in the new facility. There must have been a dozen, maybe more. Your friend Hunt gave us enough warning to beat them back, but it was close."

"Is Jeremiah all right? What about Simon?"

"The Marshal sent me to bring you in."

And that's all he would say. Every question she asked was met with the same answer.

"The Marshal will tell you."

Arriving at the new location, Dmitri had barely brought the car to a halt before Denise flung open the door and raced across the manicured lawn in search of Simon and some answers.

She burst through the front door and came to an abrupt halt, staring in shock at the destruction around her.

Gomez had said they'd been attacked, but she hadn't expected a war zone.

There were three body bags laid out in the front foyer, and men were preparing to carry them to the trucks outside even as she entered. Discarded nails and bloodstains were scattered throughout the room, and a section of the hallway just beyond was blackened from the fire that had tried to consume it.

Denise was still trying to come to grips with what she was seeing around her when Simon came down the hallway toward her; someone must have gone looking for him, must have informed him that she and Dmitri had returned.

Seeing her, he rushed over. "Did you get it?" he asked, his expression somehow simultaneously terrified and hopeful.

She nodded absently, her concern elsewhere. Seeing the bodies had made her realize that Gomez had never directly answered her question about Jeremiah.

She glanced around the room again, looking for the one person she'd expected to meet her when she'd arrived.

Where the hell was he?

Simon was still talking, explaining. "A group of Sorrows hit us somewhere around midnight. We were able to fight them off, though not, as you can see, without casualties."

That last word bounced around inside her head like a pinball, repeating itself over and over again.

No, she told herself. *He had to be here somewhere. He was just helping out and couldn't leave what he was doing just yet.*

"Simon, where's Jeremiah?"

He simply stared at her, unable, or perhaps unwilling, to answer.

Dimly, she was aware of Dmitri stepping up behind her, but she couldn't take her eyes off Simon's face.

She asked her question again, slowly and clearly.

"Where is Jeremiah?"

Simon shook his head. "We don't know," he replied, and there was real anguish in his eyes when he said it. "He was separated from us during the attack and we haven't been able to locate him. I tried scrying out his location earlier, but was unable to get anything, so I've had teams scouring the neighborhood ever since. So far, we haven't found a trace of him."

Denise wanted to throw up. *Hunt? Gone? It just couldn't be.*

"We have to do more, Simon," she said, and her voice sounded dreamy and distant even to her. In the back of her mind she knew that wasn't a good sign, but she'd worry about that later. Right now she had to find Hunt.

"Put more men on the street. Tell them to look for . . ."

Simon held up his hands, interrupting her. "I can't do that, Denise," he said.

She didn't think she'd heard him correctly. "What? Of course you can. All it will take is a few more people; we're bound to find him soon enough."

But her old coven mate was shaking his head.

"We're stretched thin as it is, Denise, and we're running out of time. The winter solstice is only a few days away. We have too much to do if we hope to defeat the Angeu."

She couldn't believe what he was saying. *He was just going to abandon Hunt? The son of a bitch!*

There was only one thing to do.

"I'll find him myself!"

She spun on her heel, intending to march back out into the streets and search them herself if that was what it took to find Hunt, but Simon caught hold of her arm and yanked her back around to face him.

"Damn it! Listen to me, Denise! Time is running out. We have to activate the knives, have them ready to use in case the Angeu strikes again. Everything else can wait."

She struggled to break free, but Simon held her tightly and refused to let go. The situation probably would have deteriorated from there if Dmitri hadn't stepped in.

"I'll find him."

Denise spun around to face him, surprised to see him flinch at the expression on her face. Did she really look that bad?

"I'll find him, Denise," Dmitri said, catching her eyes with his own, making certain she understood. "Simon is right. We need you to help activate the soul knives. If you don't, our chances of defeating the Angeu are all but nil. That's why we went to Chicago in the first place, to get the knives, remember?"

Denise stared back at him.

After a long moment of silence, she nodded. Once.

"Find him, Dmitri. Bring him back to me."

Her voice was like stone. All at once the sheer depth of her feelings for Hunt were obvious to anyone with ears to hear and eyes to see, even to Denise herself.

Dmitri didn't say anything. He just nodded, gave her a swift hug, and headed out to find their missing friend.

44

HUNT

I drifted in the darkness, unaware of the passage of time or of the steady flow of my lifeblood as it slowly leaked out of me, a drop at a time. It could have been an hour, it could have been a day; wrapped in the comforting arms of that darkness, I neither noticed or cared.

I wasn't alone, though. My dead daughter, Elizabeth, came to visit me and she brought her friend Abigail along as well. Their presence should have alarmed me, should have clued me in to just how serious my injuries actually were, but thankfully I remained blissfully unaware, unable or perhaps unwilling to face the reality of my situation.

Shock can be a marvelous thing.

The two of them kept me company for a time, laughing and playing in front of me, but eventually the joy fled from their faces and they stood there, gazing at me with solemn eyes.

"What's wrong, my love?" I asked, kneeling in front of her and placing my hands on her shoulders. "Why so sad?"

She wouldn't say, no matter how much I coaxed and pleaded with her. She just stared at me with those wide eyes, and I could see fear running through them, fear as I had never seen before.

It broke my heart just to look at it.

"We can show you," Abigail said suddenly.

Elizabeth's eyes lit up at the suggestion. She grabbed my hand as Abigail took the other. Pulling me to my feet, they led me deeper into the pipe.

We walked along way, seemingly for hours, until ahead of us I began to see a light. It grew brighter as we approached; then the pipe disappeared and we found ourselves standing on the edge of a vast cliff, looking down into a valley that stretched away from us as far as the eye could see.

In the midst of that valley a gleaming fortress rose.

But it wasn't the fortress that caught my attention, stunning though it was, but rather the massive army assembled in front of its gates.

An army of ghosts.

They stood in silence, staring not at the fortress, but toward the cliff on which we stood. They seemed unusually solid to me, almost as if they still lived and breathed, but I knew a ghost when I saw one.

Seeing so many of them together sent a cold chill scurrying up my skin.

Something was very wrong.

Elizabeth tugged sharply on my arm. When I looked down to see what she wanted, she pointed out across the valley, and I was obliged to follow the arc of her finger.

Except now the scene had changed.

The fortress was gone, replaced by a shimmering curtain of

haze, through which I could see the skyline of New Orleans lit by the light of the full moon hanging just above it. The light washed off the swelling waters of the Mississippi and, far on the other side, the rounded top of the Superdome.

Even as I watched, a rickety old cart rolled forward toward the curtain, carrying a single figure dressed in black. Behind him, the massive army soundlessly swept forward in his wake.

"Don't let him take us, Daddy," Elizabeth said. "Don't let him!"

But when I turned to tell her that I wouldn't, that she was safe with me and that no one would harm her while I was around, I found myself standing alone on that cliff, with only the wind and the silent dead below me for company.

I frantically turned around, searching for her and for Abigail, but they had vanished.

Only the army remained, marching off toward New Orleans . . .

45

CLEARWATER

Denise stumbled away from the scrying mirror and threw up violently in the corner. The room stank of vomit, sweat, and desperation, made even worse by the peculiar ozonelike scent of overused magick.

She wiped her mouth with the back of her hand and stepped away from the mess. It was no use: no matter how hard she tried she couldn't get the scrying to work. It should have been easy. She had spent months in Hunt's presence, knew how he looked and smelled and sounded. Knew just about everything there was to know about him. She had access to his clothing, his journal, even his toothbrush, for Gaia's sake! Any one of those items should have been strong enough to allow her to zero in on his location, never mind the half dozen or so items she had piled on the floor behind her.

Something was blocking her efforts, something powerful enough to dispel the energies she was raising, to keep them from homing in on her target.

Unless he's dead . . .

Not for the first time, she slammed the lid closed on that line of thought. She wouldn't believe it. *Couldn't believe it.* He was out there, somewhere. She just had to try harder.

A glance at her watch told her she'd been at it for close to an hour now. Dimly she remembered Simon trying to convince her to stop a short while before, telling her that she'd kill herself if she kept pushing so hard, especially after the amount of energy it had taken to charge the soul knives and heal the injured, but she'd warded the door before she'd begun and that had been enough to keep him from physically stopping her. In the back of her head she knew he'd been right; the ache in her bones and the worn, stretched feeling inside her head told her that she didn't have much left.

Still, she had to try.

As she staggered back over to the ritual circle she'd drawn around Hunt's possessions in the center of the room, a commotion from out in the hall caught her attention. She staggered over and opened the door, only to find Dmitri standing there, Hunt's limp body held in his arms.

Oh sweet Gaia no!

For that moment, that long, agonizing moment, she thought he was dead, but then his fingers moved and her heart began beating again.

Dmitri spoke up. "Found him crammed into a drainpipe along the canal, like he was trying to hide from something."

A drainpipe? What the hell?

But she didn't have time right now to figure it out. There was an empty bedroom next door and she led Dmitri to it, indicating he should put Hunt down on the bed.

"He's alive, but he's in bad shape, Denise. Looks like he took a bullet to the back and he's been bleeding out ever since. He needs a hospital."

One glance at Hunt told her that they didn't have time to take him to one. That he had survived this long was a miracle. His body was burning up with fever, which told her all she needed to know about the infection raging inside him, and he'd lost so much blood that he was paler than the sheets on which he lay. Moving him had caused the wound in his torso to begin bleeding in a seeping flow of blood and pus. He wouldn't make it another ten minutes if they didn't do something immediately.

She grabbed one of Simon's people who was passing in the hallway outside and sent her to scrounge any instruments, towels, and hot water that she could find. Simon was out on an errand somewhere, which meant she was going to have to do the healing on her own.

She just prayed she had the strength left to handle it.

"What can I do?" Dmitri asked, standing there looking helpless.

She knew just how he felt. "Stay right there; I'm going to need you in a minute," she told him.

Several of Simon's volunteers came hustling into the room, carrying towels, a basin of hot water, and several different medical tools, including clamps and scalpels that must have come from the clinic. Denise pressed them into service as she bent to work on Hunt.

Fifteen minutes later she knew it was no use. Hunt had flatlined once already and she'd wasted precious moments bringing him back from the edge, but that had only temporarily saved him. Dmitri had been right: Hunt had lost too much blood from the bullet wound in his chest, one from a fairly large-caliber bullet, from the look of things. It had entered through his back and exited somewhere near his ribs, which was good, since it meant the bullet hadn't bounced around inside him doing even more harm, but the wound itself had been exposed to the filthy canal water and as a result sepsis had set in. If they had caught it earlier they might have been able to do something, but at this point his system had used up too much of its reserves and the fever itself would probably kill him before the infection did.

Her healing Art allowed her to stabilize him temporarily, and in doing so she was able to clean out some of the pus within the wound itself and cauterize the smaller blood vessels that she could see near the surface, but she knew there was at least one other artery somewhere deep in the wound that needed to be sealed off. The state of the wound and Hunt's frail condition kept her from finding it, though not for lack of trying. Her hands were dark with Hunt's blood from where she had been rooting around inside his abdominal wall, trying to find the problem spot. Each time she did so, though, she seemed to push him closer and closer to the edge. The human body just wasn't designed for this kind of trauma.

She was going to have to do something a bit more drastic if she was going to save his life.

There were consequences to what she was considering. Dangerous, perhaps even deadly, consequences, not just to Hunt but to herself as well.

Still, she had to try.

Turning to Dmitri, she said, "I need you to clear the room. Take everybody with you."

"What? You need help right here and I . . ."

"Do it, Dmitri!"

Perhaps it was the urgency in her voice. Perhaps it was simply the fact that she'd never yelled at him in such a savage tone of voice. She didn't know. But whatever it was, he stopped arguing and got moving. He rounded up the volunteers who had been helping and ushered them all into the hallway outside the bedroom. She watched him go and then, as soon as the door swung shut behind him, she used some of her dwindling strength to bind the door from inside, preventing anyone from entering, even someone as powerful as Simon.

What she was going to do, she had to do alone.

In the years since she'd left the coven, she'd continued her education in the Arts, broadening the scope of her interests and learning all she could, even some of the rituals that were frowned upon by many in the mage community. She'd always been of the opinion that she needed to understand the powers of those who used such rites if she was to work to counter their influence. But magick was not something you could just learn from a book. You had to get out there and live it, channel the power, feel its effects, if you were to understand how it functioned and what you could do to work against it.

Since leaving New Orleans her traditional training had been . . . *enhanced*, was perhaps the best word, as she mixed with other practitioners and learned a wider set of skills. She knew that some of what she'd learned would be frowned upon by those with a more traditional viewpoint, like Simon, for one, but without the protection of a coven around her, she'd felt that having more tools in the tool belt was a smart move.

One of those tools was a small, forbidden ritual that had been designed to allow a mage to bind another to her will by capturing a portion of a soul and holding it as her own. But Denise thought she could turn it around, to use the same principle to bind a piece of her soul to Jeremiah's, anchoring his own soul to his body in the process and keeping him alive while she worked to heal the rest of his injuries.

She stared down at his worn and bloodstained face and used her fingers to momentarily caress his cheek.

She would do what she had to do and the consequences be damned.

46

HUNT

The pain told me I was still alive.

Which was a good thing, I guess. If I hurt this much and then I discovered I was dead, I'd have been pretty pissed. I felt like someone had run me over with a steamroller, but I'd take that over being dead any day of the week.

Cautiously opening my eyes, I found myself lying in a bed in a room that I didn't recognize. The blinds were drawn, but the lack of any light bleeding through them let me know that it was some time after dark.

Just how late, I didn't know.

I was dressed in a loose pair of sweatpants—whose, I didn't know—sans top. I turned my head and found Denise sleeping in a chair next to my bed. She'd looked better: her hair was a tangled mess and lines of exhaustion crisscrossed her face, but it was good to see that she'd made it back from Chicago alive.

Chicago . . .

It all came back to me at that moment, everything that had happened since Denise left with Dmitri to try and retrieve the soul knives. The Sorrows' attack. My encounter with Robertson. Getting shot by the son of a bitch. And perhaps most important of all, what my daughter's ghost had shown me while I lay in that drainpipe slowly dying.

I needed to talk to Gallagher.

I threw back the covers and swung my legs out of the bed without thinking, only realizing after doing so that my body should have been shrieking in agony and wasn't. Glancing down I found a wad of bloodstained bandages wrapped around me.

It hurt, sure, but no more than if I'd been kicked by a good-sized horse. It should have been a lot worse; even a healing spell couldn't repair that kind of damage.

What the hell was going on here?

My need to talk to Gallagher now all but forgotten, I reached up with a shaking hand and gently peeled the top of the bandage away from my skin.

Last week, if you'd asked me if I ever wanted to know what a bullet wound in my upper chest looked like, I would have told you no. Now, however, I was almost hoping to see it. At least then some of this craziness would make sense.

But instead of a bullet wound, the yellowish purple of an already healing wound stared back at me.

"Son of a bitch," I said.

I couldn't believe what I was seeing.

I knew I'd been shot; the memory of hot blood spilling over me was still vivid in my mind, as was the time I'd spent huddled in that pipe with only my fear and pain for company. And yet it looked like I'd been healing for months.

"How are you doing?"

I nearly jumped out of my skin at the sound of her voice. My concentration had been total; I hadn't realized she was awake.

"Not bad," I managed to croak out, as my heart rate settled back down to normal. "Considering."

I could see her nod in the darkness. "It was a bit close, I'll give you that."

There was a certain sense of satisfaction in her voice, though I wasn't sure if it was because I'd managed to remain among the living or because she'd obviously had a considerable part in my doing so.

I figured it couldn't hurt to ask.

"Did you do this?"

She rolled her head around, getting the kinks out, and then looked off into the distance. Given the room was almost completely dark, I wondered what she was seeing.

"Yeah," she replied. "And I'm sorry. There wasn't any other way."

I laughed. "Sorry? Don't be; I'd probably be dead right now if you hadn't."

She turned to face the sound of my voice, and I watched as her eyes moved slightly back and forth, trying to find something to focus on in the darkness.

"No, you would be dead. No probably about it. Which is why I did what I did."

An ugly little chill formed at the base of my spine and wormed its way up my back. Something in her tone . . .

"What'd you do? Sell my soul to the devil?"

Denise shook her head. "No, I gave you a piece of mine."

That chill crested and broke over the rest of my body. *What the hell was she talking about?*

"You did what?"

Just like that, she was wringing her hands and tears were flowing down her cheeks.

"Hey, hey," I said, reaching out and taking her hands in mine. "It's okay."

Her words flowed out a mile a minute. "I couldn't watch you die, Jeremiah. I had to do something. I didn't even know if the spell would work, but I had to try, and . . ."

"Sshh," I told her, "take it easy. Just tell me."

She got a hold of herself and, when she was ready, she told me.

The spell was ancient, she said. No one really knew where it had come from or whether it would even work, but she'd been desperate and desperate people do desperate things.

That, I understood. I was the poster child for desperation.

When it looked like I was on my way out, she'd cast the spell, grafting a small piece of her soul to mine. Doing so had kept my soul anchored in my body and had drastically accelerated the healing process.

"Sounds like a bargain to me," I said gently, but she shook her head.

"You don't understand," she told me, wiping her tears away as she got herself back under control. "It's permanent."

"So?"

Denise was probably one of the most decent people I knew. It wouldn't be so bad carrying a little bit of her around with me wherever I went.

"So now there's no going back. We are, quite literally, stuck with each other. If one of us tries to leave, the other will feel such a deep longing that they'll be forced to track the other down. The soul longs to be whole and the only way for that to happen, for either of us, is if we stay together."

She was starting to freak out, so I gave her my best smile and said, "I bet Gallagher's pissed, huh?"

She snorted, then laughed as she tried to cover it up. "Oh, yeah!" she said. "He's pissed all right. He keeps lecturing me like I'm a first-year novice. I'd like to see *him* pull it off."

No thanks. Carrying a piece of Gallagher around inside my soul was not something I was particularly interested in. But it did remind me of why I sat up in the first place.

"Speaking of the devil, I need to see him right away. Get Dmitri too. I think I know what the Angeu is up to."

Anything else and she might have told me to get back in bed and rest, but with innocent lives at stake, she knew it couldn't wait. Coaxing me back into bed, at least for the time being, she went to find Gallagher and Dmitri.

No more than ten minutes later she returned with both men in tow. Ever the considerate host, I let them turn on the lights and re-treated behind my wall of white; I was going to be doing all the talking, at least at first, and I didn't need to see in order to do so.

I filled them in on what I had seen in my vision, realizing even as I did that Denise had been right that night back at the hotel in Tennessee.

Death *was* coming for us.

And he was bringing all his friends with him.

"What about the Sorrows?" Dmitri asked, when I finished telling them about the army of ghosts the Angeu had been commanding, an army that would be headed in our direction before long.

I shook my head. "The Sorrows have served their purpose, I suspect. I don't think we'll face them again." It all even made a warped kind of sense, when you looked at it from the Angeu's view. Use the

Sorrows to harvest the souls of the dead, particularly those of the Gifted, who would have considerably more power, and then press those very same souls into service to carry out your black-hearted plans. And where was it that every lost soul wanted to go before anywhere else?

Home.

Right back to the Big Easy.

My story had at least gotten Gallagher to stop shooting mental daggers in Denise's direction, and as I finished explaining, he started in with the questions.

"You're certain it was a full moon?"

I nodded. "Absolutely."

Dmitri's voice sounded frustrated. "Well then we're really up shit's creek. The full moon's only two days away. How the hell are we going to be ready?"

But I was barely listening to him. I felt the sudden tension when Dmitri said "two days" and knew that the others had just realized something important.

"What is it?" I asked.

Denise's voice trembled as she said, "The winter solstice is in two days."

I didn't see the relevance.

But Gallagher obviously did. "Sweet Gaia!" he said. "The Curtain!"

I still didn't have any idea what they were talking about.

Denise explained. "The Curtain is the mystical barrier that separates this realm from any other, the shimmering mist that you saw in your vision. On certain nights of the year our world passes closer to the spirit world and on those nights, the Curtain is weaker. If the Angeu intends to bring an army across, he'd do it on one of those nights."

"Let me guess," I said. "The solstice is one of those nights."

She smiled weakly, telling me I'd got it in one.

While she was explaining, Gallagher was thinking about my vision. "Would you recognize it again? The place where the Angeu plans to cross over?" he asked.

I gave it a little thought and then nodded. "If I was standing there, looking out as I was during the vision, yeah, I think I could."

Denise frowned. "There have to be a million different places he could have been standing, Simon," she said. "How do you think you're going to narrow them all down?"

I was wondering the same thing. Turned out we were both way off base.

"He doesn't have to," Gallagher said, with a feral grin. "I think I already know where it is."

47

ROBERTSON

Without a body, Robertson was reluctant to believe that Hunt was dead, even with all the circumstantial evidence that suggested otherwise. He'd seen too many other agents make fools of themselves by declaring a case closed only to be forced to open it again when the killer resurfaced somewhere else a few weeks or months or even years later. He had no intention of making the same mistake.

The blood trail he'd followed to the canal had been proof that he'd struck Hunt with at least one of his shots. That was the good news. The amount of blood on the ground suggested that he'd hit something vital. But somehow Hunt had still managed to escape.

After searching the general area for two hours after Hunt disappeared from view, Robertson had been forced to call it a night. As he'd climbed back into his vehicle, his cell phone rang with a call from Doherty.

"This had better be good news," he said sourly, after answering it.

Unfortunately, it was not. By time Doherty finished explaining how Clearwater and Alexandrov had overpowered him and managed to make off with two priceless artifacts stolen from the Field Museum's collection, Robertson felt like shooting someone. Instead, he took several very deep breaths and forced himself to remain in control. He would not let Hunt get the better of him. Robertson ordered Doherty to return to New Orleans and instructed his driver to take them back to the office.

At first light the next morning, he and the cadre of men he'd brought with him, including a newly returned Agent Doherty, were back, combing the area for any trace of evidence as to where the fugitive might have gone. Help from the locals was practically nonexistent; they had their hands full dealing with the current health crisis. Not that Robertson minded. With the locals out of the way, he was free to run the investigation any way he wanted.

One way or another, he was going to put an end to the bullshit.

He was working the phone, trying to scare up a boat with which to dredge the canal, when Doherty, face flushed with excitement despite the bandage covering the wound he'd received from Alexandrov, knocked on the door of the office Robertson had commandeered.

"We've caught a break, sir!"

Robertson didn't say anything, just looked at him and waited.

"There's a CI downstairs who claims he can tell us where Hunt is. He'll only talk directly to you, he says."

"He asked for me by name?"

"Yes, sir."

Now that's interesting, Robertson thought. Very few people knew he was in New Orleans. How had the confidential informant known to ask for him by name?

Only one way to find out, he supposed.

"Bring him in, Doherty. Let's hear what the man has to say."

Robertson sat back in his chair and took a moment to straighten his tie; image was important. He toyed with and ultimately discarded several ways of dealing with the situation before deciding to play it a bit nonchalant until he knew the other man wasn't simply after the reward money. No sense in getting too excited.

Their CI turned out to be a hard-looking man in his late thirties, with dark hair and a two-day beard. He came in, glanced nervously around, and then took a seat in front of Robertson's desk when asked to do so.

The senior FBI agent studied him for a few moments, letting the other man grow a bit uncomfortable, before leaning forward and getting to the point.

"Your name?"

"Bruce," he said quickly, and then, when Robertson waved a hand in a "come on" gesture, he said, "Bruce Myers."

"What can I do for you, Mr. Myers?"

He smiled as he said it, knowing the kind of effect his smile had on people.

Myers stammered a bit but finally found his voice and said, "I'm here about the reward."

Robertson cocked his head to one side, but didn't say anything. *If this son of a bitch is wasting my time . . .*

"I know where that guy Hunt is, and I'll tell you, but I want to be sure that the reward is legit, first. Ya follow me?"

Oh, he followed him all right. And if it turned out he didn't know squat about where Hunt actually was, there was going to be hell to pay. But he didn't show any of that; he simply kept smiling as he said,

"The reward is genuine, Mr. Myers. Five thousand dollars for information leading to the whereabouts and arrest of Jeremiah Hunt, also known as the Reaper."

It was, too; the FBI had instituted the reward several years ago and had never bothered to rescind it when the Reaper's identity had become common knowledge. Robertson had at first taken it as a personal affront, a sign the Bureau didn't have faith in his abilities to catch the son of a bitch, but he was over it now. A tool was a tool; whether it was worth anything all depended on how you used it.

"When do I get it?"

Robertson's eyes narrowed at the man's bluntness, but he held his temper. *See what he's got first*, he told himself.

"You'll get your money as soon as I know you actually have information that's worth something to me."

Myers nodded then reached into his pocket and pulled out his cell phone. He played with the buttons for a moment and then passed it across the desk to Robertson.

On the small screen was a photograph. It was time-stamped from the night before and showed Hunt sitting shirtless in a bed, talking to someone offscreen. He had a few bruises on his face, but he certainly wasn't the corpse Robertson had been expecting.

Passing the phone back to his informant, Robertson said, "Talk to me."

48

HUNT

Denise had once told me that magick runs through the earth in long lines known to the practitioners of the Art as leys. The place where several ley lines meet is called a nexus and a nexus provides a wellspring of power for those who know how to access it.

As fate would have it, one of the largest nexuses in Louisiana lies on the other side of the Mississippi River, overlooking the city of New Orleans.

That it happened to be smack dab in the middle of the Fountainoute Cemetery was just icing on the Angeu's cake, for I had little doubt that he fell into the category of those who knew how to make use of such things.

Lucky for us, Gallagher knew where that nexus was and suspected that it was the location I'd seen in my vision. Two cups of coffee and a few painkillers later, I was climbing out of Denise's Charger and walking toward the tall, cast-iron gates that guarded the entrance to Fountainoute. With only two days before the solstice, we didn't have any time to waste.

The cemetery was tucked onto a gentle spit of land that looked out across the water at the Big Easy. In the old days, when the waist-high fence that surrounded the property was first erected, this area probably wouldn't have been on any developer's must-have list. All the action was across the river; why build anything this far away? But given the view that greeted me as I looked back over my shoulder at the city skyline, I knew there were plenty of people who would sell their souls to the devil to build on this spot.

Of course some people are just plain dumb, too.

I stared at the fence in front of us with more than a bit of trepidation. Fences are funny things. Most people think of them as a means to keep the unwanted out. Very few ever consider the fact that more often than not, they're really there to keep the unwanted *in*.

Like now.

Normally I wouldn't have dreamed of approaching a place like Fountainoute Cemetery at this hour of the night. There are places on earth where the dead, rather than the living, hold sway, and cemeteries like this one are definitely high on the list. There were a lot of things that could take up residence among the dead besides ghosts, and more often than not, they didn't like being disturbed.

Never mind that they were always hungry.

Tonight things felt different. As I waited for Gallagher to open the thick lock and iron chains that sealed off the entrance, I didn't get the usual sense of hungry expectation from the things that lived on the other side the way I normally would. In fact, I didn't get a sense of anything at all.

A quick look with my ghostsight confirmed my suspicions.

Even here, where they should have been packed in shoulder to shoulder, standing-room only, the ghosts were absent.

Nothing but silence greeted us as we stepped onto the grounds.

Flashlight in hand, Gallagher led the way, winding in and out among the crypts and mausoleums with the sure sense of someone who had been here before and knew exactly where he was going. It was a good thing that one of us did; I was lost after the first hundred yards, the avenues and alleys between the miniature mansions of the dead all looking the same to me.

A few yards farther and Gallagher brought us up short. We stood in an undeveloped section of the cemetery; a wide grassy lawn, empty of mausoleums, stretched ahead of us for a couple dozen yards before it sloped gently down to the banks of the Mississippi. Across the dark waters, the city of New Orleans loomed, glittering like a jewel in the night.

"Well?" Gallagher asked, a bit impatiently, but I tuned his annoyance out and took a long hard look around. I couldn't afford to be wrong. If I was, one helluva lot of people were going to die.

But no pressure, right?

I walked around a bit, moving from left to right so as to parallel the river, and then getting closer to the water's edge before backing off farther than where I'd originally started.

Eventually, the pieces of the puzzle—the view of the waterline, the location of the city against the horizon, the rounded bubble of the Superdome, even the moon, now almost full, hanging off to one side at just the right distance—all came together.

This was the spot.

I was certain of it.

"Here," I said, and as I did so I felt the nexus deep beneath my feet surge with power. The hair on my arms stood at attention and my blood seemed to race more quickly through my veins as I felt the flow of potential fill the air around me.

Gallagher nodded, his expression grim.

"Time to get to work, then."

><

On the night of the solstice, we returned to the cemetery shortly before midnight.

Over the past day and a half we'd done everything we could to prepare us for the confrontation that was coming, and now we moved with purpose, intent on the job before us.

Given Gallagher's combat prowess and my affinity for the dead, we were the logical choices to lead the attack on the Angeu. Assisting us were the surviving wardens and a small group of Sidhe. While we kept the Angeu distracted, Dmitri would carve a path forward to the Angeu's side where Denise would use the soul knives to send the bastard and his ghostly army back to where they belonged.

It sounded good in theory, but I had a feeling that things were not going to be anywhere near as easy when reality showed its ugly face.

We'd marked the location of the nexus with a brightly colored stake and had placed another marker twenty feet in front of that. As the others took up position among the crypts at my back, I walked out to that second marker and took up my position.

Because of my ability to see into both realms, I'd been assigned to act as point man.

I don't think I've ever been more scared in all my life.

My heart pounded, my throat felt three sizes too small, and as I felt my hands start to shake, one thought kept repeating itself over and over again in my mind.

I can't do this.

It was insane. Absolutely insane. We never should have come here. We should have simply packed up and headed south, away from Gallagher and the trouble surrounding him, and screw the compulsion Denise had been feeling. We would have found a way to break it . . .

I was on the verge of losing it, of turning tail and running for the hills as fast as my legs would carry me, when I felt a child's hand slide into each of my own.

They were soft, ethereal hands, and it was difficult to hold them, but I clung to them, even if only figuratively, with all of my strength.

Glancing down, I found the ghosts of my daughter, Elizabeth, and her friend Abigail, the girl I had once called Whisper, standing on either side of me, their hands in mine. They looked up at me and I found courage in their support. I was here, doing the right thing, and if I died in this life tonight, at least I knew I would not be alone in the next.

Raising my head, I found Abigail's father, Matthew, the ghost I'd called Scream, standing off to one side, as protective of his daughter in death as he had been in life. We understood each other, Scream and me, having chased our daughters' killers to the ends of the earth, and when he silently nodded at me, one long solemn nod, I felt the last of my fear vanish.

As the ghosts slowly faded away, I felt the night around me move.

The air grew heavy with a sense of anticipation, like the feeling of a summer night with a thunderstorm looming on the horizon. The sensation slowly built, growing stronger, until the air was practically vibrating around me with all that raw power running through it.

I reached into my pocket and withdrew the two items I carried there: my harmonica and a roadside emergency flare. I was going to need both of them very soon.

There was an audible crack and then the sky before me was lit with a flash of light so bright that I was forced to look away, tears streaming down my face from the sudden pain.

When I looked up again, the world had dissolved into a sea of white.

I couldn't see a thing.

Panic threatened, but I beat it back down with the sheer force of my will. I'd known this was coming and had planned for it; there was nothing to worry about, I told myself.

I reached inside my mind and the world in front of me sprang into view, lit with the pale silver blue light of my ghostsight.

The rift was directly in front of me, a shimmering curtain of power that hung down from the heavens in exactly the spot we'd predicted it would be.

Harmonica in hand, I stood there and waited for Death to come to me.

Thankfully, I didn't have to wait long.

The sound of horses' hooves reached me first.

Clip-clop, clip-clop, clip-clop.

It was a slow, steady pace, one without any sense of urgency, but it carried with it a chilly kind of inevitability, Death's steady march come to claim us all.

As the sound drew closer, I began to see a hazy figure through the glistening curtain.

Clip-clop, clip-clop.

The figure grew more distinct as it got closer to the other side of the curtain, until it resolved itself into a pair of horses pulling a cart of some kind.

Clip-clop.

Even as I watched, the curtain parted and the horses stepped into our world, dragging their cargo along behind them. One of the horses was the picture of good health, its coat gleaming, its eyes full of spark and fire, while the other looked to be at the end of its journey, all skin and bones and eyes gone filmy with age or disease.

The driver sat hunched in his seat, dressed in the same wide-brimmed hat and shimmering cloak he'd been wearing the first time we'd encountered him. In the light of the rift, though, I could see that the cloak was not the rich fabric I'd originally assumed it to be but was crafted from the very souls of his victims! Faces swarmed about its surface, eyes blinking here and there, mouths opening and closing in silent screams.

The Angeu lifted one skeletal hand and cracked a whip fashioned from human hair, urging his steeds forward, out of the way of the gate behind them so as to allow the army of ghosts to begin making its way across.

I waited, watching the cart's forward motion, trying to gauge it just right. When it reached a point halfway between the rift and the spot where I stood, I knelt and slammed the butt of the flare against the ground, activating it. As it sparked into life, I tossed it at a point in the grass a few feet in front of me.

The flare hit the ground, igniting the oil we'd poured in an intricate pattern across the lawn that afternoon. Within seconds the flames ignited the entire design, surrounding the cart.

Gallagher and his people started chanting the minute the flare left my hands, and now their voices filled the night air, rising and falling in a complicated rhythm that activated the circle's power, sealing the cart and its driver inside its confines.

With a quick jerk of the reins, the Angeu brought the cart to a halt. He slowly raised his head, staring out across the dozen or so feet that separated us. I could feel his gaze upon me, but I knew what that gaze could do, and this time I was ready for it, focusing on the center of his chest and refusing to meet his eyes.

Behind him, his ghostly army began its crossing, stepping out of the land of the dead and returning to the land of the living. As they passed through the curtain, they fanned out on either side of the flaming circle that held their master captive, moving steadily in my direction. The eldritch fire in their eyes reflected the hunger and desperation that rolled off them in waves, and I knew that if this vast host ever reached the city itself, there would soon be nothing left worth saving.

With what felt like the weight of the world on my shoulders, I put my harmonica to my lips and began to play.

49

HUNT

It was a light, whimsical tune at first, the kind of thing designed to catch your attention and draw you in with its lilting melody. I filled the night air with its intricate dance, snaring the ghosts' attention with my song, forcing them to pay attention to me and me alone.

As more and more of them turned their gaze in my direction, I added a new dimension to my tune, a secondary melody that was darker and more powerful than the first. It sang of loves lost and chances missed, of striving for but failing to reach the goal, of opportunities gone and efforts squandered.

It was the type of song that filled your heart and soul with regret and forced you to examine all that you held dear.

Like a spider's web catching a fly, my song took hold of the ghosts before me and seized them firmly in its grip, preventing them from moving even one step forward. The great army slowed and then staggered to a stop.

Surprised, the Angeu pulled sharply on the reins, bringing his cart to a halt as well. He gestured at the spirits around him, ordering them forward, but none of them moved.

As long as I played, there they would remain.

So far, so good.

In just the first few seconds of the encounter, we'd brought the Angeu to a halt and seized control of his phantom army. Now all we had to do was get Denise close enough to use the soul knives.

That's where Dmitri came in.

Out of the corner of my eye I saw him step out of hiding, Denise at his side. His berserker nature was fully in control, and in my ghostsight he appeared as an eleven hundred–pound monster covered in white fur and sporting a nasty-looking set of teeth and claws. Even as I watched, Denise seized hold of his fur and swung herself up onto his back, gripping the sides of his muscular body with her legs to keep her steady. No sooner was she settled than Dmitri lumbered into motion, headed straight for the Angeu and his cart.

Knowing I needed to keep the Angeu distracted to give the others time to reach him, I moved closer to the circle, flaunting the tune I was playing, making certain that he saw that I was the source of his troubles.

He reacted predictably, cracking his whip against his horses' flanks, urging them forward, trying to get them to cross the flames and run me down. The horses rushed forward but reared up at the last second, refusing to cross the barrier.

The circle held.

When that didn't work he turned his attention instead to disrupting the ritual that kept the circle active, staring at the men and

women assembled behind me, trying to catch them in his paralyz-
ing stare.

Our people had been forewarned, however, and all but one re-
sisted the temptation to raise their eyes from the ground before them.

Just a few more minutes were all we needed.

Unfortunately, we weren't going to get them.

From behind us came a voice blaring over a megaphone. "This is
the FBI! Remain where you are and do not move. We have you surrounded!"

It was the last thing on earth I expected to hear.

I spun around to find uniformed officers emerging from the darkness behind us, pointing guns at Gallagher and his people. Leading
them was none other than Special Agent Dale Robertson.

He walked toward me, his gun out and pointed at my face.

"Got you this time, Hunt," he said.

I couldn't believe it.

What the hell did he think he was doing? Didn't he see what was
going on? How could he think we were a bigger threat than an army
of specters just waiting to tear into any living soul they could get
their hands on? Was he that freakin' stupid?

And then it dawned on me.

He couldn't see them.

By their very nature, the Angeu and his servants were hidden
from Robertson's view. As a Mundane, he didn't have the capability
of perceiving creatures from the other side, the way the rest of us
could. From his perspective, we must have looked like a bunch of
lunatics standing around a cemetery in the middle of the night chanting and playing crazy music.

"Hands over your head, Hunt!" he yelled, brandishing his weapon.

But I couldn't do that.

If I did, I'd be forced to stop playing. And if I stopped playing, the army of hungry specters at my back would surge forward and engulf us all.

I had to hold them long enough to allow Denise to reach the Angeu.

I deliberately turned my back on Robertson and continued playing, betting that he wouldn't shoot me out of hand in front of all these witnesses.

Gambling was never my strong suit, however.

A shot rang out and a bullet whizzed past my ear, close enough that I could feel the heat of its passage.

"Last warning, Hunt. Hands up."

I could hear it in his voice. He was going to shoot me if I didn't comply.

I had no choice.

If I wanted to live, I had to stop playing.

Fuck him, I thought and played on.

I watched as Dmitri reached the outer edge of the ghostly army. He plowed into them with all the force of a battering ram, scattering them out of his way, and driving forward until he reached the flames that made up the edge of the protective circle.

Using his momentum to her advantage, Denise sprang off Dmitri's back with a huge leap, clearing the flames and landing well inside the circle's edge. Without hesitation she ran forward, vaulted the side of the Angeu's cart, and rushed toward his unprotected form, the soul knives gleaming with mystic light in each of her hands.

Just a few more steps and it would be all over.

Behind me, Robertson said, "You leave me no choice, Hunt."

That's when things went from bad to worse.

The Angeu grinned and surged to his feet. Opening his mouth impossibly wide, he threw back his head as if he were screaming, except no sound came out of his mouth, at least not in the conventional sense. Instead, the most god-awful inhuman shriek I've ever heard exploded inside my mind, reverberating around and around inside my skull like an echo through an empty canyon, driving out all rational thought in the face of its relentless attack.

The sound drove me and everyone else in front of him to our knees, our hands coming up involuntarily to cover our ears in a vain attempt to make it stop, cutting off not just my song but also the chant that powered the mystic circle.

I forced my eyes to remain open and I watched helplessly as Denise leapt for the Angeu's back, her knives out and ready for the killing blow, only to have the Angeu spin around and seize her in midair. He held her at arm's length, the bony fingers of one hand wrapped about her throat, her feet kicking helplessly several feet off the ground as he leered at her with his skeletal visage.

It might have ended there if it hadn't been for Dmitri.

He charged forward, roaring out a challenge as he slammed his massive bulk against the side of the cart, rocking it up on one side, toppling Denise and the Angeu over the other side.

They fell together, Denise on top, and, as I watched, her slim hand rose above them, the blade of a soul knife gleaming in the light from the rift at their backs, and then plunged back down.

A howling cry split the night, a scream of such misery and anguish that it seemed as if all of the world's pain was wrapped up in one blistering sound.

I saw the other knife rise above it all, saw it start to make its downward descent . . . and then lost it from view as the horde of angry specters rushed forward.

Knowing I didn't have time to get out of the way of the oncoming horde, I curled up into a ball and brought my harmonica to my lips.

I didn't have time to re-create the song I'd used earlier to keep the angry mob of ghosts pinned in place, had barely enough time to play anything at all, really, so I used what I had simply to get them to overlook me as they surged forward. Like a stream that parts around a rock, the army of ghosts rushed toward me, flowing around my huddled form, without noticing that I was there.

I could hear Robertson screaming behind me and chanced a glance in that direction. A pack of specters had surrounded him. Some were ripping and tearing at him with their claws while others had sunk their teeth into his unprotected flesh. Blood flowed, hot and bright in the night air. Robertson, of course, couldn't see what was attacking him, only the results of their efforts, and the look of horror on his face was something to behold as he fought vainly to throw them off. Beyond him, his men were also under attack, their shouts and cries adding to his own terrified screams.

As I turned away, an unearthly cry rent the air. In its wake came a shock wave that shook the earth beneath us, jolting the harmonica loose from my grasp and knocking me off my feet.

Silence fell.

Cautiously, I raised my head and looked around.

I could see Agent Robertson kneeling on the ground a few feet away, blood streaming from half a dozen wounds. He was gibbering to himself like a madman and rocking back and forth. He'd lived through the specters' assault but would probably never be the same.

In a strange way, I almost felt sorry for him.

Behind him I could see Gallagher and several of his men already up and on their feet, dealing with the federal agents who had survived the attack. Gallagher's job was made easier by the fact that there weren't many of them.

Turning in the other direction, I realized that the light was gone;

the Curtain, and the ghosts that had come through it, had vanished as if they had never been.

Over by the ruins of the Angeu's cart, I could see Dmitri, back in human form, pulling himself up off the ground. Blood ran down his face, but he didn't seem to notice it, his attention on something else lying a few feet away.

I followed his gaze to where Denise lay in the middle of a scorched patch of ground.

Of the Angeu, there was no sign.

I scrambled to my feet.

"Denise!"

I stumbled to her side, followed only seconds later by Dmitri. Falling to the ground next to her, I pulled her across my lap and into my arms. Her body was limp, but appeared to be undamaged, and I was relieved to see that I couldn't find any blood.

For a moment, I thought she had a chance.

"Denise! Talk to me, Denise!"

I gently turned her face upward so she could see into mine and my heart fell.

Her eyes were open and staring at nothing.

I'd seen that same look on too many faces since coming to New Orleans not to recognize it.

Her body might be alive, but there was no longer anyone home.

The Angeu had been forced to return to Caer Wydyr, but in the process he had taken Denise's soul along with him!

50

HUNT

We sped through the streets of the city as if the devil himself were on our heels, but I knew all too well that we no longer had anything to fear from him; the devil had already taken his due. Twice during the ride Denise's body stopped breathing and we were forced to use CPR to bring her around again, Gallagher and I huddled over her in the cramped backseat of the Expedition, alternating chest compressions and forced inhalations as we fought to get her heart started.

Dmitri roared into the emergency entrance, nearly taking out an ambulance that was headed in the other direction, and skidded to a stop in front of the doors. While we were lifting Denise's limp form out of the back of the car, Dmitri was already inside, scaring up a doctor and a team of orderlies to help us get her into the ER.

From there it was simply a question of getting out of the way and letting the professionals do their jobs. I let Gallagher handle the intake paperwork, as I couldn't see a damn thing with all the lights and wouldn't have known what to put on the forms anyway. Rather than stand there and call attention to myself, I had Dmitri lead me to the waiting room where I grabbed a chair and settled in for whatever came next.

Gallagher joined us about thirty minutes later, and in that time he looked like he'd aged ten years. His face was drawn, his eyes were red from crying, and I could see his hand shaking when he reached up to wipe the tears from his face. I knew exactly how he felt.

She's gonna make it, I repeated to myself silently. *She's gonna make it.*

But I wasn't so sure.

A nurse appeared, clipboard in hand. She surveyed the emergency room for a moment and then headed in our direction. The three of us rose to meet her.

"Mr. Gallagher?" she asked.

"Me," Simon said, then, more strongly this time, "I'm Gallagher."

She dismissed me and Dmitri without another word and focused on Gallagher, speaking in clipped, short sentences. "The intubation procedure went well. Your sister's breathing with the help of the respirator now."

Sister? I thought, then let it go. I didn't care what lie he told them as long as it allowed us access to Denise.

The nurse was still speaking. "She's stable and she'll stay that way while on life support, I'd wager. In a few hours we'll move her out of ICU and over to a private room. Any questions?"

Gee, only a couple of thousand. Like how long can the human body survive without a soul? And what in heaven's name did we have to do to get it back?

For once, I wisely kept my mouth shut.

When the nurse was gone, I turned to the other two. "Talk to me," I said. "How do we fix this?"

Neither of them said anything. I could picture them, heads down, refusing to look at me.

Suddenly, I was pissed.

"Don't give me that, you assholes," I said, my voice low and hard. "No way am I giving up and neither are you. I won't let you. We can fix this!"

But even as I said it, I wasn't so sure. Death itself, or at least his closest personification, had just sucked Denise's soul into oblivion and then disappeared with it. How the hell were we supposed to fight that?

Right now I didn't have a clue. But Denise had literally given a piece of her soul to save my life, so I was sure as hell going to . . .

Wait a minute!

Given a piece of her soul . . .

I spun to face Gallagher.

"The bonding ritual! The one Denise used to save my life! Can't we use that to track wherever the hell it is that the Angeu went?"

Gallagher shook his head. "No. It won't work."

"Why not?"

It seemed like a reasonable question to me, but Gallagher apparently didn't think so.

"You don't know what you're talking about, Hunt. Leave it alone."

I wanted to hit the stubborn son of a bitch. "Like hell I will!" I shouted, getting right in his face, politeness be damned. "Answer the fucking question! Why won't it work?"

That did it. My goading snapped whatever shred of self-control he had left. He leapt to his feet, shouting, "Because she's dead, asshole, that's why!" and shoved both of his hands against my chest.

Unable to see it coming, I had no way of bracing myself for the impact and ended up flying backward to land crashing into the row of plastic chairs behind me.

Silence fell over the room.

I climbed slowly to my feet, my anger barely held in check. I sensed someone approaching and balled my hands into fists, ready to fight back this time, but it was Dmitri, not Gallagher.

"Easy, Hunt," he said, taking my arm and turning me away from the confrontation. "Why don't we go get a coffee or something?"

I knew if I stayed things were only going to go from bad to worse, so I let him lead me out of the waiting room and through the hospital halls until we found a small lounge a short distance away. The serving area was closed down for the night, but the vending machines were still working.

Dmitri led me to a chair and then used one of the machines to fetch me a cup of coffee. It tasted like shit, but it gave me something to do with my hands to keep them from shaking.

We sat in silence for ten, maybe fifteen, minutes.

"You all right?" he asked finally.

"Fuckin' peachy."

He laughed and the sound prompted the release of some of the tension and anger I'd been holding inside.

After a few more minutes of silence, I said, "I'm not giving up."

"I know."

"Do you think she's alive?"

He thought about that one for a moment, then said carefully, "You of all people should know that there is always hope."

"Ain't that the truth," I muttered, but it wasn't the reassuring answer I was looking for. Seemed I was going to have to do this one on my own.

"I'm going to go back and see how Simon's doing. You all right here by yourself for a bit?"

"Yeah," I said, waving one hand in a sort of shooing motion.

After he'd left, I got up and began pacing about the empty room.

I was still lost in thought when the voice spoke out of the darkness behind me.

51

HUNT

"You can still save her, you know."

I knew that voice.

I'd heard it only once before, but once was more than enough to leave its gravelly timbre etched permanently in the forefront of my mind. It had been five years since I'd heard it, but the passage of time didn't matter either. It could have been ten, fifteen, even twenty-five years and I still would've known it as surely as I knew my own name. That voice had changed my life.

I spun around.

In the dim light of the lounge I had no trouble seeing. The Preacher stood on the other side of the room, watching me with those empty eye sockets of his. He was dressed just as he'd been on the night I'd first encountered him: black pants and waistcoat over a simple white shirt, a broad-brimmed black hat on his head, like a traveling preacher out of the Old West. The illusion was almost complete—all he was missing was a Bible clenched in one liver-spotted hand—but I knew him for what he was.

Devil.

Demon.

Outcast!

Under the weight of my stare a grin tugged at the corners of his thin mouth.

It was the grin that did it.

I crossed the distance between us and wrapped my hands around his throat before I was even consciously aware that I had moved. I didn't let it stop me once I had, though, but instead used my momentum to slam him bodily against the wall, knocking his hat askew. In the process, long lanky hair the color of frost tumbled free to frame his face like a burial shroud wrapped about a corpse.

With a strength born of rage and frustration, I lifted him clear off the ground, the toes of his boots dangling a few inches from the floor. A brutal cold, like an Arctic wind fresh from the depths of the frozen north, seeped off his skin, but I ignored it, concentrating instead on choking the life out of him for what he had done to me.

He didn't even try to stop me.

I stared deep into those empty eye sockets, knowing he could see me just as easily as I could see him, and squeezed, feeling his bony throat contracting beneath my fingers, watching as his face began to take on a bluish hue.

Die, you son of a bitch . . .

Only then did his words actually register.

With some effort, I opened my hands and stepped back, letting him fall to the floor in front of me.

"What did you say?"

The Preacher threw back his head and laughed, the sound

bouncing off the walls and seeming to echo in the close confines of the room.

I clenched my fists, willing myself to remain still and not go for his throat again. He was trying to get a rise out of me, and this time I refused to take the bait.

I watched in silence as he climbed to his feet, straightened his waistcoat, and adjusted his hat.

"Where was I?" he asked with mock innocence.

I took a step toward him, and you didn't need a psychic to feel the rage boiling just beneath the surface of my will. "I asked you a question, Preacher . . ."

"You can still save her." He said each word slowly and distinctly, mocking my inability to understand. "If you love her enough, that is."

I didn't know if I loved Denise or not, but I wasn't going to debate the point with him. I did know that right then I would do anything to save her, so my choice was a simple one.

"Tell me."

He pointed into the room on the other side of the glass, where I could see Denise's body lying in the bed, her chest rising and falling with each motion of the ventilator.

"The Angeu may have reaped her soul, but her body lives on. While it does, there is a chance you can save her."

I knew I shouldn't trust him. I'd listened to him once before and while he hadn't lied to me directly, he also hadn't told me the entire truth. As a result, I'd nearly gone mad from the ritual I'd conducted and the things I'd seen. If Whisper hadn't come along and saved me when she had, I wouldn't be standing here right now.

There was no sane reason for listening to him.

But I did it anyway, and maybe the fact that it was nuts was what allowed me to make that decision in the first place. After all, just about everything I'd been through since the night I'd accepted the book from the Preacher could be called insane in one way or another. Five years ago I wouldn't have even considered the existence of a creature like the Angeu or the Sorrows that he had bound to his service. I wouldn't have believed that my friendship with the ghost of a young girl would first save my life and then lead me to the answers I sought regarding the fate of my daughter Elizabeth. I certainly wouldn't have gotten involved in a mystical battle for control of New Orleans.

And I never would have met Denise in the first place.

I knew I wasn't going to like what he had to say, but what the hell. Beggars can't be choosers.

"Tell me," I said.

He smiled and there was nothing friendly in that smile.

Then he told me what I had to do.

I was right.

I didn't like it.

Didn't like it even one little bit.

But I was going to do it anyway.

52

CLEARWATER

The first thing she saw when she regained consciousness was a sky the color of wet shale that roiled and churned like something alive. It hung above her, looming there, as if poised on the edge of a long drop, and she found herself cringing from the wrongness of it, unable and unwilling to look at it anymore.

Her gaze fell first upon the wooden slats that made up the side of the cart she was riding in and then dropped lower still to give her a good look at the uncomfortable surface she was lying upon.

Bodies.

Dozens of them, men, women, and children, all naked, their bones jutting out from behind the thin covering of their pale flesh, their eyes open and staring at her.

She cried out and then tried to scramble away from them, only to discover that she was secured in place atop the pile with some kind of netting that wouldn't let her move more than a few inches at best.

She was trapped!

The discovery sent her into a panicked frenzy, thrashing against the netting, her arms and legs straining against her bonds to no avail.

After several minutes she collapsed, exhausted, only to jerk her neck upward when she realized that the back of her head was resting against the face of a corpse directly beneath her. She held her head upright for several long minutes, her muscles aching and screaming from the strain, but she knew she couldn't remain that way indefinitely. She was going to need her already depleted strength for something more important, like staying alive.

With a whimper of dismay she finally gave in and lowered her head, gritting her teeth against the scream that was building in her throat.

Easy, girl. Hold yourself together. You'll need your wits about you if you're going to get out of this.

She took several long, deep breaths, repeating a mantra to herself that she'd learned as an apprentice, over and over again until she felt her serenity return.

Good. Now think. Don't react; think.

She realized that while she might be bodily tied down, both of her hands were reasonably free of restraint. And since she wasn't gagged, that meant she could utilize both the vocal and somatic motions she needed to access her Art. She could be free in minutes!

Her excitement rising, she slipped her hands up through the holes in the netting and wriggled her fingers, making sure that she had a full range of motion. When she was satisfied, she opened her mouth and spoke a few words in ancient Sumerian while weaving her fingers in a complicated pattern.

The spell was designed to send a wave of intense cold outward from her body in a ten-foot sphere. The netting that held her down, as well as the rear of the cart itself, would instantly go from its current temperature to something on the order of thirty degrees below zero. The sudden drop in temperature would make it extremely brittle, and all she'd have to do at point was give the net a good tug and she'd be free.

At least, that's what was supposed to happen.

The reality, however, left much to be desired.

A stabbing pain shot through her skull the minute she tried to access her Art, overwhelming her senses and scattering what little power she'd begun to gather.

She shook her head to clear it and then tried again.

The pain was even worse this time, a juggernaut that roared through her skull, smashing everything in its path, causing her eyes to bulge in their sockets and blood to trickle out of her nose.

As before, the pain vanished when she stopped trying to call upon her Art.

It looked like she was going to have to do this the old-fashioned way.

Without magick.

The thought sent a quick pulse of fear through her veins.

Take it easy, she reminded herself.

She didn't know how she'd gotten here or even where *here* actually was. She needed to calm down, take stock of her surroundings, and try to understand what was going on so that she could figure a way out of here.

The first thing she noticed, aside from that awful sky, was a steady *clop-clop-clop* sound coming from somewhere behind her head, in the direction that the cart was traveling. This confirmed her suspicion that the cart was being pulled along by a horse, or perhaps a team of horses. She twisted her neck as far as it would go to one side, but all she could catch was the occasional glimpse of a tall, lean form wrapped in dark clothing sitting at the front of the cart.

That was enough, though.

She knew that form.

She'd last seen it, in fact, driving a cart much like this one, while leading a horde of ravenous ghosts on an invasion of the living world.

Denise raised her head and looked past her feet to the back of the cart, hoping there might be something to see in that direction. While the sides were made of rough-hewn slats that fit together unevenly, the rear was a single piece of wood, held in place by short strands of rope. It was clear from the way it was constructed that it functioned as a makeshift tailgate. Thanks to the way she was restrained, she couldn't raise her head high enough to see over it, so with more than a hint of frustration she turned to look at the side closest to her. At least there she could peek through the holes between the slats.

There wasn't much to see.

A gray, ash-filled landscape stared back at her, a harsh, barren plain that stretched out toward the horizon. Very little grew in that wasteland and those few trees that broke the monotony looked more like charcoal-stained skeletons than living things.

After staring at the same desolate landscape for a few minutes, she gave up and turned her attention to the netting holding her down instead. If she couldn't get free of it, it wouldn't matter where she was anyway. First things first.

The netting had a natural resiliency that let it bend slightly with her exertions, preventing her from breaking it, and it had a silkiness to it that she had never encountered before. If she could just get a closer look . . .

It was hair.

Human hair.

The need to scream threatened again and she clamped down on her tongue to keep herself from doing so, for she knew that once she started, she might not be able to stop.

Closing her eyes, she counted to ten, willing herself to remain calm. In the silence she picked out another sound, just at the threshold of her hearing. It had been there all along, she realized, but her fear and anxiety had prevented her from recognizing it.

Footsteps.

Two sets of them, actually, one on either side.

Someone was walking along behind the cart.

What kind of person would willingly serve the Angeu?

"Hello?" she croaked.

There was no reply.

She tried again. "Is anyone there?"

Still nothing.

She squirmed against the corpses behind her, trying to shift around enough that she could get a different view through the slats in the cart, but even that didn't work. With a grunt of exasperation, she gave up.

Time passed.

Eventually, her exhaustion got the better of her. The rocking motion of the cart, combined with the monotonous landscape, lulled her into a restless sleep.

She awoke with a jolt.

It was impossible to tell how much time had passed, as the sky looked exactly as it had before. They must have reached their destination though, for the cart had stopped moving. Maybe now she would get some answers.

A shuffling sound drew her attention to the rear gate, and she could sense someone approaching the back of the cart. Even as she watched, a pair of hands reached over the top and fumbled with the rope that held the gate closed.

The hands were covered with dirt and grime, but at least they were human.

Her pulse quickened and she prepared herself to take advantage of whatever opportunity the situation presented. If she could break free when they loosened the netting holding her in place she might be able to . . .

The gate at the back of the cart was lifted away and she got her first look at the two men who had been following along behind them.

Her mind processed several things at once.

The coarsely woven clothing that they wore.

The gray, waxy look to their skin.

The thick black thread that had been used to sew their eyes and mouths shut.

As they reached toward her with their dead hands, it all was just too much. Without a sound, she slipped into unconsciousness.

53

HUNT

I found Gallagher in the room they'd assigned to Denise, sitting vigil next to her unmoving form. One glance at the bed was all it took to tell me that there was no change in her condition. Not that I was expecting one; it's a bit tough to get up and walk around when your soul has been ripped from your body.

He raised his head and looked in my direction as I burst into the room.

"We're not beaten yet," I told him, but he had already dismissed me and gone back to staring at Clearwater.

"Go away, Hunt. The city can rot for all I care at this point."

"Who gives a fuck about the city?" I replied, matching him tone for tone. "I'm talking about Denise!"

That got his attention.

He turned to face me. "What are you talking about?"

"I know where to find the Angeu. There's a chance we can still save her! But you've got to keep her body alive until I get back or it will all have been for nothing."

"What?" he asked, staggering to his feet, as if he intended to join me. "How?"

"I don't have time to explain," I told him, and it was true. Every second I spent talking to him was one less that I had on the other side to search for Denise. And if I took too long, the Preacher wouldn't be there to send me in the first place. "No matter what, Gallagher, you have to keep the life-support machines hooked up. Don't let anyone turn them off or take her away. I don't care what they tell you—don't let them do it!"

He nodded and that was good enough for me; I didn't wait around to hear anything more.

I found the Preacher waiting for me in the lounge, just as we had agreed.

"All right, you bastard, let's do this," I said, as I stalked over to him.

"As you wish," he murmured.

For all I knew he was going to betray me the second I turned my back, but I was willing to take that risk if there was even a slight chance that I might be able to rescue Denise.

He grinned his trademark death's-head grin at me and then stepped closer to the wall beside us. He raised his hands to either side and said something in a language that hurt just to hear it.

He said it once, twice, three times, and then stepped back and lowered his arms. No sooner had he done so than a section of the wall in front of him split apart with a resounding crack, sending a massive tremor through the room and leaving an opening in the wall wide enough for a man to step through.

I stepped forward, until I stood just a few feet in front of the opening. I could see nothing but darkness on the other side, darkness so deep that not even my eyesight could pierce its depths.

That's when I heard it.

It was soft at first, just barely audible. If I hadn't spent years honing my hearing I wouldn't have even noticed.

A whisper.

That single, solitary whisper became ten voices whispering to one another. Those ten became a hundred. A thousand. Ten thousand, until the room was filled with the sound of them all.

To make matters worse, I recognized them, despite having never heard them before.

The voices of the dead, whispering to one another.

I glanced back at the Preacher.

"You have three days, Hunt," he told me, the empty sockets where his eyes used to be burning with an unholy light. "No more. Three days. If you cannot find her in that time, our bargain will be over."

I knew the sound of a binding when I heard one, but it didn't matter. I was going to try, no matter what.

"Agreed!" I shouted over the cacophony that filled the room and then turned to face the entrance once more. I knew if I waited much longer I'd lose my nerve, and there was no way I was going to allow that to happen.

Taking a deep breath, I stepped into the rift.

54

HUNT

There was a moment of intense cold and impenetrable darkness, a moment of being wrapped in the frozen, dead emptiness of space itself, and then I staggered through the other side of the rift and collapsed onto the dusty earth at my feet.

For a long time all I did was lie there and catch my breath. My heart was pounding like a runaway drum; I hadn't been alone in my passage through that darkness, and the things that I'd heard and seen in those split seconds would forever be imprinted on the back of my mind. It took me a bit to shake them off.

I sat up and cautiously opened my eyes, expecting to see nothing but white everywhere I looked, and so I was surprised to find that I could see just as well as I could in the old days. Not that there was much to look at. A dusty plain stretched out before me and as I turned my head, I could see that it extended as far as I could see in every direction. No trees, no bushes, no signs of life. Nothing but rocks, dirt, and dust all the way out to the horizon where a sky the color of angry thunderclouds came down from above to meet them.

I climbed to my feet and turned in a slow circle, considering my options. Somewhere in this desolate place, Denise's soul was being held captive by the Angeu. I had three days to find her and bring her home. Trouble was, without anything to guide me, one direction seemed as good as any other. I wasn't even certain I was in the right place; the truth was that the Preacher could have sent me to the ass end of nowhere rather than to Annwyfn and I wouldn't have known the difference.

Nothing to do but start walking.

Picking a direction at random, I set off, kicking up little clouds of dust with every step.

I hadn't gone more than twenty feet before I slowed and then came to a halt altogether.

You're going the wrong way.

It was just a feeling deep in my gut, a sense of wrongness that grew with each step in the direction that I'd originally chosen. Perhaps it had something to do with the fact that I carried a piece of Denise's soul bound up with my own. I wasn't sure. All I knew was that I needed to trust that feeling.

I turned in another slow circle, but this time I listened to what my soul was telling me.

Denise was . . . *over there.*

Without giving myself too much time to think about it, I turned and headed off in that new direction.

At first, it wasn't too bad.

I was eager for a confrontation with the bastard who'd stolen her away from me, and I wasn't going to give up until I found him. Each step brought me closer to my destination, and I found a certain bounce to my step that I hadn't expected.

But then the general bleakness of the place began to wear upon me. There was no sound but the crunch of the gravel beneath my boots with each step. There was no sunshine and no darkness, just that ever-present twilight that seemed to go on forever, mimicking the endless plain on which I walked.

Gradually my thoughts turned from strategies for how to confront the Angeu and rescue Clearwater to simply wishing he would show up and end this farce so that I wouldn't have to continue walking.

Minutes turned to hours, hours felt like days, and still I trudged on, step after step.

Nothing changed. There was no sign of the Fortress of Glass.

No sign of anything, really.

Just the same dim sky and the same dusty plain.

But still I continued.

Despite the passage of what felt like a considerable amount of time, I grew neither tired nor thirsty from my exertions. Like the situation with my eyesight, the normal rules of physical reality didn't seem to apply. Which was fine with me; this place was bad enough without stumbling around blind with a raging thirst to boot.

Of course, being able to see didn't stop me from nearly stepping off the cliff when I finally reached it.

I'd been walking at a steady pace for hours, my head down, my mouth closed against the dust my steps were kicking up, thinking about how I was going to get Denise away from Death himself when my next step ended in midair rather than on the rock-strewn ground.

I teetered there for a moment, one foot firmly on solid ground, the other hanging into nothing but space, and then fell backward on my ass, gasping at my narrow escape. When I had myself back under control, I crawled forward and peered over the edge.

The ground fell away before me, a sheer, dizzying drop of hundreds of feet before it met the valley floor far below. The valley itself was like a giant bowl carved into the earth; cliffs surrounded it on all sides, creating an unbroken circle around the center.

I knew there had to be a way down, for in the center of the valley floor rose a gleaming bastion of shimmering crystal.

I'd found Caer Wydyr, the Fortress of Glass.

55

HUNT

The stairs were cut right into the face of the cliff, each step worn and weathered by the passage of time. How much time, I didn't know, but something about them felt ancient, primordial.

I began a slow descent to the valley floor, taking each step with care and watching where I put my feet, knowing that one wrong step would mean not only the end of my life, but Denise's as well. The stairs were cracked and eroded in more than one place, and if there had been even the slightest breeze I would have been in real trouble: a good gust would have plucked me right off the tattered ledges of rock and sent me tumbling to my death. Thankfully the air was as dead as the land appeared to be.

Step by step I made my way downward.

When I reached the bottom I stopped and stared out across the intervening space at the tower for several long minutes. It was more a fortress than a tower, really, though one spire did rise taller than the others. It seemed to be as empty and as deserted as the rest of this place, but something about it made me uneasy. It almost seemed like the building itself was watching me.

Get a grip, Hunt. She's counting on you.

The direction-finder in my gut was calling me again, pulling me toward the tower, and I had no choice but to follow it.

Where the surface of the plateau above had been hard and rock-strewn, the ground here was covered in some kind of whitish yellow sand. Walking in it was difficult, and as I trudged my way along, my feet slipping and sliding to one side or another with every step, I fervently hoped that Denise and I wouldn't have to retreat in this direction in any kind of a hurry because it would probably prove to be near impossible.

The feeling of being watched intensified as I drew closer and I kept waiting for an alarm to be raised, for the Angeu's minions to come charging out of the central gate spoiling for a fight. But that didn't happen; I was able to march across all that open ground and right up to the entrance to the tower without being hailed or challenged in any way.

As I let my gaze drift along the wall nearest the door, I realized that what I had taken from afar to be a type of glass or crystal was in fact something vastly different; the Fortress was not constructed of glass, as its name implied, but from the souls of the dead themselves!

They had been collected and packed together, one atop another, until their wan, insubstantial forms began to take on a semblance of solidity simply from the sheer weight of their numbers. Countless generations of the restless dead had been pressed into service by the Angeu, and now those closest to the surface stared out at me from within the structure of the building itself, their gaunt faces full of pain and misery and a longing for release that hung in the air around us with a weight all its own.

I was sufficiently horrified by what I was seeing, but that didn't compare to how I felt when I realized that not only did I need to walk on these poor lost souls in order to search the Fortress for Denise, but that there was a strong possibility that Denise's soul had already been pressed into service as well.

The latter didn't bear thinking about.

It couldn't be; it just couldn't. The Preacher never would have sent me here if there wasn't some way to rescue her. Without that possibility, our bargain would be worthless, and if I knew anything it was that the Preacher desperately wanted me to be in his debt. No, she was still safe. All I had to do was enter this place and find her.

Steeling myself, I grasped the handle of the door, pulled it open, and stepped inside.

I moved quickly through the maze of hallways and rooms, searching for the central staircase that would take me upward. My instincts told me that Denise was being held in the central tower, the one that rose higher than the others, so that's where I was headed; thus far, my instincts hadn't been wrong.

The staircase spiraled around the central core of the tower, and I climbed it swiftly but cautiously. I knew the clock was ticking away, and after that seemingly endless trek across the landscape I really didn't know just how much of the Preacher's three-day deadline remained. For all I knew time operated differently here; I might be days ahead or days behind already. The narrowness of the staircase made it an ideal location for an ambush, so I kept my eyes and ears open as I climbed higher into the tower. The last thing I wanted was to stumble into a nest of Sorrows or a group of angry ghosts.

At the top of the stairs was a single door, fashioned of wood and bound with iron. To my surprise, it was unlocked. With a pounding heart, I opened it and stepped inside.

The size of the room surprised me; it seemed much bigger inside than out. But the moment I laid eyes on what it contained, I forgot all about its shape and size.

The floor was littered with the souls of the dead.

Dozens of them.

Men. Women. Children.

And my gut was telling me that Denise was among them somewhere.

I had to find her and set out to do just that. But as I moved among the dead, I realized the situation was far worse than I'd realized.

I knew in the back of my head that I was the only one who was actually present here in physical form, that the "bodies" in front of me weren't actually bodies but were just the physical representation of what was left of that person's soul after the Angeu claimed it as his own. It only took a few minutes of observation for me to realize that each soul was in the process of being broken down and consumed by the floor beneath my feet!

In some cases the person's soul was intact and whole. In others, very little remained beyond the edge of a face or a portion of a limb jutting out from the floor. Each soul that was consumed added to the solidity of the Fortress overall, making it that much stronger.

Even as I looked on, the body closest to me, that of a pretty blonde, settled nearly a half inch deeper into the floor around her. What made it so horrible, though, was the fact that she seemed fully conscious and aware of what was happening to her. She couldn't move, her arms and legs having sunk more than halfway into the surface beneath her, but her eyes were open and rolling around in her head like a panicked mare.

I had to find Denise and I had to do it fast.

Fuck being careful.

"Denise!" I shouted. "Denise Clearwater!"

Commotion off to my left pulled me in that direction.

I hurried over and knelt beside her.

"Are you all right?" I asked.

She didn't say anything, just stared up at me, her body rigid and unmoving. Her eyes were full of fear and had that round, panicky look that told me she was on the verge of losing it.

"It's okay," I told her. "I'm going to get you out of here."

But when I tried to help her sit up, I discovered that I was too late: the Fortress had already laid claim to her. It wasn't much, maybe an eighth of an inch or so, but that was enough. No matter how hard I tugged, pushed, or pulled on her, I couldn't get the Fortress to relinquish its grip.

Now what?

Panic gripped me.

For just an instant I imagined how it would all play out, how I would sit there, unable to do anything but be there for her, my hand on hers, my soft, soothing but otherwise useless words falling from my lips as she was consumed, an inch at a time, just another soul added to the Angeu's power source.

I had to do something!

As I frantically glanced around the room, looking for an answer, my gaze fell upon the faces that watched me from inside the walls, floor, and ceiling of the room itself, the ghosts that had already added their essence to the Angeu's power base.

That's when it hit me.

I wasn't trying to save Denise's physical form—that was still lying in a hospital bed in New Orleans. The only thing I was concerned with was her soul. Her spirit. Her ghost . . .

Pulling my harmonica from my pocket, I caught Denise's gaze with my own and smiled reassuringly.

"I think it's time for a little music," I said, then brought the harmonica to my lips and began to play.

Normally it takes me a few minutes to find the frequency, so to speak, to discover the right melody and tempo for my music to have any impact on the ghost I was targeting. But I'd lived with Denise for months now. I knew her as well as I knew anybody, from her quick wit to her hot temper, from her generous nature to her affinity for all living things. I didn't need time to find the right tune, I carried her song in my heart, never mind a little piece of her soul in my own. My music burst forth in a soft, gentle melody that had a core of steel, just like Denise. It filled the room, washing over the floors and walls, calling Denise to my side just as I'd called hundreds of other ghosts in the past. I closed my eyes and let the music guide me, let it build into a celebration of the life and love that Denise had given the world, until I could hear only the swirling strains of music and the call built deep within its depths.

One minute she was lying trapped on the floor in front of me, the next she stood by my side, free of Caer Wydyr's grip.

I didn't waste any time, just grabbed her hand and ran for the door.

"What about them?" she asked, but I just shook my head. I didn't know if freeing her had set off any kind of alarm or warning device, and I certainly wasn't going to stand around and wait to find out. Never mind the fact I still had the Preacher's deadline to contend with.

We were getting out of there and that was that.

Now that Denise was with me, the instinct that had guided me to her side on the way in faded, leaving me to puzzle out the path back to the entrance myself. It took us less than ten minutes to descend the central tower, make our way back through the lower floors, and exit the Fortress by way of the same door through which I'd entered . . .

. . . only to skid to a stop when we found the Angeu and his rickety old cart waiting there for us in the shadow of Caer Wydyr.

56

HUNT

You've got to be kidding me, I thought as Denise and I stopped short only a few feet from the horses that drew the Angeu's cart. This close, even they looked pissed at us.

That's when the Angeu opened his mouth and let loose a wail that would have done a banshee proud.

Agony exploded in my head, driving me to my knees before the King of the Dead, and it was all I could do to keep from curling up in a ball and weeping like a baby from the pain. I sensed Denise on the ground beside me and knew in that moment that all I'd managed to do in finding my way here and freeing Denise from the clutches of Caer Wydyr was about to be undone in a matter of seconds.

And man did it piss me off.

For the last few weeks I'd been pushed and pulled in a thousand different directions, none of my choosing. I'd been dragged halfway across the country to a city crippled by a plague that wasn't really a plague, attacked by what should have been harmless harbingers of the dead that tried to suck my soul from my still living body, been shot in the back and left for dead by an angry FBI agent, and finally made a deal with my own personal devil to travel to the land of the dead to retrieve the soul of the woman I was beginning to think I loved, only to end up on my knees in front of a horror-movie reject wailing at me like a little girl.

To put it bluntly, I'd had enough.

I let my feelings run free and felt my anger swell inside me like a tidal wave on the verge of breaking.

Deep inside me, something new responded to its call.

Maybe it was the rage.

Maybe it was something left over from the ritual Denise had used to save my life.

Maybe it was nothing more than the fact that I was one of the living here in the land of the dead.

I don't know, but I do know that it responded to me when I called it forth.

Without conscious thought, I flung a hand out in front of me, my fingers carving a complicated sigil in the air as I did so, and to my surprise a bolt of power arced across the gap separating me from the Angeu. It struck him dead center in the middle of the chest and flung him off his cart like a worn-out rag doll, cutting off his banshee wail in midstream.

Where the fuck had that come from? I wondered.

I didn't know and I didn't care. I'd use what I could get and figure it all out later.

When the Angeu's wail had stopped, so too did the pain in my head, but I knew it would only be a temporary respite unless I did something to put an end to this confrontation once and for all.

Thankfully, this time I had a plan.

For the second time that day I snatched my harmonica from my pocket and brought it to my lips, letting my music speak for me in a way that nothing else could.

This time I wasn't playing for a single ghost or entity, didn't try to tailor my song to call a solitary ghost to my side.

No, this time, I called them all.

Every last one of them.

The Angeu might be the King of the Dead, but right then and there I was the usurper waiting in the wings, and I felt the dead all around me respond to my summons.

As the music unfurled from deep inside me, the Fortress at my back began to shimmy and shake, the ghosts that formed its very foundations struggling to free themselves from its confining magick and go forth to meet the one who called them home. At the same time there came motion from deep within the shifting field of bone before me—for that was what it was, not sand at all but bone ground so finely that it took on the look and feel of sand—motion that grew until it resolved itself into shambling forms the size and shape of human beings. Behind me the great fortress of Caer Wydyr was coming apart at the seams, the ghosts flowing down around us like fog on a summer's evening, mingling with those rising from the sands.

That's when the Angeu rose to his feet, revealing himself to the ghosts gathered around me.

Like moths to a flame, they swarmed around him, burying him under the weight of their numbers.

I knew an opportunity when I saw one.

Using one hand to keep playing, I gathered my will and flung the other out before me again, this time with a different pattern of motions and a mental shout in a language I'd never spoken before.

A rift opened a few feet away, a gleaming disk of silver that hung like a curtain in the air before us.

On the other side, I could see the hospital room I'd left behind when I'd started this seemingly suicidal journey.

Shoving my harmonica into my pocket, I pulled Denise to her feet and ran for the portal as fast as my legs would carry me.

Behind me, the Angeu roared with anger, but it was too late. My ghostly army had held him occupied for long enough. With a shout of triumph, I threw Denise and myself into the portal's open mouth.

57

HUNT

Going back to the other side proved to be just as unpleasant. There was the same sensation of stepping through a curtain of intense cold, a cold so deep that for a moment my heart was shocked into stillness, and then pain exploded through my head and I staggered forward out of the rift into the empty waiting room I'd left behind what felt like years before. My head was pounding, my knees felt weak, and I only managed to remain on my feet by stumbling into a nearby chair and using that for support.

I turned to Denise to ask if she was all right, but the words died stillborn in my throat before ever reaching the air outside my mouth.

I was alone in the room.

Denise was nowhere to be seen.

I stood there, blinking dumbly, unable to process even the simplest of thoughts for a long, long moment. I'd rescued Denise from the Fortress of Glass and the clutches of the King of the Dead himself. I'd called an army of the dead to my side through magick I had no memory of having learned and used it to hold off our enemy long enough for us to dive into the rift. That I could have lost her in that final step, after surviving everything else, was just inconceivable.

When the answer finally dawned on me, I literally sagged in relief.

There was no reason for Denise to be in the room with me. I'd gone to Caer Wydyr to retrieve her soul, not her body. The minute we crossed back into the physical world the two should have been reunited, leaving me on my own.

A glance at the clock on the wall told me it was just after three, and the darkness outside the windows told me it was a.m. rather than p.m., though what day it was I didn't know. The truth was that I didn't really care either, as long as I'd come back within the Preacher's three-day window. All I needed to do now was to go find Denise and make sure that she was all right.

Given that it was the dead of night, the halls were empty and I was able to make my way to the room where I'd left Gallagher and Denise what felt like days before. I entered the room with a smile on my face, eager to wrap her in my arms and welcome her home, only to come to an abrupt halt just inside the doorway.

Denise lay on her back in the hospital bed, unmoving.

Maybe she was asleep.

I crossed to her side and put my hand on her shoulder, gently shaking her.

She didn't respond.

I touched her face, only to find her skin cold and clammy.

Nothing had changed.

I should have been angry, should have been filled with rage at having been duped by that empty-eyed devil, but I couldn't find anything but despair in my heart. Again, I'd failed to save someone I loved, despite my best efforts.

My best wasn't nearly good enough, it seemed.

"Why the long face?"

I lifted my head.

The Preacher stood on the other side of the bed, watching me closely.

"Go away, you bastard," I said, but there wasn't any heart in it. I felt completely drained, empty of every last scrap of emotion, as if I'd left my own soul behind in Annwyfn along with Clearwater's. I turned away, unable to face him or my failure.

But the Preacher's next words ignited a fire in my blood.

"You're not done yet, Hunt."

Like a puppet on a string, I slowly turned around.

"Not done?"

He frowned, like a teacher disappointed by a student's performance. "Does it look like you are finished?" he said, indicating Denise's still form with one hand.

"You've freed her soul from the Angeu's stronghold, but you haven't returned it to its proper place. Until you do, she will remain like this, trapped between worlds, neither living nor dead. We don't want that now, do we?"

I ground my teeth together in an effort to contain myself.

"What do I need to do?"

He reached inside his frock coat and removed a long-bladed knife. I recognized it immediately: it was a twin to the soul knives that Denise had used against the Angeu, but this time the blade was black rather than silver. The Preacher spun the weapon around in his hand and extended it to me, hilt first.

"It's nothing, really," he said. "All you have to do is pick up the knife and stab her in the heart."

I stared at him.

"What?" I asked, when I could find my voice again. It came out as little more than a whisper.

He smiled, revealing a mouth full of decayed teeth. "Surely you remember what you learned about knives such as these, Hunt?"

At first I didn't have any idea of what he was talking about and then, like a diver coming up for mouthful of air, a memory surfaced in the back of my mind: Gallagher explaining why we needed the weapons in order to confront the Angeu. ". . . When properly charged, they have the power to return a soul to its rightful place," he'd said.

My gaze was drawn back down to the knife, the blade reflecting the green and red lights from the life-support monitors beside the bed.

To return a soul . . .

It couldn't be that easy, could it? I wondered. That thought was quickly followed by another.

Dare I trust him?

I'd done so twice before, with mixed results. Each time he'd told me the truth, but he'd also left out some additional information that would certainly have influenced my choices. Like the fact that I would lose my normal sight by accepting the unusual abilities I'd gained. And this choice facing me now.

This time, the trap was fairly obvious. If I did as he instructed and stabbed her in the chest, I'd be causing a mortal injury. I might return her soul to her body, but that would do little good if I caused her bodily death in the process.

On the other hand, as crazy as it sounded, if I had to stab her in order to save her life, she was in the best possible place for me to do so, short of the intensive care unit itself.

Which raised another question.

Could I even do it?

I looked down at Denise's still face and thought about what it would be like to drive a six-inch blade deep into her unprotected chest, to stab her in her tender heart, all in the name of saving her life. Did I have the sheer backbone it would take to do such a thing?

Yes.

I reached for the knife, only to have the Preacher close his fist around it.

"Do you remember our agreement?"

I nodded.

"Say it."

"In exchange for your help, I will carry out a task for you at a later time and place of your choosing."

I know, call me crazy. But when he'd offered to send me to Annwyfn in order to rescue Denise's soul, I'd been ready to make a deal with the devil himself.

And apparently, I had.

Satisfied with my response, he opened his hand.

I picked up the knife.

It was heavy, much heavier than I expected, though that might have been my imagination. It also felt unusually warm to the touch. As soon as I picked it up my arm began to vibrate slightly, as if the knife was giving off an electrical current of some kind that was running up one side of my arm and back down the other, bringing to mind Gallagher's comment about the weapons needing to be "properly charged."

Was it reacting to me or the scattered remnants of Denise's soul that resided inside me? I wondered. At this point, was there any difference?

I didn't know, didn't care. All I knew was that I had to get this over with before I lost my nerve.

I'd get only one chance.

I needed to get this right the first time.

The Preacher stepped away from the bed, leaving me alone at Denise's side. I could see her chest rising slowly, ever so slowly, beneath the sheets and was suddenly overcome with my feelings for this woman. I didn't know where it had started or exactly how it had come about, but somewhere along the way I had fallen for her in a big way. I needed to hear her laugh again, to see her smile, to take her in my arms and tell her how I felt.

If this was what I had to do in order to have that chance, then it was a price I would willingly pay.

Voices came down the hall, loud angry voices, and, as I did my best to steady myself for what was to come, I could hear them getting closer, the words becoming more audible as they came down the hall.

I took hold of the dagger in two hands and raised it above Denise's chest, the point of the blade centered directly over her heart.

"You cannot do this, Doctor! I forbid it!"

That was Gallagher; his brogue got a bit thicker when he was upset, I'd noticed, and right now it was out in full force.

"Mr. Gallagher, if you do not step aside right this instant, I will have security remove you from the premises. Ms. Clearwater is beyond our help, and it is time that you acknowledged that fact and allowed someone who needs that bed to make use of it. We have a medical emergency on our hands, if you hadn't noticed."

They were right outside the door; I had a moment, maybe two, and no more than that.

It was now or never.

I focused my attention on her still face, cast a prayer heavenward, and brought the knife plunging down with all my strength.

As the blade fell toward her unprotected chest, the door beside me opened.

58

HUNT

Chaos erupted.

The air was full of sound: shouts of alarm from Gallagher, Dmitri, and several other voices I didn't recognize; the Preacher's insane laughter; and the beating of my heart so loud that it threatened to drown out everything else. I could sense people pushing into the room through the open door, but I ignored them, my attention solely on the task at hand.

With an animalistic shout of my own, I stabbed Denise deep in the heart.

Blood spurted from the wound to coat my hands where they gripped the hilt of the knife, and the air was suddenly full of its crisp, coppery scent. Power erupted from somewhere deep within the blade itself, exploding down its length and into Denise's body, slamming her against the hospital bed as if I'd shocked her with a defibrillator. For a moment I thought it had all been for naught, for there was no change in her condition, and then she gave a sudden gasp and sucked in a lungful of air.

Her eyes popped open and the first thing she saw was me standing there beside the bed, my hands wrapped around the handle of the blade that was now embedded deep in her chest.

I saw the fear and pain and disbelief cross her face at the sight of me and I desperately longed for the chance to explain, to tell her what we'd gone through to bring her back again, but time was a luxury I did not have. Hands grabbed me, pulling me away from the bed, just as someone hit the lights, stealing my sight from me as swiftly as the darkness faded.

My legs were kicked out from under me and I found myself face down on the floor with something cold and metallic shoved against the back of my head.

"Don't fuckin' move, asshole, or I'll blow your damned head off. Understand?"

I didn't recognize the voice, but I could tell from its tone that whoever it was, they were just looking for an excuse to pull that trigger. I made damn sure not to give them one.

A knee was slammed into my back without warning, shoving me harder against the floor, but I kept my mouth shut and didn't complain as I was pressed into the cold linoleum floor.

The medical equipment monitoring Denise's condition was shrieking wildly, and as I lay there I heard a doctor begin giving orders, stat this and hurry up with that. It went on for a minute, maybe two, and then the command was given to get Denise to surgery. They must have wheeled her out of the room, for it got very quiet.

Hands grabbed me, pulling me to my feet, and Gallagher was suddenly there, whispering in my ear in a voice full of murder and mayhem.

"I don't know where you've been for the last three days or what the fuck you think you were doing, but you'd better hope she lives through this," he said, "or I'll gut you like a pig and feed you to the gators piece by piece."

He turned away and said to the men holding me, "He's all yours, Officers. Get him out of here."

I knew arguing with him would be useless, so I didn't bother. Besides, I didn't care what happened to me as long as Denise pulled through. I just prayed that the doctors would be able to stabilize her long enough for Gallagher to use his powers to save her life.

My arms were grabbed by a cop on either side of me and I was hustled out of the room and down the hall to the elevator. When it arrived, they hauled me inside and waited for the doors to close behind us.

No sooner had they done so than one of them laid into me, slamming his fist into my stomach until I doubled over and then ramming his knee into my face when I had. I collapsed to the floor, blood pouring out of my nose.

"We don't take kindly to murdering sons of bitches in our town," one of them said, and then both proceeded to stomp and kick the shit out of me with their thick-soled boots. Unable to see the blows coming, I had no way to defend myself other than to curl up in a ball and wait for it to stop.

The ride down from the sixth floor seemed to take years rather than minutes, and by the time the bell dinged, indicating we'd reached our destination, I was on the verge of passing out.

The bestial roar that filled the elevator car the minute the door opened shocked me back into alertness, however. I felt the guards on either side going for their weapons and decided the floor was the safest place for a blind man at that moment. There was a short but violent struggle and then Dmitri was human again and helping me to my feet.

"Can you walk?" he asked.

"Depends on where we're going," I mumbled around swollen lips and at least one cracked tooth.

He draped my arm over his shoulders and helped me out of the elevator. As the doors closed behind us, shutting out most of the light, my sight partially returned and I could see that we weren't on the first floor, as I'd expected, but were in the dimly lit parking garage instead.

Dmitri headed for a dark-colored car parked in the last row, talking as he helped me along.

"I've known you long enough to believe that you wouldn't do anything to hurt Denise," he said, "Which means what you did up there you did for a reason."

Score one for the good guys, I thought.

"They were about to pull her off life support, so you returned just in the nick of time. Whatever you did must have worked, too, for she was conscious when they rolled her into surgery a few minutes ago."

Thank you, God.

As we got closer to the car I recognized it as Denise's Charger and wasn't surprised when Dmitri used the keys in his hand to deactivate the alarm. The chirp sounded overly loud to my pounding head and I was sure it was going to bring others running, but thankfully that didn't happen. We were still alone for the time being.

Dmitri opened the door and eased me into the driver's seat.

"It's still an hour or two before dawn. Can you drive?"

I felt like a herd of elephants had used me as a dance floor, but there was no way I was waiting around to see what Gallagher had in store for me. Not after the way his people treated me back there. It was time to get the hell out of Dodge as fast as possible. I could always reconnect with Denise later.

"Yeah," I said. "I can drive."

"Good. Take these." He thrust a small roll of bills, a cell phone, and the keys to the car into my hands. "If you hurry, you should be able to get out of the city and a good jump down the road before it gets too light for you to see. Find somewhere to hole up for the day, and I'll call you when Denise is out of surgery."

I nodded, then instantly regretted it as the pounding in my head intensified. "Don't let anything happen to her, Dmitri. And tell her I'm sorry."

He shook the suggestion off.

"You'll see her again, so tell her yourself. And in the meantime don't worry, I'll be right there with her. Nothing else is going to happen to her, not on my watch."

After that, there wasn't much else to say. He clapped me on the shoulder and then backed away from the car as the engine started with a throaty roar.

I hoped like hell that he was right, that Denise would be all right and that I'd get the chance to see her again, but right now I needed to get the hell out of there before the cops started wondering what happened to their buddies and came looking for me.

Five minutes later I was headed west, chasing the darkness ahead of the rising sun with only the ghosts of New Orleans as my witnesses and the Preacher's frenzied laughter echoing in my ears.